THE THIRD DAY

THE THIRD DAY

Book Three of the Third Peril Trilogy by
L. P. Hoffman

www.hopespringsmedia.com

The Third Day
Book Three of The Third Peril Trilogy
By L. P. Hoffman

www.TheThirdDayNovel.com
www.TheThirdPerilTrilogy.com
www.LPHoffman.com

Published by Hope Springs Media
www.HopeSpringsMedia.com
215A West 3rd Street, Farmville, Virginia 23901-1303
(434) 574-2031

International Standard Book Number (ISBN):
978-1-935375-08-1

Printed in the United States of America.

Cover and book design by Hope Springs Media and Exodus Design. Original cover artwork by L. P. Hoffman.

Dedication

This work is dedicated to God who is the same yesterday, today, and forever and to all who are thirsty in a dry and weary land.

And, to my publicist, partner, creative consultant, and soul mate, Paul Hoffman. Thank you for giving me the space to bloom. I will love you forever!

Special thanks to my talented editor, Adele Brinkley, at With Pen in Hand, the creativity of my book designer, Kristine Cotterman, and final edits by Rick Cotterman at Exodus Design.

I also want to thank my friends Annette Hertzler, Phil Hertzler, and AB Jefferson for their keen insights and encouragement.

Author's Note

The Third Peril Trilogy is a work of fiction. The author does not claim any special or prophetic knowledge, nor does the author intend to add to or take away from the Bible. The Third Peril Trilogy is inspired by Scripture and describes how Biblical prophecies might play out if those foretold events occurred in contemporary times.

The author encourages readers to hold fast to what is true and to test all things against the Bible which is the written Word of God and is the final authority on all matters pertaining to God.

Prologue

What's past is prologue...
William Shakespeare

Babbeh's bones creaked as she settled into her favorite chair, a platform rocker that had been a gift from her late husband when they were both young. Her gnarled fingers played with the tattered upholstery, and she recalled the countless little hurts she had kissed away in this spot. *Some wounds are just too deep,* she thought.

The old woman lifted a framed photo from the table beside her. In the picture, her only son las celebrating his little girl's eleventh birthday. It was the last picture ever taken of Seth.

Babbeh's eyes shifted to a promotional picture of her granddaughter, Katrina, who was now a successful network news anchor and had grown into a fine young woman. Despite the bottle-blonde hair, the image captured Katrina's olive-toned skin and her golden-brown eyes.

"Your father would have been so proud of you, my little Kitten," Babbeh whispered to herself.

Feeling weary, the old woman replaced the photo and pointed her remote at the television set. She settled back to watch a rerun of Law & Order and was just drifting off to sleep when the program was interrupted for a special announcement.

Babbeh slipped on her glasses and read the ticker on the bottom of the screen: "Alistair Dormin, Chairman of the World Reserve Bank, addresses the Global Assembly Conference."

The camera shifted to the Master of Ceremonies who recited a lengthy list of tributes. When he was finished, he stepped aside and said, "Distinguished guests, please welcome Chairman Alistair Dormin." The crowd went wild as the stately man with sable-colored hair walked across stage. He towered over the podium like a giant.

Babbeh turned up the volume as the camera zoomed in for a closer frame of the Chairman of the World Reserve Bank. Dormin's sharp features showed no hint of emotion as his intense gaze swept across the crowd.

"We are on the cusp of a better world. A bright new dawn is on the horizon!" he began. The crowd cheered, but Dormin raised a hand to silence them. "I am pleased to announce that the blueprint for economic and social stability is now complete, but there is more work to be done. Together as one, we shall raise the banner of peace as well as social and economic equity." The Chairman paused and then raised his fist. "Justice for all mankind!"

The people erupted in praise again, and this time, Alistair Dormin basked in it.

After a long celebratory pause, he said, "Absolute commitment and loyalty are essential in our quest for a better world. We must be united in our common purpose, rooting out every enemy of global peace. Tribalism, greed, and religious bigotry must fall! Rise up, I say. Let the bright new day commence!" The Chairman swept his arm upward as the mesmerized crowd launched to their feet and chanted, "Dormin, Dormin, Dormin…!"

Babbeh's heart began to pound. The pride and presumption on the man's face raised goosebumps on her aged flesh, but it was his cadence and words that made her tremble. They were terrifyingly familiar. "No!" she cried out. "It's happening all over again."

The old woman reached for her Bible and a notepad. Babbeh scribbled a message to her granddaughter, and with a trembling hand, she slipped it between the pages of her holy book. Tears streamed down her face as she petitioned God from the deep places of her heart.

Outside, the evening summer sun was casting long shadows through the windows. The resonating tick-tock of the grandfather clock marked the passage of time. The old woman's wet cheeks glistened in the amber glow.

Her soul ached when she considered the perilous days that lay ahead for her granddaughter. "God has a plan for you, little Kitten," Babbeh whispered. "You just don't know it yet."

PART 1 - The Portent

A mighty fortress is our God,

A bulwark never failing;

Our helper He,

Amid the flood of mortal ills prevailing;

For still our ancient foe doth seek to work us woe;

His craft and power are great,

And armed with cruel hate,

On earth is not his equal.

Martin Luther - 1529

Chapter 1

New York City
Thursday, August 31

In the Unified Broadcast Corporation parking garage, Katrina paused beside a white Saab and fumbled through her satchel for the keys.

"Hey, Kat!"

She turned to see the young Field Media Specialist step out of the elevator with an armload of equipment.

"Can you give me a lift?" Gar hollered. "Hey, you've done something different with your hair. You look pretty good as a brunette."

"Thanks. It's my natural color, and I was tired of that platinum blonde suggested by the producers." Katrina popped the trunk and waited for him to load his gear inside. "Don't you usually ride with the production crew?"

"Yeah, tell that to them!" Gar grumbled as he plopped into the passenger seat. "Those jokers drove off without me while I was in the bathroom."

Katrina smiled. "Maybe you took too long."

"Very funny." The Field Media Specialist stretched his

skinny legs and looked around. "New car?" he asked. "Not as sporty as your last one."

"I had to go to New Jersey to find a dealer that wasn't trying to sell water-damaged inventory."

"Yeah, I know. When that epic wave rolled through town last year, it did some gnarly damage."

"You've got a way with words," Katrina said as she turned up the air conditioner in her car.

Gar whipped out his phone and said, "Take a look at my sweet ride." He showed her a photo of a Honda Motor Scooter. "Now I can go around all those mountains of junk that are stacked up along my street."

"The cleaning crews haven't been through your neighborhood since the tsunami hit?" Katrina eased onto West 48th Street and turned right on Park Avenue.

"They've cleared a few streets, but the rats are having a field day. The city crew is still too busy spit shining upper crust neighborhoods like yours."

"Well, I'm sure your bike comes in handy."

"Right on, man! They don't call me the Scooter Dude for nothing. I'm able to navigate around massive piles of stinking debris and go where no man has gone before!" Gar gave Katrina the Vulcan salute. "Seriously though," he continued, "some of those poor peeps on the Lower East Side are still dealing with it. At least, it's warm now. Last winter, they all nearly froze in the dark."

Katrina grew quiet. The magnitude of suffering caused by the tsunami that hit the East Coast had left her feeling deeply saddened.

Gar played with his wispy soul patch. "I know we had all been warned it might happen one day, but I never imagined a big wave would rock the Big Apple in my lifetime." His face brightened. "Hey, did I tell you that I've been nominated for a Pulitzer?"

Katrina glanced at him. "Are you serious?" She slowed to a stop at a traffic light.

"For real! I've been nominated in three categories! Breaking News Photography, Spot News Photography, and Feature Photography."

"Congratulations!"

"And that's not all," Gar puffed. "My independent photo montage has been picked up by PBS for a series documenting the East Coast Tsunami, and I've also been contacted by the Time Warner Publishing Group. They are interested in a possible book deal."

"I hope this doesn't mean you'll be leaving us."

"That depends on how the Unified Broadcasting Corporation treats me now that Gar Duran is almost famous." He blew on his knuckles for emphasis.

Katrina pulled into a parking space in front of Grand Central Station that was reserved for the media as her co-worker cued up a slide show on his cellphone.

Endless haunting photos rolled across his screen: century-old caskets unearthed by the pounding fury of water, surreal images of subway tile art submerged beneath murky flood waters, a faceless mannequin lying near a row of body bags, an orange-suited Hazmat Team sifting through waterlogged debris, a sunrise against the blackened, powerless city lit by pockets of fire, hundreds of triage cots with wounded New Yorkers, shards of glittering glass that sparkled on muddy pavement, rats feeding on rotting food, and a haunting exodus of refugees making a pilgrimage across the George Washington Bridge.

Gar even had a surreal shot of a Bryant Park carousel horse lodged in a tree, but the photo that moved Katrina to tears was of the anguish on a young mother's face as she searched for her missing child.

"I tried to capture the mood. What do you think?"

There was a knot in Katrina's stomach. "You succeeded. You deserve to win the Pulitzer."

"There's still more to document." Gar popped a Tic Tac into his mouth and crunched it. "If you ask me, all those blue-collar families who left town were the lucky ones. At least, they don't have to deal with the looting and street gangs. I mean, it's a freakin' warzone in some boroughs. Even the National Guard is afraid to go in."

He's right, Katrina thought. *The disparity of the restoration efforts is hard to ignore.* The Upper East Side, Midtown, and the Financial District had been prioritized after the tsunami. Cleaning crews had wasted no time restoring electricity, removing debris, replacing shattered windows, sweeping streets, and power washing the water marks from the buildings. Meanwhile, thousands of people had fled the damaged city with no plans to return. *It's hard to not be cynical,* she thought, *when the biggest crisis discussed by Manhattan's affluent population is their difficulty finding decent help.*

Katrina was reminded of a recent memo that read, "The Unified Broadcasting Corporation chooses to focus on humanitarian efforts and the resiliency of New Yorkers. Negative issues, such as lack of food and shelter and disease, are demoralizing subjects and, therefore, should be avoided." The whole thing chaffed at her sense of journalistic integrity.

The Field Media Specialist slipped his phone back into his pocket and turned his attention to the Grand Central Station building. "Wow, look, the old edifice has had a face lift! It must have cost millions to replace all the leaded glass windows. Probably chump change for all those Rockefeller types."

Gar hopped out and did a few stretches on the city sidewalk while he waited for Katrina to pop her trunk.

"Personally, I'm glad to see Grand Central Station restored," Katrina said as Gar gathered up his gear. "This Beaux Arts structure is one of New York City's oldest landmarks."

"Yeah, yeah, blah blah," the Field Media Specialist said as he slipped through the door.

Inside, the crew was busy setting up cameras against the backdrop of golden, stone pillars and gothic windows. Katrina looked around the cavernous building, unable to shake the feeling that something was missing, and then it hit her—people! Grand Central Station, once a noisy hub, had become an eerie echo chamber. Beneath the arched zodiac ceiling and enormous bronze chandeliers, light streamed through half-moon windows and down upon newly refinished hardwood flooring.

"Hello, hello! Greetings!" someone called out.

Katrina turned to see a small-boned man striding briskly toward her.

"Isn't it exciting to know that the New York City rail and metro system is now fully restored?" He thrust out his hand and said, "Where are my manners? I'm Ansel Clapper, the Station Manager."

Mr. Clapper leaned toward Katrina with an intensity that made her want to draw back. "Tell me, are the rumors true? Will the Federal Transit Administrator be making the announcement this morning?" Clapper asked.

"That's correct." She could smell coffee on his breath. "I will also be interviewing Mayor Whitlow and the President of the Metropolitan Transit Authority."

Across the spacious room, a ladder fell over with a jarring clatter.

Mr. Clapper flashed a micro smile, nervously ran his fingers through an awkward comb-over, and said, "Sorry about that. I'll make sure there aren't any distractions during your interviews." He excused himself and rushed over to have a word with the renovation crew.

Katrina thumbed through her satchel, found her talking points, and went over them once more as the dignitaries began to arrive.

After brief introductions, the interviewees were each directed to their respective places to await the signal to begin.

Katrina positioned herself in front of the camera and watched for the flashing light. On cue, she said, "We have gathered here today to celebrate the reopening of Grand Central Station. As you know, New York City's transit system, along with this beautiful hub, was structurally damaged by the powerful forces of nature that devastated our fair city one year ago." A brief video clip was inserted into the feed, show-ing a missing wall of the old building, smashed train cars and buses, as well as flooded subways.

When the clip was finished, Katrina began the interview with the President of the NYC Metropolitan Transit Authority. "Mr. Lentini, can you elaborate on the challenges you faced during the restoration efforts?"

The man's haggard face filled the camera frame. "Yes, Katrina. The task of repairing our transit system to a pre-tsu-nami state has been monumental. Not only did our subways get flooded, but the pump systems were overwhelmed and ir-reparably damaged, and our entire fleet of metro buses and trains was wiped out. To make matters worse, the command center that controls lighting and train crossings was also destroyed. Yet, despite all this, we have made remarkable progress. State-of-the-art pump trains were introduced to the subway tunnels. These generator-powered marvels pumped over ten-thousand gallons of water a minute back into the harbor. Thanks to the World Reserve Bank and their generous donations, we now have a new fleet of metro buses and trains.

One year later, I'm proud to say that our rail systems and tunnels have been fully restored. It is my honor to announce that Grand Central Station is scheduled to reopen early next week, and all trains and subway system will be rolling again!"

"Very impressive Mr. Lentini," Katrina said and turned her attention to an older woman with stylish glasses. "Margaret Satterfield, Federal Transit Administrator, has joined us today. Ms. Satterfield, what role has the federal government played in the efforts to get New York City running again?"

"Thank you, Katrina." Margaret smiled for the camera. "I'm sure you are aware that after President Ira Corbin declared the East Coast a natural disaster area, Congress promptly allotted the funds needed to start restoring hard-hit areas. FEMA immediately set up a mobile command center to distribute food, water, and shelter. The international community has also been impacted by New York City's wounds. As one of the world's major trade centers, the economic ripple of this disaster has been felt across the globe. We are profoundly grateful to the Chairman of the World Reserve Bank for his generosity. Thanks to Alistair Dormin and the World Fortress Institute, New York City has now been restored to her former glory!" Margaret Satterfield laced her fingers together and smiled, signaling the end of her statement.

The cameras shifted to the left and locked on Mayor Eugene Whitlow, a balding, ruddy-faced man. "I echo Ms. Satterfield's heartfelt gratitude to Chairman Dormin and the World Reserve Bank. Without their help, we would not be gathered here to celebrate the reopening of Grand Central Station."

"Mayor Whitlow," Katrina said, "as a fellow survivor of the catastrophe that struck our city last summer, can you elaborate on the collective impact that this disaster has had on our community?"

"As you know, Katrina, the tsunami tragically claimed the lives of nearly 100,000 residents, and countless others lost their homes and livelihoods. When the waters finally receded, the Con Ed Power Plant had been destroyed, and most of Manhattan's infrastructure was gone. Our first course of action was to restore power and clear roadways of debris so that we could aid our citizens." The mayor nodded to the news crews who cued up some brief aerial footage of the damage. "The Red Cross set up triage units," he continued. "The seriously wounded were transported to inland hospitals by helicopter. Shelters quickly opened to house displaced citizens, and a list of survivors was posted on a cloud network to help reunite families."

Katrina's thoughts flashed to Brody Hays who was among those unaccounted for and presumed dead. Last she had heard, his widow and son lived somewhere in Arizona.

The mayor cleared his throat and continued. "Cross-contamination of sewage and water systems necessitated the deployment of water trucks. The National Guard was mobilized to help keep order, and extra fire crews flew in to battle fires sparked from gas mains and electrical shorts. And then there was the financial toll. Revenues from the Metropolitan Transit system ground to an abrupt halt and our once thriving investment centers, including Wall Street, were forced to relocate to continuity-of-operations facilities. To complicate matters further, thousands of our taxpayers have fled the city, many with no plans to return."

The camera shifted to Katrina. "Can you give me a rough estimate on how many displaced citizens have joined the city's homeless population?"

"I don't have those numbers, but as I mentioned earlier, our shelters remain open to anyone who needs provisions." Katrina nodded. "In retrospect, do you believe that the impacts of this tsunami could have been mitigated?"

Eugene Whitlow slowly shook his head as the cameraman zoomed in for a closer shot. "A contingency plan had been in place for years but given the logistics of the city and the magnitude of the natural disaster, we found ourselves at the mercy of an unstoppable act of God."

Chapter 2

Ithaca, New York
Monday, September 11th

On the short plane ride to Ithaca, Katrina reread her grandmother's obituary, "Babysta Katz, a Holocaust survivor, was born in Czechoslovakia after her parents fled persecution in the Soviet Union. In 1938, when she was six-years old, her father's cobbler shop was confiscated by the Nazis, and Jewish children were banned from public schools. In the winter of 1944, Babysta and her family were forcibly removed from their home. They were stripped of their belongings and loaded onto crowded railroad cattle cars headed for Auschwitz, Poland. Babysta's mother, father, and younger brother, Aaron, perished at the death camp."

Aaron had always been a mystery to Katrina, for even the mention of his name seemed painful for her grandmother.

The plane began a slow descent and landed smoothly on the runway at the Ithaca Tomkins Airport. Grief welled up in Katrina's heart as they taxied toward the terminal. Never again would she hear her grandmother's voice saying, "Everything will be all right, Kitten, for even a sparrow can't fall to the ground without God knowing it."

Katrina collected her suitcase and stopped briefly at the Hertz desk to collect her keys. Outside, a soft, humid breeze skimmed over Cayuga Lake, the longest of the New York Finger Lakes. With bag in hand, she located her rental car and headed for town. Driving past the tree-lined streets, green hills, and rock walls brought waves of nostalgia.

Katrina was twelve when she came to live here with her grandmother. It took a while to learn to trust, but in the safe shelter of Babbeh's love, Katrina eventually found her footing and later her sense of purpose.

Even as a child, Katrina was fascinated by the stories that Babbeh told. The atrocities that her grandmother had endured in Poland had a profound effect on Katrina. As a young woman, she developed a gift for interpreting current events through a historical lens. By the time Katrina had entered high school, she had chosen a career path. After being accepted to the Cornell University Journalism Program, Katrina pursued her education with single-minded determination, that is, until she met Benjamin and fell in love.

Just over the Lake Street Bridge, Ithaca Falls came into view, and that old familiar grief fell across her soul like a shadow.

Ithaca Falls was the last of a series of waterfalls along the hanging valley that was formed where Fall Creek intersects the Cayuga Lake glacial trough. But to Katrina, the sight of those white waters tumbling over shale filled her eyes with tears.

She drove on and turned down the tree-lined street to

her grandmother's gingerbread-style house. The Honey Locust tree she used to climb still shaded the grass with its lacy bows, but Babbeh's prized petunias had withered from lack of care.

A rusty van positioned diagonally in front of a double garage forced Katrina to park on the street. She gathered her things and made her way up the brick path that led to the porch. She climbed the steps, drew in a deep breath, and went inside.

Judging from the cardboard boxes stacked everywhere, Great Uncle Shem, her grandfather's peculiar, younger brother, had wasted no time laying claim to Babbeh's things.

Katrina hung her jacket on the coat rack and locked her gaze on Babbeh's favorite chair. The sight of the empty rocker brought a lump to her throat.

"You startled me!" Shem yelped from the doorway of one of the bedrooms. He placed the loaded box he was carrying next to some others. "How long have you been here?"

"Nice to see you too, Uncle Shem." It had been nearly a decade since Katrina had seen her eccentric great-uncle. He had grown an impressive belly, and his hair had disappeared on top of his head leaving a clownish-looking half-circle above his ears.

Katrina lowered herself onto her grandmother's platform rocker that still smelled of lavender, talc, and love.

"I know how busy you are with your career and all, so I just popped over to clear away some clutter for you." Shem wiped sweat from his brow and offered his best long-suffering look.

Katrina scanned the once tidy room and spotted Babbeh's family photo albums along with a hatbox where her favorite mementos were stored: handmade trinkets, sentimental cards, and a jar with some baby teeth. "There are a few things that I would like to keep," Katrina said. "Have you come across any of Babbeh's old journals?"

Shem licked his lips. "If you're talking about her Auschwitz diaries, I figured the Holocaust Museum in DC would pay good money to have those, so I just assumed…"

"Babbeh wanted me to have them."

"Oh, I wasn't aware." Shem rifled through a box and handed them to her.

Katrina placed the diaries inside a storage box where her grandmother kept her photo albums and some of her special treasures. "Where is Babbeh's Bible?"

"Oh, that old thing? It was about to fall apart so I tossed it in the trash." He motioned to a plastic bag. "Don't tell me you've converted too?" Shem shook his head as he watched his niece sifting through the contents of the garbage bag.

"It just seems wrong to throw it away, that's all." Katrina pulled the dog-eared Bible from the bag and clutched it to her breast.

Shem swept his hand around the room. "What about the rest of this junk? I'd be happy to take the whole mess back to my Corning building and sort through it there."

Katrina had been to her great uncle's place of business only once, and that was enough. He lived in the cluttered backroom of a commercial warehouse that was stacked to the ceiling with used furniture and accessories. Aside from being a firetrap, the building reeked of mildew, urine, and body odor.

"Of course, if I find anything of value, I'll let you know," he added.

Babbeh's words came to Katrina's mind: *Life's true treasures can never be bought or sold.* "That's fine," she said, glancing at her watch. "We should head over to the church."

"Oy vey!" Shem bellowed. "Where did I put my suit?" He racketed about the room moving boxes and looking under piles of clothing and between stacks of books.

Katrina's phone buzzed with a text message from her boss, Otto Benedict. "I need you back at the studio ASAP!" She silenced the ringer and gathered her grandmother's special mementos.

"I'll see you over at the service," Katrina called out as she headed out the door.

A few blocks from downtown Ithaca, she arrived at her grandmother's church. The Messianic Congregation met in an unpretentious brick structure with arched windows and a gabled tower.

On the sidewalk in front, a small group was loitering. As Katrina approached, a man wearing a scotch cap lifted an anti-Semitic sign and yelled, "The Holocaust is a hoax!"

A cluster of women and children began to chant, "Expose the lies! Jews are deceivers not victims!"

Katrina felt sickened as she walked past the vile gathering. "Where is your sense of decency?" she yelled. "This is my grandmother's funeral!"

A young woman with a baby perched on her hip shrieked, "One less Jew!" The infant began to wail.

The Messianic church doors opened, and a short round woman ushered Katrina inside. "I'm so sorry you had to see this ugliness, Hon." She stepped back and said, "Aren't you Katrina? I've seen you on the news. Your grandmother talked about you all the time! My name is Hannah. Let me take your wrap, Hon."

Katrina mustered a smile. "Thanks."

"Your grandmother was a great woman of God," the round lady said as she slipped the coat onto a hanger. "It was a privilege and an honor to know her."

I could use a little of Babbeh's faith right now, Katrina thought as she entered the sanctuary.

Just inside the double doors, the Rabbi stood. Beside him, on a stand, was a basket. "Are you family?"

Katrina nodded. He pinned a black ribbon to her right lapel and tore one of its ends. "This Kriah symbolizes the rending of the garment in grief." His eyes met hers. "Babysta will be missed, but if you believe, then one day, you will see her again in paradise."

As Katrina walked down the aisle, she pondered the Rabbi's words. *If only that was true,* she thought as she took her seat in the pew reserved for family members. Her grandmother's faith had always puzzled Katrina. *How could Babbeh possibly believe in a God that allowed the kind of suffering that she had experienced?*

The room soon filled with church congregants and

friends—men in dark suits with heads covered by traditional caps and women dressed conservatively. Young and old had turned out to honor Babbeh. It deeply touched Katrina to see that so many people loved her grandmother.

The Rabbi began his memorial remarks by reading from the obituary that Katrina had written before he added, "Babysta Katz endured the trials of her life with courage and grace. She has run the race as a child of God, and now she has received her reward."

A clamor rose from the back of the room. Heads turned as Uncle Shem hurried up the aisle and plopped down beside Katrina. He pointed to his cap and said breathlessly, "I couldn't find my kippah."

The Rabbi had paused, and he then read from the book of Psalms before reciting the Mourner's Kaddish.

Katrina parroted, "Amen," at all the appropriate places, but the words did little to lighten her broken heart.

"May He give reign to His kingship in your lifetimes and in your days. May His great name be blessed. May there be abundant peace from Heaven." When the Rabbi was finished, he invited family and friends to go to the graveside. "A reception in the church hall will follow the burial," he announced.

"Mind if I ride with you?" Shem asked. "No sense wasting gas."

All the way to the cemetery, Katrina's uncle prattled on about nothing.

Katrina found a parking spot on University Avenue,

near the entrance to historic Ithaca Cemetery. They strolled along a footpath with those who had come to pay their respects. Walking past retaining walls and grassy knolls covered with mossy gravestones, they finally stopped at the plot where Babbeh would be laid to rest beside her husband.

"Did you know that the locals refer to this place as the old burying ground?" Shem whispered as they waited for all the mourners to gather. "There's some really famous people laid to rest here, but I can't remember who."

A firestorm of powerful emotions raged inside Katrina as they watched the casket being lowered into the ground. *How can I say goodbye to the person who saved my life?* Katrina's thoughts drifted to the day her grandmother and a social worker had arrived at the foster home. Babbeh wrapped the twelve-year-old in her ample arms and cried. "My precious Kitten, I have been searching for you, and I've come to take you home."

With the casket in place, the Rabbi instructed family and friends to engage in a last act of charity. One by one, he handed each of the mourners the shovel filled with dirt. Katrina held back tears as she dropped soil upon the casket.

The ride back to the church was a blur. She parked along the curb. "Why don't you go on ahead Uncle Shem?"

"I can keep you company," Shem said. "Besides, my feet are killing me."

"Really, if you don't mind, I'd like to be alone for a few minutes."

"Suit yourself. I am getting hungry anyway." Shem

adjusted the kippah on his bald crown and climbed out.

Alone at last, Katrina wept.

She was trying to muster strength to face the crowd when an old Rambler station wagon idled slowly past and backed into the space in front of her. The engine shuddered to a stop and backfired like a rifle shot, and a curious-looking little man with a snow-white beard stepped out. He was wearing a colorful Hawaiian shirt and oversized Bermuda shorts. He fluffed his long white beard and spotted Katrina sitting in her car.

She cringed as the stranger made his way over and tapped on the window.

"Are you here for Babysta's memorial service?" he asked. "Hope I'm not too late. I had to make a little detour, and it took longer than expected."

Katrina emerged from the car. "The service is over, but there's a reception in the church hall." The man looked vaguely familiar, but she couldn't place where she'd seen him. "Were you a friend of my grandmother?"

"I certainly am. There's a big party going on in Heaven right now; I can tell you that!" He thrust out a hand and shook hers. "I'm Zeke."

"Katrina," she returned. "Babbeh was my grandmother."

"She's still your grandmother!" he said with a broad smile.

"Have we met before?" she inquired.

"That's entirely probable." Zeke offered his arm. "I'll escort you inside."

As they strolled into the church, Katrina struggled to place this odd, little man. Something about him was disturbing, yet at the same time, comforting.

In the reception hall, Zeke made a beeline for the buffet table, but Katrina was flanked by congregants and friends offering comfort. She listened carefully to each story they shared about Babbeh. Everyone who knew her grandmother had loved her deeply. Finally, Katrina excused herself to join her uncle, who was grazing on a massive plate of food.

"They really put on a great spread!" Shem reloaded his fork and took a big sloppy bite.

Katrina touched her finger to her chin, "Uncle Shem, you've got a little something…"

He snapped open a napkin, wiped away a dribble of gravy, and shoveled more food into his mouth.

"How can you possibly eat all that?" Katrina asked.

Shem swallowed hard. "I always carry zip-lock baggies, just in case."

Zeke appeared with a plate in hand and said, "I believe a feller could get fat just off all these heavenly smells. Mind if I join you?"

Katrina introduced the little old man to Shem who mumbled something that passed for politeness.

Zeke looked comically out of place in his casual attire. He tucked his beard inside the collar of his Hawaiian shirt and closed his pale eyes. "Thank you, God, for this meal and the loving hands that prepared it." He savored each dish like a restaurant critic. "I think my taste buds might explode from happiness!"

Katrina smiled, but there was something about this joyful little man that still troubled her. "How long have you known my grandmother?"

Zeke pressed a napkin to his lips and said, "Can't remember when I didn't know her!"

"You talk about her as though she's still alive."

"Didn't you get the memo? It's all written down in the good book." Zeke's pale eyes twinkled. "Everybody's gonna face death sooner or later, Missy, but your grandmother found the true secret to life."

The old man pulled a little box from his pocket and placed it onto the table in front of Katrina. "Babysta gave this to me a long time ago," he said. "I believe she'd want you to have it."

Katrina searched the old man's face. "How did you know my grandmother?"

Across the table, Shem abruptly stood, knocking over his chair in the process. He began to claw at his throat.

"He's choking!" someone yelled. People rushed forward to help.

"I know the Heimlich maneuver?" A large man pushed through the crowd, wrapped beefy arms around Shem's brisket and squeezed sharply.

Katrina watched helplessly as her uncle's brown eyes bulged with fear.

"He's turning blue," one of the church women screamed.

The large man thrust his fists harder, again and again, until a piece of un-chewed kuegle jettisoned across the room. Shem gasped in air and cried out, "Thought I was going to die! I really thought that was it!" Everyone gathered around to fuss over him.

Katrina turned back eager to continue her conversation with Zeke, but he was gone. Only the little wrapped package remained, right where he had placed it.

Chapter 3

Hope Springs, Arizona
Friday, October 6th

It was still dark outside when Paige rose from her slumber. As her husband slept, she quietly dressed and slipped into the compact bathroom of the Airstream. Paige fluffed her short red hair and applied a few spots of concealer under her green eyes, but the woman's reflection in the mirror still looked tired.

All night long, Paige had tossed and turned as she tried hard to embrace the coming changes. Brody insisted that the move to Tucson would be good for their family. *Why then,* she wondered, *does it feel so wrong?* Paige tiptoed to the other end of the camper and lingered over the couch where her thirteen-year-old son slept. She reached out and touched Connor's crimson hair that glowed softly in the nightlight. He was small for his age, still a boy in his mother's eyes. *Will he be accepted at his new school?* she worried.

At Hope Springs, no one rolled their eyes or called Connor a freak when he spoke about his visions from God, not even the children. In this tiny desert community, Paige never had to put on airs, for nobody knew or cared that she came from old money.

Paige slipped on her jacket and quietly stepped outside. A faint glow appeared on the horizon. Paige lingered for a moment to enjoy the aroma of desert blooms that hung in the crisp morning air. A beautiful sunrise spread across the sky as she strolled along one of the dirt roads that ran between eclectic dwellings: rows of RVs, vintage trailers, wall tents, teepees, and even a school-bus conversion lined the primitive streets.

Many of the campers, including the Hays' family Airstream, had been equipped with solar panels and tin roof shelters that helped to manage the extreme summer temperatures of southern Arizona. Other dwellings used straw bales or adobe for added insulation to protect against the seasonal extremes.

Paige committed every detail to memory as she walked. The water system began from an artesian well that was tapped uphill from the dwellings, routed through a generator to produce electricity and then was divided into two channels. One filled a cistern with gravity-fed lines that delivered drinking water to campsites and livestock. The other channel was diverted to the pavilion for cooking, washing dishes, and a nearby solar-shower hut. From there, half of the wastewater went to a drip system to water greenhouse vegetables, and the other half flowed through irrigation pipes. Each dwelling was also involved in water conservation. A shallow trench ran from each camper lot to capture greywater for the fruit trees that were planted below. The resourcefulness of the people here never ceased to amaze. They had even engineered a refrigeration system that was designed to work through evaporative cooling.

Nearing the pavilion, Paige was startled to see many of her friends and neighbors gathered there. "Good morning!" she called out.

Randy Bales looked up from stoking the fire pit and said, "Hey, everybody, look who's up with the roosters!"

Pricilla's head turned so fast her blonde ponytail slapped her pretty face. She hoisted her toddler, Hari, to her hip and hurried over to greet Paige. "What a surprise! We didn't expect you to be up this early."

"Did you see that beautiful sunrise?" Paige asked.

"Sure did." Randy poured coffee from an enamelware pot, offered it to Paige, and turned his attention to a skillet of sizzling bacon.

"So, this is what I've missed by sleeping in." She took a sip of coffee. "Where's Kay?"

"Oh, she's around here somewhere," Priscilla said.

Travis arrived with a massive load of firewood in his arms and dropped it into the crib near the fire pit.

"Look who surprised us by getting up early," Randy said.

The young carpenter tipped his John Deere cap. "Morning, Ms. Hays." The way he said Ms. made it sound like "Mizzz."

"I didn't know you and Pricilla were such early risers," Paige said.

"Well," Travis drawled, "y'all know how it is with a young'n."

Pricilla shot her husband a look. "That's right. Little Hari never lets us sleep in."

Pulling a garden wagon full of paper goods and decorations, Jim and Bonnie Sanders entered the pavilion. The silver-haired village patriarchs spotted Paige, and one of them said, "I think the jig is up, Mama."

Bonnie rushed over for a hug. "Dear, I'm delighted you're here. It gives us more time to spend with you."

"We've been planning this surprise going-away party for a few weeks now," Jim said. "Ever since we learned that that husband of yours accepted a teaching position at the University of Arizona in Tucson."

"Brody will be very surprised!" Paige said, hoping that he wouldn't be annoyed by the disruption of his plans for an early departure.

The Ortega family filed into the pavilion carrying gifts: a wooden bowl for bread dough, dried flowers, and rocks that the kids had painted by hand. "We made these for you," their oldest daughter announced. "Vaya con Dios!"

Paige fought back tears as the Ortega children left their gifts on a picnic table.

As more friends and neighbors began to arrive, Jim volunteered to fetch the rest of the Hays family.

"Great idea!" Paige said.

"Tell them to bring an appetite!" Randy hollered. Beside him, Sue Brewster tied an apron around her pudgy frame and slid a batch of her famous sourdough biscuits into the brick oven.

"The Fillmores are here!" someone yelled, and Paige turned to see her brother and his family walking up the trail to the pavilion.

David gave her a big hug. "Wish you didn't have to move so soon. I've really enjoyed having my big sister around the store."

"I second that!" Elita placed a grocery bag on the table, kissed her sister-in-law's cheek, and said, "We threw in a few staples for your pantry."

Joy, an eight-year-old version of her pretty Hispanic mother, tugged on her aunt's jacket. "Where's Connor?"

Paige pointed. "Here comes your cousin now."

Joy ran to meet Connor who was hurrying up the path ahead of his dad while Jim trailed along behind them.

When Brody sat down at a table, Paige joined him.

"Wasn't this nice of everyone?"

"Very thoughtful," he flatly replied.

A few yards away, Jim Saunders rang the dinner triangle and said, "Let's pray. Lord, thank you for this food we are about to receive and may abundant blessings follow the Hays family as they begin their new big adventure. In Jesus name, Amen!"

Everyone lined up for a hearty breakfast. Cheerful banter filled the pavilion, but Brody ate in brooding silence.

When the plates were finally cleared away, Jim approached Brody and handed him a scroll of paper. "I made this to remind you that you've got a place to come if that new teaching position at the University of Arizona doesn't work out."

Everyone watched as Brody untied a leather string and unrolled a large sheet of graph paper and looked at a detailed map of Hope Springs.

"This is fantastic!" Paige said, admiring the drawing that included the community greenhouse, drip system, hydropower plant, spring-fed refrigeration, evaporative cooling, and composting stations.

"Yes, nicely done," Brody agreed.

At the far end of the pavilion, Raymond Lee settled his dark lanky frame onto a stool, tuned his guitar, and began to pick a melancholy bluesy tune.

Bonnie leaned close to Paige and whispered, "Ray wrote this song for your family, and Mr. Mike made a recording."

Against the backdrop of music, the residents of Hope Springs quietly streamed forward with gifts in hand: rustic handmade coasters; a colorful cross crafted from old pieces of architectural molding; a woven table runner; a basket filled with jam, applesauce, and bread; raw honey; and a wooden plaque with a scripture burned onto it, "As for me and my house, we will serve the Lord." – *Joshua 24:15*.

Brody stood and cleared his throat. "I'd like to thank you all for this thoughtful send-off, especially for the support you gave my family during a very difficult time." He reached for his wife's hand. "We will always be grateful."

As she rose from the picnic table, Paige felt swamped by sadness. "I wish that we could take you all with us."

"Connor, gather your things. It's time to go." Brody snapped his fingers, and his son reluctantly did as he was told.

Kay Bales helped pack the gifts into cardboard boxes. "Remember that I'm here if you need prayer or someone to just listen."

Paige threw her arms around her best friend. "I'm going to miss you most of all."

"Daylight's burning!" Brody barked as he headed for the truck with a load.

David grabbed a box and walked with Paige as the good people of Hope Springs waved goodbye.

Fussing with some suitcases in the back of the truck, Brody grumbled, "I don't know why we bothered to pack last night." He climbed behind the wheel and fired up the engine.

"Oh, I almost forgot!" David said. "A letter came addressed to you." He pulled a folded envelope from his jacket pocket and handed it to his sister. "It came in care of the General Store."

Paige glanced at the return address. "It's from Katrina Katz! I can't believe it!"

"Why is that name familiar?"

"She's a network news anchor in New York City and also a friend." Paige ripped the letter open and began to read.

"Oh no, she thinks that Brody died in the tsunami!"

The truck horn blared.

"Is everything okay?" David asked. "Brody doesn't quite seem like his old self."

"He's just anxious about his new job." Paige climbed into the cab of the truck and tried to convince herself that that was all it was.

Chapter 4

New York City
Monday, November 6th

Alone in the elevator, Katrina tried to focus on the momentous task that lay ahead, but her thoughts kept returning to the mysterious stranger named Zeke. All night long, he had invaded her dreams, leaving vivid impressions of a colorful Hawaiian shirt, a long white beard, and crystal-blue, smiling eyes. In the dream, the old man opened her hand and placed an object there, an enamel pendant shaped like a shield. The back was inscribed with "Genesis 31:49".

The elevator doors opened to the Unified Broadcasting Corporation, and the smell of fresh paint and carpet glue assaulted Katrina's senses. The reception area had been redecorated with gaudy wallpaper and matching designer carpet.

The receptionist looked up from her station and chirped, "Good morning, Ms. Katz!" Amber, a perky redhead, ran her fingers through her pixie haircut and said, "Isn't it exciting? I still can't believe that Alistair Dormin is going to walk through these doors in a few hours. I had to pinch myself when I woke up this morning. Do you think I could get a selfie with the Chairman? It probably wouldn't be appropriate to ask, would it? I bet you are a nervous wreck. I would be a basket case if I was the one interviewing him. What am I saying? You're a professional!" The receptionist drew a breath, and Katrina seized the moment.

"Are there any messages for me?"

"Let's see...," Amber tapped her fingernail across her touch screen. "Yes, Mr. Benedict left a note on your desk, and Ms. Shiff wants to speak to you ASAP."

Katrina headed to her office just past a cluster of producers and their assistants. Everyone she passed was dressed as though they were headed to a White House luncheon.

She read the sticky note from her boss that had been posted on her computer monitor. "ABSOLUTELY NO AD LIBS!" Katrina tossed it into her wastebasket and then made her way to Studio One.

The large news theater was bustling with activity. A troupe of technicians adjusted LED lighting to display a rainbow of hues designed to coordinate with the news feeds that had been cued up on a dozen wall-mounted monitors.

To her left, the staff engineer was kneeling behind one of the robotic cameras with a tool in hand. "Good morning, Jeff. Don't tell me we're having Cyborg problems?"

He looked up, slicked back a runaway strand of hair, and said, "I was told to give the bots a checkup. They were just serviced, but hey, it all pays the same." Jeff closed the door that had revealed the robot motherboard and moved his toolbox to the next one.

A man with a clipboard arrived. "We're here with the new chairs," he hollered. "Somebody needs to tell us where to put them!"

Gloria Shiff, the News Director, rushed over and directed them to the In Depth News set. "I need you to take away the old furniture."

"Okay, lady, but that'll cost ya extra."

As the deliverymen trudged past with their load, Gloria spotted the UBC Co-anchor and said, "I have been looking all over for you, Katrina. I expected you to be here early like everyone else."

Katrina gave her News Director a deadpan look. "I didn't get the memo."

"Well, there wasn't an actual memo, Dear." A flash of pink spread across Gloria's face after she realized the jest. "Well, the important thing is that you are here now." The News Director rifled through her brief case and retrieved a stack of papers. "Chairman Dormin's public relations staff faxed this over last night. Here is your copy of the script. It has already been fed into the teleprompter, and the video clips are cued up. Everything is in order, Dear, so you're good to go. Just remember to stay strictly on message."

"No ad-libs, I know," Katrina returned.

"Oh, I almost forgot. I've scheduled an appointment for you at the Media Image Booth—orders from upstairs." The News Director held up a hand, and said, "I know you dislike heavy makeup, but we all must make sacrifices." Gloria looked over Katrina's shoulder, let out a gasp, and hurried over to the In Depth News set to supervise the placement of the new furnishings.

Katrina flipped through the script with growing unease. The prearranged questions read like a political lovefest. As far as she was concerned, Alistair Dormin could have arranged this interview with any news outlet, so why had the Unified Broadcast Corporation been chosen? It was common knowledge that Katrina had crossed Dormin and the World Fortress Institute, so why had she been asked to conduct this interview?

Feeling uneasy, Katrina headed to the Media Image Booth.

Raquel, a black-haired beauty with a swath of lavender for added color, motioned her inside. "I've been waiting for you, Ms. Katz!" The stylist waited for Katrina to settle, snapped open a nylon cape, and fastened it around her neck. "Are you ready for me to work some magic?" Raquel cooed.

"Do I look that bad?"

The stylist studied Katrina's face with a furrowed brow. "Looks like somebody didn't get much sleep last night. No worries. When I get done, you will look like a movie star."

"That's what scares me," Katrina said, but the stylist was busy rifling through her bag of paraphernalia.

Raquel whipped out a pink bonnet and gingerly covered Katrina's brown hair. "Would you consider going blonde again? I thought it looked stunning on you."

"It sounds like you've been talking to the executives. Platinum blonde doesn't suit my complexion."

The stylist shrugged and loaded her airbrush with silicone foundation. "Close your eyes and relax. You're in the hands of an artist." The small compressor purred as Raquel went to work on her human canvas.

The fine mist of face paint felt cool against Katrina's skin and then came a bead of wetness on her eyelashes. "What are you doing?"

"Hold still. I've got my orders, and you wouldn't want me to lose my job, would you?"

Finally, after what seemed like ages, Raquel spun the chair around, and said, "Ready for the big reveal? Open your eyes! I chose a shimmery copper pallet for your eyeshadow because it really highlights your lovely brown eyes! What do you think, Ms. Katz?"

Katrina stared at the fake eyelashes and heavy makeup. The word "garish" came to mind, but when she looked at the young woman's beaming face, she didn't have the heart to be negative. "Wow!"

Raquel removed the bonnet, picked up a large barrel curling iron, and went to work creating loose twirling curls that had become popular among celebrities. After engulfing Katrina's head with a liberal dose of hairspray, the stylist stood back to admire her work.

Gloria Shiff poked her head into the Media Image Booth and said, "Looking good, Dear! Oh, by the way, there's a designer suit waiting for you in the Wardrobe Department."

"Let me guess," Katrina said sarcastically, "I bet it has a short skirt with matching stiletto pumps."

Ms. Schiff's cherry lips pursed. "Do I detect an attitude, Dear? That just won't do!"

"Why should Alistair Dormin be treated differently than any other interview?"

"Did those words actually come out of your mouth?" Gloria slid her purple-framed glasses up her button nose. "The Chairman of the World Reserve Bank is NOT just anyone!"

Gloria whirled around, clapped her hands, and yelled. "Listen up everyone—chop, chop! Alistair Dormin's security team will be here in a few minutes to do a sweep."

She glanced over her shoulder and shot Katrina another disapproving look. "Honestly, Dear, you should be grateful that the most influential man on the planet has selected you to conduct his first personal interview. Every other news anchor in this nation would kill to be in your position!"

That much was true, Katrina thought, but there was another side to this man and his cronies at the World Fortress Institute, and she had good reason not to trust any of them.

⁂

Feeling a bit ridiculous in her sleeveless designer sheath and stiletto pumps, Katrina returned to Studio One.

Gar whistled as she passed by. "Nice pins."

Katrina stopped. "This isn't your turf. What are you doing here?"

"Same as everyone else; I came to see the Big Cheese himself." Gar looked around the studio and said, "Man, look what they've done to this place. Talk about rolling out the red carpet. He lowered his voice and added, "Looks a little like a Las Vegas casino if you ask me."

Katrina silently agreed. Every detail, from timing and video clips to technical nuances, had been checked and double-checked. The atmosphere was electric with anticipation.

According to the studio clock, the anchorwoman had a few minutes, so she settled onto one of the new couches to review her media packet. Katrina was scanning her scripted interview questions when someone let out a gasp. She looked up to see Alistair Dormin strolling through the studio door with his entourage in tow.

Towering over everyone around him, he was much taller than Katrina remembered. Dormin's deep-set eyes swept across the room, briefly stopping on Katrina, just before he was engulfed in a flurry of top-brass introductions.

After Dormin was escorted to the In Depth News set, Katrina rose to shake his hand.

As they settled back into their respective seats, an awkward silence passed between them.

Katrina drew a deep breath as the numbers on the teleprompter wound down, and the UBC logo flashed on the screen, signaling the lead-in announcement.

She turned toward the camera. "This is In Depth with Katrina Katz. Thank you for joining us for an exclusive interview with Alistair Dormin, Chairman of the World Reserve Bank." The camera frame drew back to showcase her guest looking relaxed in his gabardine suit.

"Welcome, Chairman Dormin."

He crossed his long legs and said, "Thank you, Katrina. I'm delighted to be here. Please call me Alistair."

The teleprompter rolled discreetly into view. "Alistair, in just three remarkable years, you have managed to broker agreements that no one has ever before accomplished. Some say that your powers of persuasion are nothing short of miraculous. Here is a recap of just a few of your achievements."

From the control room, the pre-arranged news feeds played along with a voiceover. "The Global Unity and Economic Recovery Treaty, known as GUERT, has opened the door and ushered in a bright new dawn for mankind." On the screen, a conference of world leaders—heads of state—appeared, all smiling as they shook hands. The image shifted to a vast array of signatures on the document. "Alistair Dormin has garnered international goodwill on an unprecedented scale."

Next the video feed transitioned to heartbreaking images of human suffering in third-world countries: starvation, disease, and poverty. The digital images morphed into happy children drinking clean water, new housing, and jobs. "Thanks to the Chairman's leadership and the work of the World Fortress Institute, free general education and trade schools that equip people with practical skills are bringing hope and prosperity to their countries."

Katrina spotted a fleeting look of self-satisfaction on her guest's face as the altruistic video clips continued. "Under the umbrella of economic justice through agreements like the

North American Coalition Treaty, known as NAC, cultural walls are crumbling. Nations are linking arms in the common bonds of global brotherhood."

The camera light signaled that Katrina was again live. She followed the script on her teleprompter. "Alistair, as Chairman of the World Reserve Bank, you have been called a man of vision and a harbinger of international peace. Where do you get your inspiration?"

"That is a wonderful question, Katrina." Dormin tilted his chin upward, striking a subtle visionary pose. "As the only child of a diplomat, I witnessed the oppressive divide between extreme poverty and opulent wealth. At a very early age, I yearned to see our world stabilized by social and economic reforms." The Chairman paused briefly and then added, "Destiny has smiled upon me. For these dreams are fast becoming a reality."

"Can you elaborate on your international policies and how these policies have impacted countries that have refused to sign the Global Unity and Economic Recovery Treaty?"

The Chairman's long fingers clenched the armrest of his chair, but his face showed no hint of irritation at the unscripted question. Without missing a beat, Dormin said, "I pity the nations that lack vision and fail to see the virtue of these peaceful precepts. Blinded by tribalism and nationalism, these small-minded leaders are marching their people over the precipice to poverty and suffering."

The deep rhythmic cadence of the man's voice was mesmerizing as he danced around the question like a prize fighter.

"Our universal policies include sound fiscal programs and generous stimulus monies for infrastructure, schools, health-care, and work incentive programs. Tell me Ms. Katz, how could any competent leader not embrace such benefits?"

He avoided any mention of sanctions or trade embargoes, Katrina thought. "Social justice seems a bit more challenging. How do you plan to address that issue?"

"It's quite simple, Ms. Katz. Universal peace can only be realized in a culture of absolute equity. Ideologies that promote division must be replaced with absolute unity. One mind—one people, if you will. We have made great strides toward peace though the NAC Treaty, the World Reserve Bank Charter, and GUERT. Citizens across the world are being re-educated through multicultural initiatives, sensitivity training, and edicts of diversity, equity, and inclusion."

Katrina's mouth felt dry as she formed her next question. "Alistair, the Seven Year Treaty has granted you temporary economic sovereignty and authority over a large coalition of nations. These countries, as a block, are now pressuring Israel who says that you broke the treaty when you announced that the newly rebuilt temple in Jerusalem was to become an ecumenical place of worship. Do you intend to seize control of the temple? If so, how will this further your plans for brokering peace in the Middle East?"

Alistair Dormin stared at Katrina with an intensity that unnerved her. "That is an interesting question, Ms. Katz. The Global Unity and Economic Recovery Treaty has given me broad authority to negotiate international agreements. The

Seven Year Treaty was ratified by ten of the most powerful nations on earth, not to mention the hundreds of third-world countries that have also placed their trust in me by signing the treaty. For the good of all mankind, all nations must work together in the spirit of cooperation." The Chairman of the World Reserve Bank looked straight into the camera and added, "Simply put, the enemies of peace are the enemies of humanity."

Katrina was stunned. Alistair Dormin spoke volumes by his omission. Her earbuds exploded with orders to wrap things up, and video clips venerating Dormin promptly played on the monitors. After a few brief words, the interview was concluded.

The Chairman of the World Reserve Bank rose slowly from his chair. He leaned his towering frame over Katrina as if to intimidate. "This has been a very informative interview, Ms. Katz. Very informative indeed."

"I'm curious," Katrina said as he turned to walk away. "Why did you request that I conduct this interview? Did it have anything to with the fact that I did an op-ed piece implicating you and the World Fortress Institute in the Brody Hays scandal?"

Alistair Dormin stopped abruptly. He turned to face Katrina. The darkness in his eyes made her shudder. He spoke not a word, but the message was received. Katrina knew that she had just made a very powerful enemy.

Chapter 5

Tucson, Arizona
Saturday, December 16th

Paige and Connor sat in the backseat of the real estate agent's Suburban listening to the woman gush over Brody. "I am so excited to show you and your lovely family this property. I know you'll fall in love with it!"

After passing several upscale estates, the agent turned down a winding road that led to a Spanish-tile driveway. She parked in front of the massive iron-clad doors, hopped out, and threw open the car doors for her passengers. "Welcome to Casa Palacia!"

The air was dry but chilly. Paige buttoned her sweater and waited as the woman fiddled with the lock box. She leaned close to Brody and whispered, "Are you sure this is the best time to purchase a home?"

"Absolutely. It's a perfect time," he replied. "My job is going swimmingly well, and besides, I'm tired of renting."

The real estate agent opened the doors wide and waited just inside the tiled entryway. "You're going to adore this fabulous estate. It boasts over 6,000 square feet of luxury living. I must warn you, though, it won't be on the market long."

She led the way into an airy grand room. Sunlight streamed through the floor-to-ceiling windows providing warmth against the December chill. "Isn't this panoramic view of the desert simply breathtaking? May I draw your attention to the exquisite fireplace and hearth crafted from Arizona Onyx? You will see this stunning design feature repeated throughout the home."

"That's awesome!" Connor exclaimed. "That rock looks layered, just like the Grand Canyon."

"Yes, very nice indeed," Brody said with a nod.

Paige's first impression of the modern house was that it was vast and cold, but she tried to keep an open mind.

The agent guided them into a home office and gushed over the custom-built shelves and state-of-the-art electronic ports. "I'm so excited to show you the sunny heart and soul of this beautiful home."

The Hays family followed the woman through a stone-arched doorway into a spacious open-concept family room and kitchen.

The real estate agent kept her eye on Paige. "Isn't this kitchen just to die for? It comes fully equipped with an Italian gas range, two convection ovens, and the stainless-steel refrigerator is a high-end, commercial-grade unit."

Connor ran his hand along the countertop. "Look, Mom, same stone as the living room hearth."

"As you can see, the polished Arizona Onyx countertops provide ample workspace."

"Very nice," Paige agreed.

"I have a surprise for you all!" The agent hurried over to the window, flipped a latch, and slid the windows apart. "These glass pocket doors disappear, and voila, your indoor space expands to embrace nature!"

Connor hurried outside for a better look. "Is that an infinity pool?"

"Yes, it is." The realtor beamed. "I'm sure you'll have loads of fun there with all your friends."

Brody admired the water feature and the veranda landscaped with massive boulders, ornate paving stones, and succulents against a sunny desert backdrop. "This is exactly what I envisioned."

They lingered in this space for a few minutes before the woman suggested they head to the master bedroom where she gushed over the twin luxury baths, a cedar-lined walk-in closet, and a sitting room with a gas fireplace.

This house seems to go on forever, Paige thought as they wandered down a sunny hallway for a quick tour of two smaller bedrooms complete with on-suite baths.

Lastly, the Hays family was shown a home theater room, a salt cave sauna, and an indoor gymnasium with a lap pool. "What do you think?" the agent pressed. "This is one of Tucson's most prestigious neighborhoods, so this house won't be on the market very long. In fact, there is another showing scheduled for this afternoon."

Paige leaned close to her husband and quietly said, "We really don't need this much space."

"Nonsense! I see this as a fresh start for our family."

Without further discussion, Brody turned to the real estate agent and said, "Let's talk."

⚙

Arroyo Seco, Arizona
Thursday, December 21ˢᵗ

On the front porch of the old General Store, David cupped his hands around his mug and leaned against the antique Coca-Cola cooler that radiated heat. The soft glow of the Christmas lights that hung in the window behind him cast a warm glimmer on the weathered porch.

David took a sip of coffee and waited for the sun to rise over the sleepy little town he had come to know as home. Rising early in the border town of Arroyo Seco gave him a sense of peace, a peace that he once found illusive. There had been a time when David believed that his life would end in a motorcycle crash or drunken brawl, but God had other plans. Gratitude rose in David's heart as fiery colors fanned across the horizon, and soon the town was bathed in the soft glow of morning light.

Litter was strewn about the crumbling asphalt along with several broken bottles. For a Thursday night, it had been unusually raucous at the Watering Hole Bar, wakening the household with a few rounds fired from a pistol.

David spotted something in the middle of the street. It took him a few seconds to realize that it was the only Arroyo Seco stoplight that had been dangling precariously for years. *Someone finally killed it!*

His thoughts shifted to some shady characters who had recently rolled into town. It seemed like no coincidence that Alvaro Garcia and his crew arrived just after the discovery of a mass grave in the desert. According to the news, the victims were immigrants who had all been butchered for their sub-dermal passport chip.

The rise of criminal activity along the border deeply concerned David. Law enforcement was understaffed and overwhelmed.

He surveyed the old, wooden porch with an eye for mounting a new security system. The walls were lined with bumper stickers and decals from decades of travelers, and Elita liked it that way. "You can't get more Americana than that," she would often say.

Even the old metal door and screen sported vintage political lapel buttons. Some dated as far back as Eisenhower.

David settled on mounting a video camera just inside one of the store windows.

The screen door burst open, and eight-year-old Joy burst out to model her new pink cowboy boots and t-shirt. "What do you think, Dad?"

"You look like a pop star."

"Really?"

David put his arm around his daughter and said, "Don't grow up too fast."

"Guess what, Dad? I wrapped a present for you this morning and put it under the Christmas tree. I'll tell you what it is if you'll tell me what you and Mom got for me?"

"What was it you wanted again?" David tapped his unshaved chin. "Oh, I remember. A big lump of coal."

"A laptop!" Joy rolled her eyes and sighed. "Mom says breakfast is ready."

David followed his daughter upstairs and opened the door of their little apartment to the smell of sourdough pancakes. He took his place at the table and asked a blessing.

Elita watched their daughter drowning her pancakes in warm syrup. "Wish I still had her metabolism."

Grabbing the jug, David said, "Hey, save some for us, sports car!"

"Have you talked to Paige lately?"

"No, why?" David asked his wife.

Elita shrugged. "Your sister has been on my mind lately, that's all."

After breakfast, David cleared the table, and his wife did the dishes. He leaned over her shoulder and whispered "Have I told you lately that I love you?"

"I'm glad you love me lately," Elita replied and then got busy fixing a sack lunch for their daughter.

"Mom, we're making Christmas decorations in art class today, and I don't want to be late."

Elita put the lunch in with Joy's books. "What is this?" She pulled an envelope from the backpack.

"Oh, just something the teacher wants the parents to read," Joy said as she slipped out the door.

Elita read the note and handed it to her husband. "I can't believe this."

"The school will be closing January 1," David read aloud. "The building has been sold!"

"I don't understand what's going on around here. Who is buying up all the properties in this area, and why all the secrecy?" Sparks flew from Elita's Hispanic eyes. "I'm going downstairs to knead some dough or something!"

David followed her from their apartment. He turned the sign in the General Store window to read "OPEN" and unlocked the door.

Over at the lunch counter, Elita had retrieved a large metal bowl from the commercial fridge, sprinkled flour onto the counter, and began to work her frustrations out on a large lump of risen dough. "Who would want to buy out this town? I know of several buildings on this street that recently sold, and at least a dozen families have moved away. There won't be anyone left if this keeps up."

David settled at the counter and thought about all of the rumors that had been circulating: speculations of some evil corporate taking over, a secret bio-laboratory, or maybe a drug cartel was setting up a nefarious money laundering operation.

Elita dropped the pummeled lump of dough back into the metal bowl.

"Feel better now?" David grinned.

"Actually, I do." She covered the bowl with cheesecloth and left it to rise on the counter.

David rose from the stool and made his way to the heavy tapestry curtains that hung in the doorway of the storage room. "I'll be working on the books."

In the storage room, David booted up his computer and settled down at his plywood desk to go over the store inventory and reconcile the recent discrepancies. A lot of merchandise had gone missing lately, mostly small items like candy bars, canned goods, and batteries, but the losses added up.

An hour later, the smell of fresh-baked bread enticed David from the back room.

His wife was behind the lunch counter cutting into a warm loaf. David was just about to talk her out of a slice when the sleigh bells on the front door of the General Store jingled. He looked up to see Alvaro Garcia saunter through the door with Lola Mendoza hanging on his arm. Garcia's motley minions followed close behind.

Lola's dark eyes briefly swept the room and then she fixed her gaze upon the display cabinet near the register.

David kept a watchful eye on the group in the convex mirror. They fanned out and fingered merchandise as they perused the store.

Miss Mendoza slammed her palm on the service bell at the counter. "Hola, hola! Can I get some service over here?"

David hurried over and nearly choked on her musky perfume. "What can I do for you?"

She tossed back her thick black mane of hair. "Jewelry! What do you think?"

"Anything in particular?" David patiently unlocked the display case, and Lola tapped a long red nail on the glass countertop. He reached inside and pointed to an ornate coral and turquoise bracelet. "This one?"

"No, no, estupido! I'm talkin' about that big fat necklace next to that."

David removed a massive silver and turquoise squash blossom and handed it to Lola. He stood patiently as she inspected the heavy piece of jewelry.

Lola snapped her fingers at her man to summon Alvaro Garcia who rushed over and dutifully fastened the clasp. She admired her reflection in a nearby mirror for a few seconds as she fondled the stones that hung near her cleavage. "Cuantos?"

"This is authentic Native American jewelry made from the finest Bisbee Blue," David explained.

"You talk like a commercial," Lola snarled.

"Mi mujera asked you a simple question, Gringo," Alvaro Garcia hissed.

"It retails for forty-nine hundred."

Lola threw her head back and laughed. "This thing? Chafa!" She snapped her fingers again, and Alvaro unfastened the clasp and tossed the necklace back across the counter.

David could not let the slight pass. "All our jewelry is certified by the Indian Arts and Crafts Board. Every piece is authentic and of premium craftsmanship. Definitely not chafa." David put the necklace back in its place and locked the counter display cabinet. "Will there be anything else?"

Lola waved her hand dismissively, rattled off a couple Spanish insults, and stormed outside to wait on the porch.

Alvaro Garcia leaned his skinny frame against a post and glared at David. He slid a buck knife from a scabbard on his belt and began to clean his fingernails. "She doesn't like you, Gringo." Garcia wiped the blade on his red leather vest and returned the knife to its place. "What are we going to do about that?"

"You can always take your business elsewhere," David said.

Garcia's eyes turned black and menacing. "Yo hombres! Senor merchant suggests we find another store to shop at."

Edwardo Romaseco approached. He leaned his sweaty girth across the countertop and sneered at David. Behind him, the short one they called Moppy began to laugh.

Garcia raised his hand. "Take it easy hombres. I'm sure we can find a civilized way to work out our differences." He pulled a huge roll of cash from his pocket. He peeled off five one-thousand-dollar bills and said, "I'll take the necklace. Keep the change."

David wrapped the squash blossom in a box and rang up the sale.

"We are through here for now, Gringo." Garcia flashed a crooked smile as they headed for the door. "But we will be back."

The room grew quiet, except for the ceiling fan that squeaked overhead.

Seconds passed before Elita spoke. "David, I've got one of my bad feelings."

Chapter 6

Tucson, Arizona
Monday, January 1ˢᵗ

By 11:00 a.m., Monday, the moving truck had come and gone. The sunlight pouring through the windows had taken away the morning chill. Paige stood among stacks of moving boxes filled with personal items from their Manhattan residence. Most of their furnishings had been sold along with the Tribeca penthouse apartment, and the new furniture had arrived yesterday. All modern minimalist, the living room, dining set, and bedroom furnishings were well suited for the sprawling Southwestern estate.

Paige pushed up the sleeves of her old sweatshirt and went to work trying to make the place feel like a home.

"Mom, I'm hungry." Connor stood in the doorway, his wet swimming trunks dripping.

"Where's your towel?"

"Out by the pool," he said. "Can we go get some burgers or something?"

Paige glanced at a clock on the mantel. "I completely forgot about lunch. Maybe later we'll go to the store. In the meantime, let's see what we can find."

She followed Connor into the kitchen and opened the commercial-grade refrigerator. Aside from condiments, there was a pat of butter, a nearly empty milk carton, and some restaurant leftovers destined for the trash can.

"I know!" Connor said. "There's a can of Spaghetti-O's that came in the bag of groceries that Uncle David and Aunt Elita gave us."

"That'll have to do." Paige found the can in the cupboard, popped the tab, and emptied it into a microwavable bowl. "Are you enjoying the pool?" she asked as they waited for the meal to heat.

Connor shrugged. "It gets kind of boring after a while. When can we go back to Hope Springs for a visit?"

The microwave beeped. Paige gave the spaghetti a stir and placed it on the counter in front of her teenage son. "I miss them all too. Are you making any friends at school?"

The door chimes rang. "Who could that be?" Paige wondered aloud. She hurried from the kitchen, dodging packing material as she went.

Paige opened the iron-clad doors to see two women with a couple teenage girls. "Can I help you?"

An attractive blonde wearing a tennis outfit stepped across the threshold and said, "We're the welcome wagon, Darling!" The woman, followed by her entourage, breezed past Paige. "Where are my manners? I'm Jolene Thorne, and this little beauty is Bella, my clone."

"Stop it, Mom!" The pretty blonde teen gave her mother an exaggerated eye roll. "That's so embarrassing."

Jolene motioned to the women beside her. "This is Ellie and her daughter, May."

Paige suddenly felt awkward in her oversized sweatshirt and ripped jeans. "It's nice to meet you. I'm…"

Jolene interrupted. "Darling, that handsome man of yours has told me all about you. My husband is the head of the economics department where Brody works."

The woman named Ellie peeked from behind a large gift basket that she held, "We understand that you love to cook, so we picked up some special spices at our local gourmet shop."

"I would absolutely adore taking a peek at your kitchen, if it's not too much trouble," Jolene interjected.

"Of course. Please excuse the mess." Paige led her visitors through the maze of moving boxes, past the home office, and into the open-concept family room and kitchen.

Paige introduced her son who was sitting at the counter in his swim trunks.

The two girls giggled and exchanged whispers as Jolene gushed over Connor's red hair. "It's fabulous, just like your mother's," she cooed and turned her attention to his bowl. "What delicious culinary dish has your gourmet mom prepared for you?"

When Connor told her, Jolene's mouth froze in a plastic smile. "Oh, well, I'm sure your mom has been very busy."

"That's right." Paige began to feel annoyed. She had navigated around snobby women all her life. Jolene was the type who probed for weakness and could even make a complement sting. "Ladies, thank you for your visit and these thoughtful gifts. As you can see, I have a lot of unpacking to do."

"Yes, Darling, of course," Jolene said as they were escorted to the door. "Oh, I almost forgot the main reason I came by! We're throwing a little dinner party for my husband's birthday next Friday. I wanted to personally invite you and your family." Jolene slipped an envelope from her purse and handed it to Paige. "All of Brody's colleagues will be there."

Tucson, Arizona
Friday, January 12th

Brody drove his brand-new Mercedes past a long string of vehicles that were parked along the yucca-lined driveway.

"Look at all these cars," Paige said to her husband. "Maybe we should park here and walk."

"Relax. The invitation says that valet parking will be provided."

Paige glanced at her son who was in the back seat drawing on his sketch pad. "Connor, did you bring a jacket? There is going to be fireworks later in the evening."

Just over a series of outcroppings, a sprawling Southwestern ranch home came into view. They passed beneath a rustic entrance gate that was fashioned from massive logs and native stone. Across the top of the gate, words were burned into a sign that read "Welcome to Hacienda del Sol."

They stopped behind a string of cars idling near a pergola. After receiving a valet ticket, Brody and his family were directed inside for a warm welcome to Hacienda del Sol.

Paige and Brody were each offered a glass of champagne from a silver tray, and Connor was invited to join the children and teens who gathered in the basement for supervised fun and games.

"Go on Connor," Brody said. "You'll have fun."

At the top of the basement stairs, the boy looked back anxiously and then made his descent.

"That boy needs to man up," Brody said under his breath.

The irony of the statement was not lost on Paige. Even Zeke had noted Connor's serious nature when he nicknamed him "Little Man."

With champagne flute in hand, Brody escorted his wife into a cavernous grand room with massive exposed beams. Several dozen people milled about in their formal attire. Jolene spotted them and sashayed over in a body-con lavender dress. "Marvelous to see you both! I'm so glad you could make it."

Brody smiled and said, "You have a very beautiful place."

Paige fingered the single strand of pearls around her neck and echoed her husband's compliment. "Yes, it's very lovely."

"I like to think of Hacienda del Sol as our little piece of paradise." Jolene leaned close to Paige, engulfing her in a cloud of expensive perfume. "My husband has just been dying to meet you." She motioned to a pudgy man with a thinning crown. "Dear, come meet Brody's darling wife."

"Brody, you didn't tell me what a gorgeous creature you married. I don't blame you for keeping her a secret."

Brody made the introduction. "Paige, this is my boss, Gavin Thorne. He is the head of the University of Arizona Economics Department."

Jolene, who was looking over Paige's shoulder, waved at another guest. "Excuse me Darling," she said as she hurried off to coo over another guest.

Paige stood beside her husband, who was busy talking about university business with his boss. She glanced around the room full of strangers and was just about to wander off when a man wearing a clerical collar approached.

"I saw you from across the room, and something told me that you are newcomer to our fair community." His warmth was disarming.

Paige returned the smile. "We're still settling in."

Their host cued in. "Let me introduce you both to our local holy man," Gavin said. "Brody and Paige Hays, I'd like you to meet Max Nellaf."

"Yes, of course." Max reached out and shook Brody's hand. "You're the new university recruit that I've been hearing so much about. Nice to finely meet you and your lovely bride."

Gavin slapped Max on the back and said, "If you want to know anything about God, Doctor Nellaf is a theological

Rhodes Scholar."

"I won't hold that against you, Father." Brody teased as their host wandered off.

"Don't let the collar fool you. My parishioners call me Reverend." Max laughed. "So how are they treating you over at the ivory tower?"

"No complaints so far," Brody said.

"Let me know if they give you any problems." Nellaf ran a finger down his neatly trimmed goatee and winked. "I know all their secrets."

A formal-looking butler announced that dinner was being served in the dining tent, and as they moved along with the crowd, Max engaged the couple in interesting conversations. He listened attentively and spoke with the ease and charm of an old friend.

"I'd love to hear about your church," Paige said as they entered the party tent.

A smile spread across the man's pleasant face. "My favorite subject! It's called the Memorial Interfaith Assembly, MIA for short." The Reverend paused to make eye contact with the couple. "If you don't already have a church home, I'd like to invite you to come visit."

Paige squeezed her husband's hand. "That would be nice, wouldn't it?"

Spotting his coworkers, Brody said, "I believe that's our table. It was very nice to meet you, Max. Maybe we'll give your church a try."

Paige followed her husband to a linen-covered table,

adorned with crystal and bone china settings. Like a perfect gentleman, he offered her a seat and made introductions. A few social niceties were exchanged, but soon Paige again found herself excluded from the conversations. *It's going to be a long evening,* she thought as her mind began to wander.

The wait staff delivered plates of honey-glazed pork, new potatoes, and broccoli to the guests. Paige asked a silent blessing and quietly ate her meal.

Finally, after the dessert plates were cleared and the coffee poured, their host rose from his seat. Gavin tapped a butter knife on his crystal goblet and said, "May I have everyone's attention please? Many of you know that it has become a tradition to cap my birthday with fireworks. Please join us on the veranda for after-dinner libations and pyrotechnic fanfare!"

Everyone cheered for their host, and they all went outside into the chilly winter air to wait beneath the brilliant canopy of stars.

A group of kids arrived, and Paige looked for Connor among the crowd. Her heart sank when she saw him standing alone. She hurried over, and said, "Hey, let's watch the fireworks together."

Overhead, the sky burst forth in an ostentatious display of color.

Connor shrugged, and said, "Mom, can we go home now?"

Paige spotted Jolene's daughter, Bella, standing among a cabal of other girls. Their laughing faces were softly lit by the glow of a cellphone.

Seconds later, Connor received a text message, and they all looked his way.

Paige snatched her son's cellphone.

"Mom, don't!"

She read the text captioned, "What a looozer!" Paige opened a video clip and was horrified to see Connor standing shyly on the edge of a group of teens. A boy approached from behind. He pulled Connor's pants down to his ankles, and all the kids roared with laughter.

As the mean girls disappeared into the crowd, the humiliation on Connor's face raised something fierce inside of Paige.

⬳⬳⬳

New York City
Saturday, January 20th

Katrina arose early to the smell of brewing coffee. She padded to the window of her Morningside Heights apartment and threw open the curtains allowing light to flood the room.

The skiff of snow that had fallen yesterday had already melted, and the temperatures were slated to be in the mid-fifties. *Perfect time for a brisk run through Central Park,* Katrina thought. She dressed in her thermal running togs, scraped her hair into a ponytail, and followed the scent of coffee into the kitchen.

Katrina poured herself a cup of black coffee and reread the letter that had arrived yesterday. *What a relief it is to know that Brody survived the tsunami, and that Paige and their son, Connor, are doing well.* The news buoyed Katrina and lifted the burden of guilt she had carried all these months. She made a mental note to send Paige a note of thanks, grabbed her ball cap, and headed out the door.

It is shaping up to be a wonderful day. Katrina stepped onto into the elevator and nodded politely to a man with wispy red hair. The stranger pulled a red ballpoint pen from his pocket and pointed it at Katrina.

When the elevator doors opened, she burst into the lobby looking for the friendly face of Floyd, the building's security officer. Not seeing him, she hurried from the building.

Trying to put the strange encounter out of her mind, Katrina began her usual route to Central Park. She cut through Morningside Park at a brisk pace and fell in behind a cluster of track students from Columbia University. By the time she reached Frederic Douglas Circle, Katrina had put the threatening incident in the elevator out her thoughts.

Near the blockhouse in Central Park, Katrina stopped, stretched, and then resumed her usual weekend run on the six-mile trail. The park had been cleaned up since the tsunami, but she still recalled what it had looked like. Uprooted trees and shrubs had been washed away by the fierce waters. The Central Park Conservatory had generously replaced trees and shrubs, and philanthropic funds had been raised to repair many of the structures, but it wasn't quite the same.

Katrina tried to focus on the cheerful sound of birds and

the warm winter sun upon her shoulders as she ran. A few things had returned to normal: dog walkers, Columbia students, and fellow joggers, but nothing like the crowds that had frequented Central Park before the East Coast disaster.

Below Nutter's Battery, Katrina sprinted around Laser Rink and spotted a couple of skaters. She jogged past ballfields, tennis courts, and eerily quiet playgrounds.

A little farther down the trail, Katrina passed one of her favorite places, the Conservatory Gardens. There was a new fountain there, but it wouldn't be working until the threat of a winter freeze-up passed.

The dancing girl statue was gone, and it had been replaced by bronze waves. *Fitting,* Katrina thought.

At the wrought iron fence near the reservoir, Katrina spotted a woman sitting on a park bench. Her wild salt and pepper hair billowed in the winter breeze. The woman turned as Katrina approached and held up a piece of cardboard draped with Heishe necklaces. "Five dollars each," she said.

Katrina sprinted past, but something in the sound of that voice sent an involuntary shiver down Katrina's spine. Without responding, she continued her run.

In the center of the park, Katrina spotted some teenagers gathered near the Alice in Wonderland Statue. A tall African American kid called out, "Hey Lady, would you take a picture of us all together?"

When Katrina agreed, the teenager handed her his phone and scrambled over to pose with his friends.

A boy with short-cropped, brown hair and a pierced ear

crouched under one of the toad stools, and a couple of blondes who looked like sisters perched on top. A dark-haired beauty hugged the bronze figure of Alice in Wonderland, and a few feet away, a kid with a man bun leaned casually against the Mad Hatter. The African American teen took his place beside the dark-haired girl. "Okay, everybody," he yelled, and the group flashed their best selfie smiles.

"Ready?" Katrina positioned the phone and gasped as she looked at the screen. All the teenagers held red pens! The cellphone slipped through her fingers and hit the ground.

"Hey bitch, I paid good money for that!" The kid raced over to examine his iPhone. "Lucky for you, it's not broken!" Clicking their pens, the rest of the group climbed from the statue and began to form a circle around Katrina.

"Who put you up to this?" she demanded.

The African American boy kid jabbed his pen at Katrina and said, "I guess you're a marked woman."

The boy with the man bun chuckled. "Careful bro, you don't want to be charged with assault with a deadly ballpoint." The group of teenagers roared with laughter as Katrina made her escape. She hurried toward a shortcut known as the Rambles as their taunts echoed in her ears.

⸻

Kirby, Arizona
Wednesday, January 24th

David and Elita climbed the steps of the county courthouse. He opened the door for his bride and followed her inside. After going through security, they made their way to the office of the Clerk of the Court.

They stood at the desk, waiting while an officious-looking clerk punched vigorously on her keyboard and pretended not to notice them.

David cleared his throat. She looked over the top of her reading glasses and said, "Can I help you?"

"Yes, someone is buying up properties in and around Arroyo Seco," Elita said. "A couple of huge warehouses are being built just outside of town, and…"

David cut in. "We would like to look at the property deeds."

"Next door," the woman said and turned her attention back to the computer.

The handsome young man at the Office of the County Recorder was very helpful. "There's been a lot of activity down your way. It has been keeping me busy." He retrieved some files from the cabinet, laid them on the table for the couple, and lingered while they opened the files. "I've been curious. So, what's going?"

Surprised by the question, David looked up. "That's what we're here to find out."

"I don't think you'll find any answers here," the man said as he watched David thumbing through the files. "Alpha

& Omega Corporation is the name on all the deeds."

David shook his head as he studied the documents and title deeds. "The corporation has practically bought up the whole town and most of the land in between the town and Hope Springs."

"Right." The title clerk nodded eagerly. "So, do you think they're a shill?"

"Whoever it is has gone to great lengths to remain anonymous," David replied, "and I'd like to know why."

CHAPTER 7

New York City
Monday, February 5th

Katrina arrived early for the morning news briefing and joined the assignment editors at the UBC conference room, also known as the "nerve center" of the station. She made small talk around the long table, but her thoughts drifted elsewhere.

"Yo, Katrina, what planet did you fly to?"

She snapped to the present and forced a smile as Gar, her Field Media Specialist, plopped into the chair beside her.

"Suup with you?" he asked. "You look like you've been through a zombie apocalypse or something."

"It's not quite as bad as that," Katrina muttered.

"Well, I'm a pretty good listener." Gar unwrapped a candy bar and took a bite. Before Katrina could respond, the UBC News Director breezed into the room with her briefcase in hand.

"Good morning, everyone," Gloria Shiff chirped as she took her place near the head of the table. "I hope you're all rested and ready to work." Gloria pushed her purple glasses up her button nose and turned her attention to the Head Assignment Editor of the station. "Jeff, what do you have for us today?"

The thinned-boned man straightened a stack of papers, cleared his throat, and said, "We've got some interesting happenings."

"Wonderful!" Gloria glanced around the conference table. "Has anyone seen Richard this morning?"

As if on cue, Katrina's co-anchor, Richard Ross, waltzed into the room with a steaming cup of mocha. "Hold the drumroll everyone," he said.

"He's such a rooster," Gar whispered. "Hey Ross, what are those red marks around your mouth?" he jabbed. "Did someone finally smack you in the chops?"

"Very funny!" Richard whipped out his iPhone and examined the results of his latest cosmetic procedure.

Otto Benedict's blocky frame filled the doorway. He glanced at his watch and said, "Okay, people, we don't have all day, so give me some good news."

Gloria waited for her boss to take his seat at the head of the table and nodded to the Head Assignment Editor.

Jeff flipped through his clipboard, nervously cleared his throat, and began, "Dozens of dolphin carcasses have washed up on shorelines along the East Coast. The Outer Banks and Virginia Beach, mainly. The reasons are unclear. The carcasses are being tested for a virus known to affect dolphins, but scientists believe that the aftermath of the tsunami may have stressed the marine mammals. Also, as a sidebar, there's a religious fringe group who is claiming that this is some sort of divine sign."

Laughter rippled around the table. Gloria pursed her lips. "Let's focus, shall we?

"Alistair Dormin and the World Fortress Institute have convened a global round table to discuss the challenges of peace in the Middle East." Jeff paused briefly to consult his notes. "President Ira Corbin has announced an impromptu visit to Manhattan this week to laud the generosity of the international community during the rebuilding efforts."

"Let the political pandering begin," Gar mumbled under his breath.

Jeff cleared his throat. "The Signature Killer has resurfaced. His latest victim is a young woman named Janie Lamont. Like the others, a message was left at the scene, but authorities aren't releasing details."

"What an evil creep." Gar popped a Tic Tac into his mouth.

"Mr. Duran!" Otto Benedict growled, "You are on the UBC payroll as a Field Media Specialist, so spare us your editorial comments." The boss snapped his fingers signaling Jeff to continue.

"A private, non-denominational church group has organized relief efforts for NYC neighborhoods that are still without food and clean water since the tsunami." The Head Assignment Editor ran his index finger down the page. "The Manhattan Health District is investigating an outbreak of cholera." Jeff drew a breath, cleared his throat, and said,

"Lastly, there are several noteworthy community events to report. The Metropolitan Museum is having a patrons ball to celebrate the restoration of fine art that was damaged during the tsunami. The city animal shelter is hosting an adoption fair, and a group who call themselves Constitutionalists have organized a protest. They claim that our civil liberties are being systematically eroded to accommodate the advances of globalism. Governor Folgate has asked the National Guard to stand by in case violence erupts."

"I've read about Constitutionalists," Katrina interjected. "They advocate for limited government intrusion, but their protests have always been peaceful."

Mr. Benedict glowered at her from beneath his hooded eyelids. "Ms. Katz, it's commonly known that all rightwing groups like this promote dissension. That makes them enemies of the collective mindset that unifies us!" A murmur of agreement rippled around the conference table.

Katrina stared at her coworkers in amazement. *What about freedom of speech and the right to protest?* she thought. *Can't they see that such oppressive rhetoric is precisely why the Constitutionalists are marching?*

⸙

"Can you believe all those lemmings? They really kissed up to the big boss man." Gar shot his co-worker a grin as she climbed into the passenger seat of the WUBC news van. "By the way, Kat, welcome to the Otto Benedict hit-list club!"

"What do you mean?"

Gar affected his best Otto Benedict impersonation. "Rightwing groups who promote dissension are enemies of the collective mindset." He plugged an address into the navigation system and then looked over at Katrina. "Seriously though, it's obvious the man is gunning for us both. I mean, Mr. Botox gets all the plum assignments while you get fish kills, animal shelter adoptions, and a psycho killer."

"What has Benedict been doing to you?" Katrina asked.

"Remember when I told you about all those photojournalism publishing offers?" Gar asked. "Well, now, I'm getting doors slammed in my face. Just last week, three of my montages were scrapped because, and I quote, 'They showed a negative side of New York City's recovery efforts.'"

Katrina recalled all the recent stories that had been pulled from the lineup: A cholera outbreak in one of the poorer boroughs and the generous relief efforts of some church group. *It's true that information is being tightly controlled,* she thought. *The whole thing smacks of censorship.*

"So, how did you get in Otto-man's crosshairs?" Gar asked, and then he slapped his forehead. "Oh snap! I bet it's because of your interview with Alistair Dormin. The whole studio was buzzing about how you went off-script. But, man, I thought you rocked!"

"I was taught that a good journalist should remain objective and seek the truth," Katrina replied.

As they neared the Brooklyn Boerum Hill address where the Signature Killer's latest murder had occurred,

Katrina noted the impacts left by the tsunami and the signs of the great exodus that followed: abandoned brownstones, graffiti, and littered streets.

"You have arrived at your destination," the navigation system announced.

Gar pulled up to the curb in front of a brownstone apartment. He hopped from the UBC van, threw open the back doors, and began sorting through gear.

Katrina took a moment to look through her notes while the Field Media Specialist positioned his camera on the sidewalk. A few moments later, Gar rapped on the van window.

"Okay, let's roll! I want to get the brownstone door in the background, so I've set the frame in the middle."

Snowflakes fluttered from the grey sky as Katrina climbed the stairs and waited for the signal to begin.

A rusty Volkswagen idled slowly past, and the driver caught Katrina's eye. *That's the woman I saw in Central Park, the one selling Heishe necklaces!*

"Yo, Kat, daylight's burning!" Gar said as the woman sped away. "Where did your brain fly off to this time?"

"Sorry, I'm ready now." Gar gave the signal, and Katrina began. "In this quiet Brooklyn neighborhood, the Signature Killer has claimed his latest victim," she said somberly.

"Behind this door, the body of twenty-eight-year-old Janie Lamont was discovered by a relative. Just like a string of other recent murders, a unique signature was left at this crime scene. This is the trait that has caused the perpetrator to be nicknamed the Signature Killer.

Authorities are not releasing specific details, but Detective Arcolla, of the Brooklyn P.D., is asking anyone with information to contact him." She paused, "This is Katrina Katz reporting live for UBC."

"That's a wrap. You nailed it," Gar said.

Katrina sighed. "A thirty-second news piece seems like a shallow tribute to the life of a vibrant young woman."

"Sweet. Look what I found. It's an expensive one, too!" Gar scooped an object from the gutter and held it up like a trophy.

Katrina felt faint and her breathing quickened. Gar's grin vanished when he looked at her. "Hey, what's a matter with you? It's a red ball-point pen, not a bloody hatchet."

Katrina hurried to the news van and climbed into the passenger seat. Once there, she struggled to compose herself.

"So, what's going on?" Gar said after loading the camera gear. "Don't tell me you've developed some kind of ink phobia."

"If I told you, you would probably think I was crazy," she said as they headed to the next assignment.

"Not a chance! I already know you're nuts." He gave her a sideways glance. "Hey, Kat, remember, you're talking to your old pal, Gar. What have you got to lose?"

Katrina told her colleague about the series of strange events that began the morning of her most recent Central Park run. "Sometimes, when I arrive at work, there is a red pen sitting on my desk, and I didn't put there. A couple of times, while I'm driving, a stranger pulls up beside me and holds up a red pen. The other day at Whole Foods, a man tried to give me a red pen. He said that I dropped it. And now, that strange woman…"

Gar was unusually quiet.

"Say something!" she said.

"I could roll out one of my usual quips." His tone was serious. "But, I really don't think this is a joking matter. There's an old saying, 'Just because you're paranoid, doesn't mean you don't have enemies.'"

"Very funny!"

"Have you ever heard of gang stalking?"

"You've got to be kidding! That has been debunked as nothing more than the chatroom delusions of conspiracy wing-nuts."

"Yeah, yeah, I know, but think about it. It's a brilliant strategy for psychological warfare." Gar steered the van onto a one-way street. "Besides, I've never known you to make up stories. Let's face it, Kat, you just don't have that kind of imagination."

"I think I've just been insulted!"

"It's obvious that someone is trying to mess with your head." Gar pulled into the SPCA parking lot and turned off the engine. He looked at her. "So, who have you pissed off lately? Someone with resources. Someone who wields a massive amount of power!" Without waiting for an answer, Gar continued, "You should listen to this podcaster, Joel Sutherland. This guy has quite a following. He mostly deals with political and cultural stuff, but he recently did a cool episode about gang stalking, cyber stalking, and other stuff like that."

Joel Sutherland? Why is that name familiar? Katrina wondered.

"The Podcast is titled, 'Beyond the Fall,'" Gar added. "Check it out."

North Dakota
Wednesday, February 28th

"Wake up America!" Joel began his Podcast. "While you were sleeping, political opportunists used the assassination of President Thomas Atwood to push through gun-control legislation, thus weakening our Second Amendment rights. Citizens are now required to register all firearms or turn them in for money. Such government overreach would have horrified the founding fathers who penned the Bill of Rights as a safeguard against tyranny.

"While you were dreaming, our leaders ratified the Global Unity and Economic Recovery Treaty, known as GUERT. This massive wealth redistribution program not only compromises the economic strength of developed nations, but it poses a direct threat to the sovereignty of all. History teaches us that those who have been given power seldom relinquish it. In the three and a half years since GUERT was instituted, Alistair Dormin and the World Fortress Institute have garnered the support of a vast network of international powerbrokers. Sovereign nations have cast their crowns at Dormin's feet in exchange for the promise of prosperity and world peace. Where will it end?"

Joel paused for a moment to collect his troubled thoughts. Outside, snowflakes floated past his window.

"While you slumbered, the North American Coalition Treaty was ratified," he continued. "Despite claiming to protect and promote international freedom, the NAC mandates have compromised the safety and freedom of immigrants and Americans. Currently, all who travel across North American borders are required to receive a subdermal passport chip. Identity theft and murder are rampant. Pirated passport chips are sold on the black market to criminals.

"While America slept, political and social propaganda has soaked into the fabric of our society. Free thought is being replaced by a post-modern groupthink. We are being pummeled by cancel culture, woke messaging, and corporate virtue signaling.

"Education, healthcare, welfare, and social justice programs are cultivating compliance and dependence. We are being conditioned to accept unprecedented levels of social control. Corporations are now encouraged to track employee productivity and attendance by using microchip implants, and soon it will be required in schools for vaccination records.

"Is our quest for a manmade, global utopia leading us all over a precipice?

Arise and shine America! Wake up before it's too late!"

Joel ended his weekly Beyond the Fall Podcast and then posted the link on his Twitter account, @beyond_the_fall.

It didn't take long for comments to start rolling in from his thousands of loyal followers, but also from the rabid Twitter mobs.

Joel scrolled through the comments and froze when he read, "How is that delicious young wife of yours?" Despite blocking these Twitter snipers over and over, their offensive statements would resurface under different account names.

"You're up early," Coco said.

He turned to see his young bride standing in his office doorway.

She yawned and said, "How long have you been up?"

"Couldn't sleep," Joel said. "I've got a lot on my mind."

Coco ran fingers through her silky hair. "Anything you want to talk about?"

"Not really." Joel dreaded telling her about all the vile tweets.

"Guess what?" she said. "I checked my Gossamer Threads webpage, and I've made three sales!" Coco's brow furrowed. "What if I get so many orders that I can't fulfill them all?"

"First world problem." Joel looked at his delicate bride standing before him. "You should put on your robe."

"I thought you liked my baby-doll nightie." Coco approached her husband and began to rub his shoulders.

"Yes, I just thought you might be cold."

Coco smiled sublimely. "If you're worried about that, then you can always come back to bed and keep me warm."

Joel rose from his desk and took Coco in his arms. He kissed her, and she responded with a passion that sent shock-waves through his body. Joel pulled his wife closer and could feel her trembling. "You are so incredibly beautiful." He swept her up and carried her to their bedroom…

In the quiet afterglow, with Coco nestled in the crux of his arm, Joel considered his good fortune. Once, he had been a fugitive from the law with no hope for a future, and now as Coco's breath brushed softly across his chest, Joel felt invincible.

From the heap of clothing on the floor, Joel's iPhone began to vibrate.

Coco lifted her head.

"Shhh," Joel whispered. "Whoever it is will call back or leave a message." As he nuzzled Coco's neck, he smelled the faint woodsy aroma of her sage perfume.

From the other side of their small apartment, Coco's cellphone began to ring with a familiar tone. "That's your mom's ringtone!" she said. Coco rose and dashed into the living room to answer the call.

A minute later, Coco returned with a stunned look on her face. "Something bad has happened," she said and handed her phone to Joel.

Chapter 8

Delmont, North Dakota

Saturday, March 10th

Joel drove his Jeep through the streets of the small farming community of Delmont, North Dakota. Just past the granary, he turned left and slowed to a stop in front of the largest building in town. The Delmont Hotel had once been built to woo the railroad, but the old Burlington Northern Railroad ultimately chose a different route. For years, the old building languished like a jilted lover, until it was purchased and repurposed as a pancake house. By the time Joel entered the scene, his birth mother had inherited the building and turned it into a second-hand clothing store.

The street in front of Nora's Bargain Bin was jammed with cars.

"Wow!" Joel said as he maneuvered his jeep into a tight parking spot. "It looks like the whole town turned out for the wake."

Joel's wife shook her head. "I still can't believe that Gertie is gone. She always seemed so invincible."

"I know what you mean. She was a character for sure,"

Joel said. "Old Gertie was the closest thing I've ever had to a grandmother."

When they stepped from the jeep, Coco zipped up her puffer jacket. "Wow, that wind is icy."

Joel and Coco were just about to head up the porch stairs, when a florist van screeched to a stop behind them. A gangly teenager jumped out and threw open the side door of the delivery vehicle. "Hey man, if you're goin' in there, would you mind taking these flowers?"

When Joel agreed, the kid said, "Thanks man. Sorry for your loss." He hopped back into the van and sped away as the young couple made their way up a snow-packed trail. They walked across the porch and entered Nora's Bargain Bin.

"It looks different," Coco said.

To make room for Gertie's wake, all the racks of used clothing and household items had been pushed to the back of the old hotel lobby. The spacious room was now filled with people who had come to pay their respects.

There must be over a hundred people here, Joel thought as he placed the flower arrangement on the counter.

J. J. O'Shay hurried over and said, "Oh, you shouldn't have. How did you know that I just adore Day Lilies?"

"Bro, you're really not my type." Joel glanced around the room. "Looks like Gertie will be missed by a lot of folks."

"Either that or they turned out just to make sure that the old broad is really gone," O'Shay replied with a wink.

"You don't fool me," Coco said to the big man. "Everybody knows how much you loved Gertie."

"It has been way too quiet around here without that blue-haired biddy barking orders at me." The former circus clown pulled a tissue from his colorful hemp beanie and wiped a tear from his eye. "Guess I always figured that that old Norwegian was just too mean to die!"

"Where's Nora?" Joel asked.

J. J. cocked his head toward the kitchen. "She's been hanging out in there and cooking all morning, but I think that your mom just needed some space."

The young couple found Nora standing in front of the stove stirring a large pot of stew.

She turned as they approached, offered a faint smile, and said, "I'm so glad that you're here."

Joel put his arm around his birth mother's shoulder but offered no platitudes. He had learned from personal experience that, in times of sorrow, words did little to ease the pain of grief.

"What are you cooking?" Coco asked. "It sure smells delicious."

"I've been trying to make some of Gertie's Norwegian Lapskaus stew…" Nora suddenly began to cry. "It just doesn't taste right."

"Things won't ever be the same around here," Joel said. His thoughts flashed back to the tragic events that had altered the course of his own life.

The kitchen door cracked open, and J.J. O'Shay poked his head into the room. "Nora, there's a dude out here asking for you." A squat little man shoved past O'Shay and into the kitchen.

"Hey Cue Ball, where do you think you're going?" J. J. hollered.

"Ms. Meyers, I really apologize for the intrusion, especially at a time like this, but it's extremely important that I speak with you." He pulled a handkerchief from his pocket, dabbed his brow, and offered a limp handshake. "My name is Regis Letterbuck. As Gertrude Bell's attorney, I have been instructed to allocate her assets with speed."

"Can't you see we're in the middle of a freakin wake here?" O'Shay growled.

Letterbuck ignored him and pressed on. "Ms. Meyers, I understand that it's an emotional time; however, before I can submit the will for probate, I need to update the addresses of a few of the beneficiaries."

Coco leaned close to Joel and whispered, "Awkward."

"Nora, we'll be in the other room." Joel took Coco's hand, and they slipped quietly into the lobby, dragging J. J. with them.

The young couple made small talk with the folks who had come to pay their respects. An overall-clad farmer was saying, "You didn't want to get on Gertie's bad side." He laughed. "I called Gertie 'she who must be obeyed.' But, beneath it all, that woman had a heart of gold."

"Yeah, she was like an overly toasted marshmallow," another local interjected. "Crusty on the outside, but a big softy on the inside."

The manager of Delmont's bank said, "I'm really going to miss those Norwegian Fattigmann cookies that she delivered every Christmas."

A group of church ladies breezed into the room leaving a wake of perfume. Joel cleared his throat and leaned toward Coco. "I need to get some fresh air."

Outside on the porch, he checked his phone for recent activity from his podcast; #beyondthefall was trending on twitter. Comments were tweeted and retweeted thousands of times. Joel was scrolling through positive remarks when his eyes locked on an alarming post.

Joel's breathing quickened as reread the words. "I'm thirsty for a hot cup of Coco." *Could this be the same malicious troll that I have already blocked so many times?* Joel curled his fist in anger at the thought of anyone harassing Coco. *Now it's personal!*

New York City
Wednesday, March 21ˢᵗ

Feeling unusually exhausted, Katrina sat down at her desk. She popped the tab on her energy drink and began sorting her mail. A package had arrived that contained a new set of red pens. She took a photo with her iPhone and angrily tossed the box of pens into the trash. Then, she turned her attention to her voicemail. One message in particular caught her interest.

"This is Detective Arcola," the gruff voice said. "Give

me a call." There was no name on the caller ID, only a number.

Why now? Katrina wondered as she dialed the number. All her previous attempts to get a comment from the Brooklyn P.D. had been stonewalled.

Detective Arcola picked up on the fourth ring. "Thanks for returning my call, Ms. Katz."

"Of course," she replied. "What have you got for me?"

"Are you aware that the Signature Killer claimed another victim last night?"

"Yes," Katrina said, "a young woman named Jennifer Dunkirk from Chelsea. Just like the other murder scenes, a signature was left behind, but the details aren't being released."

"There have been some developments that may interest you."

"I'm listening."

"Okay, but this conversation is strictly deep background. Do I make myself clear?"

"Perfectly." In journalistic terms, deep background means that the information could be used, but only anonymously and without attribution of any kind. Katrina grabbed a pen and notepad. "Go on."

"Miss Dunkirk worked as a copy editor at Taft Publishing House, along with her roommate, Mazie Bell."

Katrina jotted down the information and waited for more. "Have you found any connection between the earlier victims?"

"That's a line of inquiry that needs to be followed." There was a long pause on the other end of the phone. "I have a daughter the same age as these victims. Those poor girls deserve justice."

"How can I help, Detective Arcola?" Katrina pressed. "What is it that you're not telling me?"

"I have been pulled off this case. In fact, I've been warned not to pursue further inquiries."

She could hear the frustration in Arcola's voice.

"Look, Ms. Katz, I'm throwing you a bone with some meat on it. Just follow the lead," he said and hung up.

Katrina was puzzled by the strange call. *No suspects had been named, so why is this investigation being hindered?* She looked up a number and dialed.

"Taft Publishing House. How may I direct your call?" a young man said.

"Mazie Bell please."

The switchboard operator rang the extension, and a woman picked up. "Copy Editing Department."

"This is Katrina Katz from UBC. I'd like to speak with Mazie Bell."

The woman gasped. "Oh my gosh, really? Mazie isn't here. I really shouldn't have answered her phone, but I've been so worried about her, since… I would be an absolute basket case if I found my roommate that way. I was at Mazie and Jen's apartment days before the murder happened. Poor Jen was showing off her new dress. One minute she was so happy, and the next..." The woman's voice broke with emotion.

"Do you know where I can reach Mazie?"

"Last I heard, she went to stay with her mom in Tribeca. Who could blame her? I wouldn't want to go back to that apartment."

"Do you have Mazie's phone number?"

"Oh, I'm not supposed to give that information out..."

"It's very important." Katrina bit her lip, and to her surprise, the woman blurted Mazie's contact information.

A moment later, Katrina shot Gar a text. "I've got a hot lead. Let's roll ASAP!"

Katrina took her usual place at the news desk. She kept a steady eye on the camera and waited as the lead-in voiceover was announced.

"Live from Studio One, at UBC headquarters in New York City, this is the six-o'clock news."

The camera pointed in her direction and began to blink. "This is Katrina Katz with tonight's lineup.

"A serial arsonist is targeting churches in the South." She paused as a video a clip played on the screen of an Arkansas investigator poking through the remains of a smoldering building.

Next, a clip was run of a geologist with the USGS Yellowstone Volcano Observatory saying that the crust of the Yellowstone Caldera was rising at an alarming rate.

Finally, the lead in for the scoop was played for the viewing audience. "I'll never forget the words that were written in Jennifer's blood on the wall. 'For Coco,'" Mazie Bell sobbed. "We've never met anyone named Coco!"

"The Signature Killer's calling card is finally revealed," Katrina said as the news camera shifted from her to the co-anchor.

"I'm Richard Ross. Newly instated Mexican President, Pirro Millan, promises to root out government corruption. The global drought continues, and Mega Church Pastor Max Nellaf weighs in on the two self-proclaimed prophets in Jerusalem." He looked directly at the camera, "These stories and more after this."

After a commercial break, the journalists elaborated on the rest of the evening lineup, and finally, it was a wrap. Katrina was just about to remove her earbuds when they crackled with the sound of Gloria Shiff's shrill voice.

"I don't recall clearing the piece about the Signature Killer," the News Director barked. "I want to see you in my office right now!"

Chapter 9

Tucson, Arizona

Sunday, April 1st

"I can't believe that I let you talk me into this," Brody complained as the Mercedes inched along behind a long line of slow-moving traffic.

"And I can't believe that you agreed to go to church with your family." Paige glanced in the back seat at Connor who gave his mom the thumbs up.

The Memorial Interfaith Assembly was perched atop a large plateau overlooking the city of Tucson. "It's a beautiful building," Paige marveled as they approached a massive white edifice that seemed to shimmer beneath the desert sun.

Brody followed the line of cars around the back to a vast open-air parking lot. They found a parking space about half a mile from the church.

Paige said, "We should have come earlier. I didn't wear proper walking shoes."

"According to the MIA webpage, they provide shuttles," Brody explained.

Connor pointed. "Here comes a bus now!"

Brody looked mildly annoyed as they boarded the shuttle. "This seems more like a theme park than a church," he grumbled as they disembarked near the side of the building.

The Hays family joined the pilgrimage, and they strolled together beneath a covered footpath.

"What a lovely spring morning," Paige said as they moved along the beautifully landscaped grounds. Joshua trees, fountain grass, and fiery desert coral nestled among carved sandstone structures that resembled Stonehenge.

In front of the sprawling edifice, they were met by greeters dressed in white robes and welcomed inside. Three double-glass doors etched with the trinity symbol opened automatically as people approached.

Paige gasped when she entered the vestibule. The black marble walls, ivory-colored pillars, and red carpeting was all meant to impress.

A tuxedo-clad usher handed them each a program. "Is this your first time here?"

"Yes," Brody replied. "Reverend Nellaf invited us to attend."

"Oh, well then, you are very special guests." He took their names and escorted them into a cavernous three-tiered sanctuary that more closely resembled a stadium or a concert hall than a church. The usher led them down the center row to some cordoned-off seats just below the stage. Once there, the man unfastened a thick velvet rope and invited them to sit in row that was reserved for special guests only. The ritual was repeated as other VIP guests began to arrive.

"This isn't what I expected," Brody said as he perused the program.

Paige looked over her shoulder as the sanctuary filled with congregants. "I had no idea there were so many Christians in Tucson."

"According to the program, visitors travel from all over the country to attend."

A countdown appeared on the large screens, and a team of musicians ambled onto the stage.

"Are you ready to celebrate?" The worship leader shouted into his microphone as a rousing song began. "Everyone, stand and clap your hands!"

The people launched to their feet and sang along with the words that appeared on the big screens. The music pulsed through the atmosphere, overpowering the voices of the congregation.

Connor remained seated and quietly turned the pages of his Bible. Brody poked his son. "Stand up and show some respect." The boy did as he was told.

Before long, the upbeat tempo of the songs shifted, and the music turned somber and reflective. Paige glanced at her maudlin son. "What's wrong, Honey?"

"Nothing," Connor replied. "It's just that minor keys always make people want to cry."

The song ended, but one of the musicians played a soothing melody on a harp as the congregation settled back in their seats.

The worship leader lifted the mic to his mouth. "Saints, I've been given a word from our Lord," he began. "There is a powerful anointing in the sanctuary this morning. The Lord has chosen a few select believers to give a special offering of $6,000! If you feel God's favor on you this morning, then rise up! Step out in faith and receive double from God's hand."

The congregation shouted, "Glory!" as an elderly woman struggled to her feet and made her way down the aisle. One by one, others soon followed and gathered on the stage where they were met by a team of ushers with portable credit-card processors at the ready. The worship leader uttered long-winded blessings upon all who came forward, and the music erupted into a triumphant song. The congregation stood to applaud the givers as they returned to their seats.

Church announcements were made, and the ushers stepped forward to collect the usual tithes. The lights dimmed for a moment of contemplative silence while the music team disappeared from the stage.

An air of expectancy filled the sanctuary. In the center of the stage, black silk curtains and then silver panels parted to reveal the Reverend Max Nellaf, clad in a red-silk clergy robe with a gold vestment. The people stood respectfully as the reverend walked onto the stage.

An ebony podium rose from the center of the stage floor, and Nellaf took his place there. "Welcome, precious saints!" Praise exploded through the sanctuary.

After a few seconds, the reverend instructed his congregation to be seated. "Dear ones, many of you have come here today bearing the true yoke of divine fellowship. Selflessly, you have submitted yourself to the covering of this fellowship. What is this yoke I speak of? It is a supernatural commission to be set apart for service and to be unified in common purpose and vision." He drew in a long breath. "This yoke will never be found among narrow-minded religious zealots, nor can it be discerned through endless scriptural debates. The true yoke of fellowship is realized in covenant and community. Beloved, with arms linked in purpose, we march toward a world redeemed from ignorance and division. Jesus discovered his divinity and pointed the way. Now, dear ones, we are seeing others realizing their divinity through leadership. Just like Jesus, Alistair Dormin is blazing a new path to a bright new day."

Paige felt a catch in the pit of her stomach as Reverend Nellaf wove snippets of scripture into his message. *Did I hear him right?* she wondered. *What did he say about Jesus?*

Brody seemed mesmerized, and even Connor was busy taking notes. *Lord, help my unbelief,* Paige prayed.

When the message was over, Nellaf pronounced a liturgical blessing over the congregation and slipped off the stage through the parted silk curtains. Pleasant music was piped through the speakers as the congregation made their way from the sanctuary.

"Well, this certainly wasn't what I expected," Brody said as he stood and nodded to the usher who had unfastened the velvet cord.

"What did you think, Connor?" Paige asked. She was

interrupted before he could reply.

"Mr. and Mrs. Hays," an usher said, "Reverend Nellaf has requested that your family join him for refreshments."

Brody glanced at his wife. "That sounds wonderful."

The usher unlocked a door beside the stage and led them down a long hallway. He opened another door and invited them into a spacious room with chandeliers and mirrored walls.

There a uniformed staff member greeted them personally. "Mr. and Mrs. Hays, may I interest you in a cappuccino or a latte?" He turned to their son and said, "We have fresh-squeezed orange juice, or soda. How does that sound?"

After taking orders, he directed the Hays family to a banquet table where dainty morsels were arranged around an elaborate ice sculpture of the world.

Trying to gauge his mood, Paige glanced at her teenage son. "Are you hungry? There is plenty to choose from here." She selected some finger food and settled at a table with her family.

"Darlings! Lovely to see you here." Jolene sashayed across the room in her tan silk suit and matching stiletto heels. "I was so thrilled when I heard that Max invited you to join us!" She air-kissed Paige, but made contact with Brody's cheek. "Oh dear, I left a smudge of lipstick on you." Jolene pulled a tissue from her handbag, licked it, and rubbed the spot of fuchsia from Brody's face. "There, that's better," she cooed.

Jolene turned to Paige. "You look simply adorable in your little spring dress."

The veiled slight flew right over Brody's head, but old social-survival instincts stirred inside of Paige. *Refuse to play the game,* she told herself.

"Where is your family?" Paige asked Jolene.

"Bella was at a sleepover last night, so Gavin had to sneak out of church early to pick her up. They'll just be green with envy when I tell them that you were here."

Connor was busy sketching something in his notebook when the waiter arrived with drinks in hand.

"Oh, those cappuccinos look so delicious. I'll have to order one for myself," Jolene gushed.

"Here, take mine," Brody said. "Would you like to join us?"

"I wouldn't want to intrude…"

"Nonsense." Brody rose and pulled out a chair as Max Nellaf entered the room. He made the rounds giving individual attention to each special guest. When Nellaf approached their table, Brody said, "I really enjoyed the sermon, Reverend."

"Please, call me 'Max.'" Nellaf clasped Brody's hand with a firm grip and shook it. "I recently learned that you and your lovely bride, Paige, are both Ivy League graduates. Yale and Harvard, I believe." A smile spread across the reverend's pleasant face. "It's not every day that I am privileged to visit with a man who served in the White House as an advisor to a president." He ran a finger down his neatly trimmed goatee and nodded. "Very impressive!"

"Yes, isn't it!" Jolene chimed in.

Nellaf turned his attention to Paige. "My dear, you look lovely." His gaze shifted to Connor. "Young man, I understand that you are a gifted violinist and that you studied at the prestigious Julliard School. Maybe one day soon you will agree to perform for our congregation." It was more of a statement than a question.

Connor looked up from his notepad but didn't respond.

"Don't be rude, Son!" Brody said. Turning to the reverend, he added, "I'm sure that he would be honored."

Nellaf watched Connor drawing in his sketch pad. "I see that you're an artist too. Mind if I take a peek?" The reverend studied a pencil drawing of a dark and brooding sky. "I see you've drawn eyes in the clouds. How clever."

Connor looked at the man and said, "That's right, Reverend Nellaf. Because God sees everything."

"It's been delightful, and I hope to see you next Sunday," Nellaf said as he moved on.

Paige kept an eye on the reverend as he continued making his rounds. He knows a lot about my family. *But what do we really know about Max Nellaf?*

━━⊶⊷━━

Arroyo Seco, Arizona
Monday, April 23rd

Ready to begin his usual morning routine, David descended the apartment stairs. When he opened the door to the General Store, he froze. Something wasn't right. The air was cold. *Maybe the furnace finally gave out,* he thought as he reached for the light switch.

The fluorescent lights flickered on, and David scanned the store. At first glance, everything seemed in order, but then he realized that the front door was wide open.

David hurried to the front of the General Store, and that's when he noticed that the glass display case near the register was empty.

After instructing Elita and Joy to stay in their apartment, David phoned Sherriff Hodges. Next, he grabbed a hammer from the hardware section and did a quick sweep of the store before turning his attention to the deadbolt on the front door. It looked like a hacksaw had been used on it.

How did we sleep through it? David shuddered at the thought of what could have happened if the robbery had been interrupted.

Twenty minutes later, a cruiser pulled up in front with lights strobing. The sheriff climbed from the vehicle and lumbered inside. He looked around, pushed up the brim of his cowboy hat, and said, "Yup, looks like you've had a break-in."

Brilliant deductive reasoning, David thought. "Did you notice they used a glasscutter to get into the display case?

Our Native American jewelry is gone, about $85,000 worth."

"Got any idea who did this?" Hodges asked.

Without hesitation, David said, "I suspect Garcia and his boys."

The sheriff nodded. "That's probably a pretty good guess. Hope you've got insurance 'cause the chances of recovering any of these stolen items are slim to none."

David was beginning to get annoyed. "Especially if you don't plan on apprehending any suspects."

"Word is the cartel is spooked. Garcia and his boys are probably in Wyoming by now."

"What's going on?"

"Where have you been?" Hodges said as he leaned over to examine the door lock. "Alistair Dormin has ordered troops into Mexico to clean up government corruption. The cartel has scattered like a bunch of cockroaches when someone turns on the lights."

The sound of helicopters met their ears, and the men stepped outside to see a fleet of military choppers. "The cavalry has arrived," Hodges chuckled. "It's a mighty bad day to be a corrupt Mexican official."

The porch began to vibrate, and a line of U.S. military vehicles rumbled onto the main street of Arroyo Seco. Flags sporting the emblem of the World Fortress Institute fluttered in the breeze as the tanks rolled past.

The sight unsettled David. *How can one man amass the power to command the military forces of the United States of*

America and have them fly the flag of a Non-Governmental Organization? he wondered.

Chapter 10

New York City
Saturday, May 26th

The apartment intercom buzzed, and Katrina answered on the first ring.

"Wow, I didn't know you lived in such a swanky neighborhood," Gar said. "Do you really want to mingle with us peons?"

"I'll be right down." Katrina slipped on a light jacket and reached for her work satchel. It wasn't on the bench near the entryway where she usually placed it. Katrina dashed around her Morningside Heights apartment searching for her satchel and finally found it on the kitchen floor leaning against the breakfast counter. *I'm sure it was on the entryway bench last night,* she thought. Katrina retraced her steps. She came home exhausted and went straight to bed without going into the kitchen. An alarming thought passed through her mind. *Was someone in my apartment?*

The buzzer rang again. "Coming," she said and hurried out the door.

Gar was pacing in the lobby when Katrina stepped off the elevator.

"It's about time!" he grumbled as they walked outside. "I didn't want to spend another second with that creepy door-man of yours. He's a real lurch!"

"He's new," Katrina replied, still troubled about her satchel.

They took a shortcut through Morningside Park and walked together in silence for a while. Katrina could feel Gar staring at her, and she gave him a sideways glance.

He popped a Tic Tac into his mouth and asked, "What's got you so introspective? Is Otto Benedict being toad again?"

"That's a good guess," Katrina said. "Since the last executive meeting, all of my news packages must now be personally approved by Otto Benedict."

"Tightening the old muzzle, eh?" Gar chuckled. "Just don't let them bring out the choke chain and jerk you around. You're nobody's b…"

"Enough with the dog metaphors," Katrina cut in.

Gar rubbed his soul patch. "Seriously though, are you okay? You're looking a bit green around the gills these days."

"From dog to fish imagery? Gar, you'd better quit while you're ahead."

They approached the Cathedral Parkway Subway station, descended the stairs, and moved through the turnstiles. They waited for the subway with the rest of the commuters.

Once on board, she settled onto the hard plastic seat. As the train pulled away, Katrina thought she caught a glimpse of the same mysterious Heishe woman. "Gar, did you notice that woman standing on the landing? Kind of heavy with wild salt and pepper hair?"

"Can't say that I did," he replied, without looking up from his iPhone. "Why?"

"Just somebody I keep seeing," Katrina said as they entered the tunnel.

Gar looked at her. "The same biddy you saw at Boreum Hill? You should get a photo because she might be part of this gang-stalking thing." He offered Katrina a Tic Tac and then shook another one out for himself. "Speaking of pics, I would love to capture the look on Benedict's mug when you crack the Signature Killer case."

Crack the case? Katrina thought as the subway rattled down the tracks. "These friends of yours must really think they've got something. Tell me more about them."

"Spud and Tiki created a viral podcast known as the Dark Muse, mostly true crime and stuff, but they also dabble in a bit of conspiracy."

"Are those their real names?"

Gar shrugged. "I have no idea, but it suits them. Anyway, lately, they've been focused on the Signature Killer. You know, reaching out to family and friends of the victims. They've been creating quite a buzz. Tiki believes that she has uncovered a common link between the murders..." Gar's eyes widened. "Yo, Kat, your nose is bleeding!"

She fumbled for a tissue in her satchel and pressed it against her nose.

Gar gave his friend a sympathetic look. "Maybe you should tilt your head back or something."

"If your friends found a connection, shouldn't they be telling this to a homicide detective?" Katrina asked.

"They tried, but the Popo looks down on citizen sleuths and crime podcasters. Now they won't even take their calls."

Katrina's thoughts drifted to Detective Arcola, and she wondered why the case wasn't even being investigated. She leaned back in her seat and stared at the subway ceiling. When her nosebleed finally stopped, she said, "You realize that I could lose my job for looking into the Signature Killer case?"

"Yeah, risky, I know." Gar flashed a grin. "That's what makes the whole thing such an adventure."

"Next stop: Bowery," a monotone voice announced. The train slowed and rattled to a halt. The door slid open, and they moved with the crowd to the Bowery & Delancy Street exit. They headed West on Delancy.

"It has been ages since I've been on the Lower East Side," Katrina said as they turned right on Chrystie Street.

"Really? You've been living a sheltered life. The best Chinese and Italian food in the city is found here."

They strolled through the bustling neighborhood between graffiti-covered buildings, Asian eateries, and piles of garbage. A tiny woman hurried past with her loaded shopping cart in tow. On the other side of the road, there was a long, narrow, tree-lined park. Katrina spotted a homeless person sleeping on a park bench.

"Here we are." Gar stopped at an apartment building with scaffolding out front. "Looks like their landlord is finally getting around to repairing the water damage. About time!"

After they were buzzed into a small lobby, Katrina followed her friend up two flights of stairs.

He knocked on the door, and a chocolate-skinned beauty, wearing a colorful turban, let them in. "I'm Tiki. Welcome to our humble abode." She directed Katrina to an uber-modern couch. "Can I get you anything? Coffee, tea, vodka maybe?"

"A cup of black coffee would be great." Katrina stifled a yawn and made a mental note to pick up some energy drinks on the way home.

"Do you happen to have any IPA in the fridge?" Gar asked as he followed Tiki into her tiny kitchenette.

Katrina looked around the modest living room. It had been freshly painted, but still it carried the faint odor of mildew.

Tiki returned with a tray of milk, sugar, and coffee mugs. She placed it on the table in front of Katrina.

Gar unscrewed a bottle cap and took a swig of beer. "So, Tiki, where's the old Spud Meister?"

"He just ran over to the corner convenience store for some bagels and cream cheese."

"I like your tribal décor," Katrina said and then pointed to a particular piece of art. "That painting looks just like you."

Tiki laughed showing a perfect rack of teeth. "Compliments of TJ Maxx."

The door opened, and a young man entered with a bag that he dropped onto the coffee table.

"This is the ugly dude I was telling you about," Gar said and then introduced him to Katrina.

Spud wiped a hand on his t-shirt and shook her hand. "Thanks for coming."

Katrina sat across from the young man, with his ball cap on backward, baggy low-riding jeans, and a scruffy beard. She couldn't decide if he was a wigger or a redneck.

Gar landed a playful punch on Spud's arm, and they began to wrestle.

"Behave yourselves, boys!" Tiki yelled. "We've got some serious business here."

Katrina seized the opportunity. "Yes, I understand you've been looking into the Signature Killer case?"

"That's right." Tiki retrieved her laptop from the coffee table and booted it up. "How much has Gar has told you?"

"Only that you have talked with people who knew the murder victims, and you found a link."

"Wait 'til you see this." Tiki's long nails flew across the keyboard. "All of the victims were found wearing a designer outfit that they had each purchased online."

"A lot of people shop online these days. That could be a coincidence," Katrina said carefully.

"That's what I thought at first," Tiki said, "but then I realized that all of these dresses were purchased from the same designer."

Katrina was stunned. "Are you positive?"

Spud looked at his girlfriend and said, "Reel it in Bae."

Tiki pulled up the website and turned her screen toward Katrina. "All of these poor girls were murdered while wearing one-of-a-kind creations with the label Gossamer Threads."

Katrina was stunned by what she was learning. "You've got my attention."

"There's more." Tiki scrolled down the webpage and pointed to the name of the designer.

A chill snaked down Katrina's spine when she read the name: Coco Sutherland.

North Dakota

Monday, May 28th

Joel leaned against the kitchen sink, scrolled through his email, and stopped to read one. "You got to be kidding!" he said.

Coco looked up from her bowl of cereal. "What?"

"Remember when the Patriot Review was de-monetized because they featured my articles? Well, now the 'thought police' want to de-platform my Beyond the Fall podcast."

Coco poked at the Cheerios in her bowl and a tear rolled down her cheek.

Joel hurried to her side. "Hey, it's no big deal! Really, it doesn't matter…" He looked into the deep pool of her sad eyes and said, "Talk to me."

"I can't believe what is happening to us." Coco cried.

"Your career is being destroyed, and I can't even go outside anymore without worrying that someone has seen those skanky images of me that are circulating all over the Internet."

Joel wrapped his arms around his bride and longed to tell her that everything was going to be all right, but he knew that once photos reached the net, they were almost impossible to reel back in.

Coco stared out the kitchen window, past a flowering lilac bush. "That creep could be outside watching us right now."

Frustration and guilt came crashing down on Joel. *If only I'd been more careful,* he thought. The malicious troll had hacked into his webcam and used it to take photos of Coco.

"We can't let that bottom feeder steal our freedom," Joel said. "We need to get out of here—maybe take in a movie—anything to get out of this little apartment."

Coco fingered the amber cross that hung around her neck. "You're right," she agreed, "but let's go check out the Sheepherder Wagon. We haven't been there since Gertie left it to us."

Joel kissed tears from his bride's cheeks. "That's my girl. Why don't you go get ready?"

As she headed for the bedroom, Coco's phone rang. "Would you get that for me?"

He answered on the third ring. "Gossamer Threads. How may I direct your call?"

"This is Katrina Katz. I'm calling for Coco Sutherland."

"She's busy right now. May I take a message?" Joel said, trying to sound officious.

"This is a personal matter. I need her to phone me as soon as possible. It's extremely important."

An ominous feeling rose inside Joel. "I am her husband, Joel. I would like to know what this is about."

There was a pause on the other end of the line. "I'm developing a story, and I'm trying to run down a lead."

"Wait—Katrina Katz from UBC news?"

"Yes, I've been chasing down some leads regarding the Signature Killer, and Coco's name recently came up."

"The serial killer? I doubt if she can help."

"Your wife's name was written on the victims' walls," Katrina said.

"But Coco has never even been to the East Coast," Joel scoffed.

"Mr. Sutherland, there's more. All the murdered women were found wearing one of your wife's fashion creations."

Joel felt the blood drain from his head. "What? Are you sure?"

"Gossamer Threads, by Coco," Katrina said. "Your wife's name was written on the walls in the victims' own blood."

"What's being done about this?"

"Law enforcement says they are pursuing inquiries, but I have reason to believe that someone is hindering the investigation. Look, I'm going to sit on this story for a while to give the authorities a chance to follow through. In the meantime, I thought you should be aware of the situation." After a long pause, Katrina asked. "Does your wife have any enemies?"

Joel's fingers gripped the phone so hard that they began to throb. "We've been dealing with a cyber stalker, but this… " His words trailed off.

"Maybe I can help. I want you to gather all your information and send it to me ASAP. Every detail matters, no matter how small. You can reach me at this number."

"Okay."

"And one more thing, Mr. Sutherland," Katrina said. "Since the killer seems to be obsessed with your wife it might be prudent to find someplace safe and lie low for awhile."

When Coco emerged from the bedroom, Joel said, "There has been a change of plans. I need you to pack some clothes."

"Why?" she asked.

As calmly as he could, Joel said, "I'll explain on the way."

Chapter 11

New York City
Monday, June 4th

Katrina could hardly believe her eyes as she thumbed through thirteen pages of new corporate guidelines being implemented by the United Broadcast Corporation. "All news packets and opinion pieces must be reviewed prior to airing and must conform with the parameters outlined by the World Fortress Institute," read a particularly egregious part of the guidelines.

As a trained investigative journalist, Katrina found these new policies offensive. *How can I reconcile these mandates with the ethical journalistic standards I learned at Cornell University?* she wondered. *What about objectivity, impartiality, or even accountability?* Tightly scripted propaganda was rapidly encroaching on the tenets of free speech.

Katrina thought about her grandmother's stories about the political censorship that foreshadowed the despots, first in Russia and then later in Nazi Germany.

Alistair Dormin's political allies were in place around the globe and willing to promote his agenda. The man seemed unstoppable as evidenced by his recent military campaign in Mexico.

While everyone was celebrating a planet being systematically cleansed of corruption, and Dormin was neatly positioned to become the chairman of the world, no one seemed to notice that it all signaled the end of national identities and possibly freedom. A chill ran down Katrina's spine.

She glanced at her watch. It was less than forty minutes to airtime. *I need to work fast,* Katrina thought, and she emailed the scripted news packet to her boss. Knowing what it would cost her, Katrina began working on some editorial remarks of her own before heading to the studio.

Co-anchor Richard Ross began the evening live broadcast with breaking news. "A network of global peace-keeping troops just seized control of the newly constructed temple and secured a perimeter around the Temple Mount. Chairman Alistair Dormin is pleased to announce the future dedication of the New World Religion Center."

Katrina was stunned, but the news only strengthened her resolve.

A news clip of an interview with Reverend Max Nellaf played for the viewing audience. "For years, the Holy Land has been plagued with discord fomented by religious zealots, such as the people who have referred to a pair of charlatans as the Two Witnesses of scripture fame. Alistair Dormin, as the harbinger of peace, is the long-awaited answer to our prayers!" The news clip ended.

Katrina drew in a deep breath as her camera blinked.

"Drought conditions that began in the Middle East are now spreading across the nations," she began. "Rivers such as the Nile and the Euphrates are drying up at an alarming rate. There have been outbreaks of plagues and pestilence across the planet, exactly as the two prophets in Jerusalem have proclaimed. Perhaps these warnings should be heeded…" Katrina's feed was suddenly cut off, and the camera shifted to her co-anchor

"The opinions just expressed do not reflect the views of the United Broadcast Corporation," Richard Ross said as he parroted the disclaimer with an air of indignation. "We apologize for any offense my colleague may have caused."

Canned, feel-good footage of global humanist efforts rolled across the screen, and Katrina braced herself for what she knew would soon come.

As expected, Otto Benedict stormed into the studio followed by two security guards. With his red face quivering with rage, he leveled a finger at Katrina, and shrieked, "You're fired!"

The security guards whisked Katrina to her office to collect her personal items. She was then stripped of her UBC access badge and escorted to the parking garage. In her rearview mirror, Katrina spotted the guards who watched like sentinels as she left the building.

⸙

Arroyo Seco, Arizona

Friday, June 8th

David shot up in bed and gasped for air, and Elita reached out with concern.

"Honey, what's wrong?"

"A bad dream, that's all." David kissed his wife's cheek and said, "Go back to sleep."

He laid still beside Elita until the soft sound of her breathing became rhythmic, and then he slid quietly from beneath the covers. He grabbed his clothes from yesterday and tiptoed into the living room.

The wall clock indicated that it was a little after 3:00 a.m. when David settled into a chair by the window. There, he replayed the nightmare. *Stepping carefully to avoid the cactus, he walked alone in the Arizona desert. He paused to look at the stars above. When his gaze fell on the horizon, he saw a city of white dwellings laid out as far as his eyes could see! Suddenly, he heard a roaring sound and turned to see that a wall of water was racing down the valley toward Hope Springs and Arroyo Seco.* The dream abruptly ended there, but the imagery remained so vivid in David's mind that his hands shook. *Just a nightmare,* he reassured himself.

Elita's Bible lay open on the table beside the chair. Seeking comfort, David took the book in hand and began to read from the Book of Revelation. "But she was given two wings like those of a great eagle so she could fly to the place prepared for her in the wilderness. There she would be cared for and protected from the dragon for a time, times, and half a time. Then the dragon tried to drown the woman with a flood of water that flowed from his mouth."

He tried to tell himself that it was just some strange coincidence. Needing some air, David opened the window and looked down upon the street. The nights had been quiet since the Watering Hole Bar had closed its doors for good. The whole place was beginning to look like a ghost town.

David recalled a recent conversation he had with his wife. He had said to her, "We are the last holdouts, and most of our customers have moved away. Maybe we should consider selling to the mystery buyer."

"This store has been in my family for generations," Elita had replied. "Besides, I believe we're supposed to be here."

If it wasn't for dividends paid from my family trust, we would be in trouble financially, he thought.

Something down below caught David's attention. He spotted a light inside the old Roadkill Café. Someone was moving about in there with a lantern! David stood and watched with growing concern. *What if the banditos have come back?* Without hesitation, he made his way downstairs, retrieved the baseball bat from behind the register, and slipped into the night.

Through the window of the Roadkill Café, David observed a person. The man placed his lantern on one of the tables, sat down, and bowed his head as if in prayer.

Definitely not a bandito, David thought.

The stranger turned and looked straight at the window as though he had sensed David's presence. He stood and hurried over to unlock the door. "Come in my friend. I welcome the company," he said with a thick foreign accent. "I recognize you, Mr. Fillmore. You and your lovely family live across the street. Please join me, won't you?"

As David followed him to a table, light from the lantern fell across the stranger's disfigured face. "Yes, I'm David Fillmore, and you must be the one who is buying up property around here."

"Very perceptive of you." The man flashed a distorted smile. "My name is Ezra Hamburg. Can I offer you a turkey sandwich?"

"No thank you. Don't let me interrupt your meal."

"A cup of coffee perhaps?" The stranger retrieved a mug and filled it for him. "Have you reconsidered my offer to buy the General Store?"

"All our customers have moved away since you came to town," David said. "I'd like to know what you're doing here in Arroyo Seco."

The stranger wiped his scarred lips with his napkin and looked at David with kind, hazel eyes. "Yes, of course. I'm genuinely sorry if my business dealings have caused trouble for you and yours," Ezra said. "I imagine there have been many rumors, but I can assure you that my interests are not nefarious."

"Then why all the secrecy? Just what are your 'interests' here?"

"Do you have faith, young man?"

"That sounds like another cryptic deflection," David replied impatiently. "How about giving me a straight answer?"

"Fair enough," Ezra said, "but first, will you tell me how you came to oversee the remarkable community of Hope Springs?"

David eyed the stranger with growing lawyerly suspicion. "Are you some kind of federal bureaucrat?"

Ezra laughed. "Good heavens, no!" He pushed his plate aside, leaned forward, and said, "Please, pour yourself another cup of coffee, young man, because I've got quite a story to tell you."

❦

North Dakota

Thursday, June 28th

Joel rolled over on the lumpy mattress. He reached for Coco beneath the paper-thin, motel blanket and bedspread. "You asleep?" he whispered.

"Who can sleep with that rattle?" Coco's responded.

Joel rose and made his way across the filthy carpet of the motel room to turn off the noisy air conditioner. He returned to bed and held his bride close until he felt her body relax.

They had just drifted back to sleep when a banging noise awakened them. Through the walls, private sounds were heard until they grew to a crescendo.

"I don't like it here." Coco buried her face in Joel's shoulder and began to weep.

Frustration grew inside Joel as her tears fell softly on his skin. They had both agreed not put anyone else in danger while the Signature Killer was at large. *Still, there must be a better place to hide than this dive motel,* he thought.

As the night wore on, Joel considered their options until his anxiety finally gave way to exhaustion. When he opened his eyes again, it was morning, and Coco was standing beside the bed with two Styrofoam cups in her hand.

"Rough night, eh?" She handed her husband a cup of fresh brewed coffee. "We'll get through this." Coco mustered a smile. "We're together, and that's all that really matters."

Joel reached for her hand. "I love you so much…" *So much it frightens me*, he thought.

A text came in. Joel plucked his phone from the charger and began to read the message.

"What is it?" Coco said as she read his face. "Is it something bad?"

"It's from Katrina Katz. They have discovered the identity of the Signature Killer. Some IT guy named Theron Hunt."

"That's good news, isn't it?"

"Katrina says that this guy left town four days ago. Apparently, he took a leave of absence from work, saying that was going to North Dakota to help a sick relative."

Coco gasped. "Then he could be here now!"

A rush of adrenalin ran through Joel's arteries. He shot to his feet and began jamming their belongings into a duffel bag. "We need to find a safer place to hide out."

"Where?"

"I'll figure something out." Joel buttoned his shirt and slipped into his tennis shoes.

Ten minutes later, with Coco and their dog, Moses, loaded into the Jeep, they left the seedy motel behind. To make sure they weren't being followed, Joel kept a vigilant eye on the rearview mirror.

"What about our sheepherder wagon?" Coco asked. "Maybe we could hide there?"

"No, we'd be sitting ducks there," Joel replied, "but that gives me an idea. Do you remember Sergeant Rudd's bunker?"

Coco gave her husband a skeptical look, "The whole place was torched when the ATF raided it. Most of those shipping containers melted."

"I know that, but Gertie once mentioned that Rudd had built a bomb shelter there. His aunt was sure that the sergeant had lost his mind. It's worth checking out."

After a brief stop at a convenience store for supplies, they merged onto Highway 2 and headed toward Delmont. Twenty minutes later, Joel turned off the main highway onto a bumpy dirt road. They traveled between cornfields that hadn't yet tasseled and angled up a county road that ran along a creek shaded by cottonwood trees.

Joel slowed to a crawl as they neared the sheepherder wagon. He grabbed his wife's hand and smiled. "We made some sweet memories there, didn't we?" Coco smiled that sublime smile of hers, and Joel fought an impulse to stop at their little love shack.

Just over a rise, the burnt-out remnants of Sergeant Rudd's bunker came into view. All that remained were concrete slabs with twisted rebar jutting out and melted skeletons of shipping containers that had once served as a fortress wall. Most of the structures had been reduced to melted masses of steel, but a couple of containers had somehow survived the inferno.

Joel parked far enough away to avoid any sharp hazards that might puncture a tire.

"Where do we begin?" Coco asked as they surveyed the ruins.

"Let's start in the middle and work our way out." Joel found a couple of pieces of rebar and handed one to his wife. "I'll go to the left. You go to the right. Tap the ground as you go and listen for something that sounds hollow or like a metal hatch."

They took their time, and the minutes turned into hours. Every probe proved disappointing. By the time they completed the search, Coco and Joel were both covered in soot and discouragement.

Coco held a finger to her lips. "Did you hear that?"

Joel listened. The sound of hammering met his ear.

She pointed to one of the surviving shipping containers.

"We've already looked it over. There was nothing in that container but some sheets of metal and an old stove pipe."

"Maybe it's coming from the one we didn't check," Coco said. She took a few steps in that direction, stopped, and pointed to the one they had already looked in. "No! It's coming from that one. I'm sure of it."

"Wait here," Joel said. With rebar in hand, he cautiously crept through the opening and stood to let his eyes adjust to the dark.

Suddenly, a small animal sprang from beneath the pile of scrap metal and dashed past Joel. "It's only a rabbit!" he called out over his shoulder. He turned to leave, but the sound of a rusty hinge stopped him.

Joel spun around just in time to see a piece of scrap metal lifting from the floor. Light streamed through the crack, and before Joel had a chance to react, a familiar head popped through the opening.

"I was wondering when you kids would arrive?" Zeke motioned to the young couple. "I've got some Dinty Moore stew simmering on a little gas stove. Come on down."

Once inside the bomb shelter, Coco hugged the old man and said, "It's so good to see you, Zeke."

"Mighty good to be seen, little lady!"

"How did you get here?" Joel asked.

The old man grinned. "That's a silly question. The old Rambler, of course."

Joel looked at his wife. "We didn't see it."

"You kids should have looked in the other shipping container. That's where she's parked." Zeke ran his fingers down his long white beard. "A mutual friend told me that you two were headed this way, so I thought I'd pop over and tidy things up a bit. Sergeant Rudd had his strong points, but cleanliness wasn't one of them."

The old man pointed to a pitcher of water and a bowl. "I'll set the table while you kids wash up."

After cleaning up, Joel and Coco looked around the cozy space. The bomb shelter walls were concrete, and the dirt floor was covered with a braided rug. In one corner, there was a mattress on some wooden pallets. There were shelves all around stocked with paper products, canned goods, blankets, and batteries.

Zeke turned the camp stove off and ladled stew into some plastic bowls. "Come and get it!"

The couple joined him at a crude table made from an old wire spool.

Zeke bowed his head for a quick prayer and then said, "There's two kinds of people. The quick and the hungry."

"I can't believe this place. There is even a wood-burning stove down here," Joel said.

"Works pretty good, but it'll drive you out in the summer months." Zeke polished off his bowl of stew and offered them each a second helping. "Poor Sergeant Rudd was always fighting an invisible war, even as a boy, but the good Lord must have had you two kids in mind when this place was built. You'll be nice and cozy here."

"God is so amazing," Coco said. "I still can't believe that we found you here."

Zeke chuckled. "Didn't know I was lost." He rubbed a drop of stew from his Hawaiian shirt and sprang to his feet. "I'll be going now."

"Wait! So soon?" Coco protested.

"Places to go and people to see." Just before he climbed the ladder, the old man turned and pointed to the far side of the shelter. "I found that wall plaque at a flea market, and it made me think of the big adventure you kids are on."

The sign featured a vintage picture of Betty Davis along with the words, "Buckle up, it's going to be a bumpy ride."

Chapter 12

New York City
Saturday, July 7th

Katrina stared out the window of her Morningside Heights apartment as she tried to summon the energy to tackle the bills that piled up. *This can't go on*, she told herself. There was barely enough money in savings to cover the utilities next month, let alone the rent. Most alarming of all, Katrina believed that her career prospects were being sabotaged. The interviews she had been granted felt doomed before they began. The whole thing had Dormin's fingerprints all over it, but this time, Katrina felt too exhausted to fight back.

"Get a grip," she muttered. Still dressed in the sweatpants, t-shirt, and wooly socks that she wore yesterday, Katrina padded to the bathroom, raked a comb through her tangled hair, and stared at the woman in the mirror. "You're pathetic."

Back in the living room, Katrina plopped onto her couch and turned on the TV. She tried to take her mind off her problems, but the PSA announcements constantly reminded her of the coming changes. Soon, monetary implants would be mandatory. Without a subdermal chip, citizens would be unable to buy, sell, or even seek medical attention.

Katrina switched off the TV, lay back, and closed her eyes. She was just drifting off to sleep when her lobby bell rang. At the door, Katrina pushed the video intercom button and saw Gar mugging for the camera.

"Hey, man, you're alive!"

"Barely," Katrina responded.

"I came by to cheer you up." Gar dangled a gift bag in front of the camera.

"I'm not really feeling up to company."

"Hey, Kat, you might as well buzz me in 'cause I'm not leaving."

Katrina pressed the button, and a few minutes later, Gar sauntered into her cluttered apartment. "I see you've let your maid go."

"Very funny. I never had one," she replied.

Gar's gaze shifted to his friend, and he gasped. "Man, you look like you're auditioning for a horror flick or something!"

Katrina returned to the couch. "I thought you came by to cheer me up?"

"How are you really doing, Kat?" Gar asked, his voice filled with concern.

She shook her head. "My career is over, I'm about to get evicted, I'm broke, and I don't want to get out of bed, but other than that…"

Gar handed Katrina the gift bag. "Go ahead. Open it."

She unwrapped tissue from the item inside and was puzzled to find an enormous pair of cotton panties—at least sixty inches around. Katrina stared at the gargantuan undergarments and said, "What's this about?"

"Think about it Kat. It's time to get your butt off that couch and put on your big girl panties."

"That's hilarious," she said flatly.

"Kat, you've really got to shake this off." There was a rare look of seriousness on Gar's face. "It's a beautiful day outside. Let's get out of here and go for a walk."

He's right, Katrina agreed. "Just let me freshen up a bit."

"Capital idea!" Gar called out as she disappeared into her bedroom to change.

Katrina threw on a NYC Hard Rock Café t-shirt, a pair of jeans, and her white tennis shoes. In the on-suite bathroom, she fluffed her shoulder-length brown hair and dabbed on some lip gloss.

"Ah, there's the feisty Czech girl I used to know!" Gar opened the door and followed her out.

"Thank you for being such a good friend," Katrina said as they rode the elevator to the lobby.

"It's nice to know I'm good at something." Gar held open the main door of the lobby and followed Katrina outside.

They strolled through Riverside Park and walked along the Hudson River. "Do you have a destination in mind or is this just some random stroll?" she asked.

Gar gave her a sideways glance. "You don't like surprises, do you?"

"Not particularly."

"Yeah? I bet that, as a kid, you were a real buzzkill at birthday parties."

Katrina's thoughts flashed back to a haunting childhood memory, and she shuddered.

"Earth to Kat!" Gar snapped his fingers. "I just realized that it's almost noon. Let's grab a bite. My treat."

"Tom's Restaurant?"

"Naw, there's a new place I'd like to try. I heard their coffee is strong enough to make you slap your granny!" Gar gave his friend an apologetic look. "Sorry, bad joke. I forgot you lost your grandmother a little while back."

They walked in silence for a few blocks, and then Gar stopped in front of a narrow storefront that had gingham curtains hanging in the windows. "Happy Trails" was painted on the glass along with "Best Camp Coffee Around!"

The door was locked. Gar knocked and then peered through a crack in the curtains.

"If they're closed, why don't we just go back to Tom's," Katrina said.

"Wait. Someone's coming."

The door swung open, and a man with a wide-brimmed cowboy hat said, "Howdy pardners! Come on in."

They followed him past a coffee bar with stools made from old saddles. The man directed them to some canvas chairs placed around an imitation fire pit. "Kick off your spurs 'n make yourselves at home. I'll be back before you can say Howdy Doody.

"I bet he's rustling up some grub," Gar whispered. Katrina shook her head. "Seriously?"

"I think it's kind of campy," Gar said. "Give it a chance, Kat. I think you'll find it very interesting."

A set of saloon doors parted near the back of the coffee shop, and Katrina turned to see Tiki and Spud.

"What's going on here?" Katrina asked as they entered the room. "Is this some kind of intervention?"

Tiki giggled.

"Why not?" Spud said. "Let's call this an intervention for our way of life."

"I apologize for all the cloak and dagger stuff," Gar said, "but we had to be careful. Remember when you told me that you believed someone had been inside your apartment?"

"Your place is probably bugged," Spud cut in.

Their cowboy host returned with a platter of coffee and some feed bags of trail mix.

Suddenly, an older gentleman with a leather-fringed vest pushed his way through the saloon doors. He locked eyes on Katrina and briskly strode across the room with an out-stretched hand. "Ms. Katz, I've been looking forward to this meeting. My friends call me Butch Cassidy."

Katrina stifled a chuckle. On the wall behind the man was a poster that read, "This May Not Be the Hole in the Wall, But It's as Close as You'll Get in Manhattan!"

"Now, I know I'm being punked!" Katrina looked around the room at the eclectic mix of people gathered: a lanky cowboy, an African American woman, her overweight redneck boyfriend, a beatnik photojournalist, and now this stranger whose leathered face looked like something out of a Clint Eastwood movie. "Where is the hidden camera?"

Mr. Cassidy sat down beside Katrina and studied her from beneath a busy ledge of eyebrows. "Ms. Katz, have you ever heard of the Shadow Riders?"

"Are you talking about the 1980s movie? Surely you haven't brought me here to discuss old westerns?"

"We are a tight-knit network of concerned citizens united to defend our way of life and our freedoms. Our identities are protected by code names and rigid protocols. We are hiding in plain sight," he explained. "We could be your neighbor, physician, delivery man, or grocer, but the one thing we all have in common is a deep concern about the political future of our country because of the current trend to muzzle free speech and independent thought."

"You've got my attention," Katrina said.

"The Shadow Riders' mission statement is very simple: To defend our Constitution, national sovereignty, and religious liberties. Our objective is to expose oppressive political policies and propaganda by providing an open channel for the free exchange of information."

Mr. Cassidy placed his mug onto a wagon-wheel table and clasped his leathered hands together. "We've been observing you for some time, Ms. Katz. It took tremendous integrity and courage to confront Alistair Dormin the way that you did. Those qualities are very rare in today's mainstream media. Wouldn't you agree?"

Katrina recalled the ethical standards for journalism that she was taught at Cornell University: *Truth & accuracy, Independence, Fairness & impartiality, Humanity, and Accountability.*

"Ms. Katz, I'm offering you a position with the Shadow Riders. We believe that you would be a great asset to the organization."

"Doing what exactly?"

"We hope to engage you as an undercover investigative journalist. You would also be a vital contact for some of our core team members."

"Cool, huh?" Gar interjected. "And guess what? I'll be your wingman!"

"Would I be free to report without bias?" Katrina asked.

"Absolutely!" Cassidy replied.

"Then, I accept your offer."

Amidst a chorus of whoops and hollers, the head of the Shadow Riders raised his coffee mug to toast the occasion. "Welcome to the posse, Sundance! Now, let's talk about your first assignment..."

Hope Springs, Arizona
Monday, July 9th

David drove his old pickup truck down the dirt road with Ezra Hamburg. The mystery man who'd been buying up properties around the area was finally ready to share his vision with the people of Hope Springs.

Ezra poured his heart out as they went. "The political climate in Israel is very bad these days. The national legislature, the Knesset, is imploding. The infighting has been fierce between the Conservative Zionists and the Progressive Party. The Zealots who had reinstated the daily sacrifice are furious because the World Fortress Institute recently put a stop to that practice when they seized control of the temple.

"Now, the members of Liberal International are putting great pressure on our Prime Minister, urging him to recant his earlier statements that Dormin broke the treaty. They see the temple only for its historical significance and are seeking peace at the expense of our heritage." Tears filled Ezra's hazel eyes. He raised hands that were missing several fingers and uttered a prayer in Hebrew.

"It definitely sounds like a country in crisis," David said as he bounced over a series of ruts.

"Yes, between the drought, the sanctions, and the collective rage of nations, my people are suffering greatly." Ezra grew quiet as they turned down the road that led to Hope Springs.

David pointed ahead and said, "All of this land was designated for special use by a local rancher named Rupert Sims."

"Ah, the one who believed that God instructed him to set this land aside for the people who would come." Ezra looked earnestly at David. "Do you share this vision?"

"I didn't at first, but when believers from all over the country began showing up…" He glanced at his passengers scarred face. "Mr. Hamburg, may I ask you a personal question?"

"Of course, young man."

"Do you remember the explosion?"

"Very little of it."

David didn't press the issue, and they traveled in silence for a few miles along flowering Brittlebush that lined the dirt road. Across the terrain, Ocotillo plants and desert sage dusted the landscape with subtle shades of green.

"Those buildings are the milking sheds," David said as they passed by, "and the sheep pens are up ahead." Next, he drew Ezra's attention to the irrigated pastures to the left of the road. "The water is channeled from an aquifer and used for drinking and cooking. Some of it is diverted to generate electricity and for washing. All wastewater is captured for the greenhouse and then routed to the fields for irrigation. Even the grey water from individual households is used to water fruit trees."

"Fascinating," Ezra said. "It reminds me of an ancient Middle Eastern water delivery system that I've read about."

"Very similar, but we added the hydroelectric generator."

"How do the people of Hope Springs sustain themselves?" Ezra asked.

"Some local artisans sell their wares at festivals around the state. Others supply eggs, raw honey, and herbs to organic grocers and restaurants over in Kingston. We used to sell a lot of their goods at the General Store." David shot a look at his passenger. "But that was before you bought out all of our customers."

"I believe that will soon change," Ezra replied.

David pulled into a parking space near the pavilion where a crowd had gathered.

As they approached, Jim Saunders, the silver-haired patriarch of Hope Springs, stepped forward and shook the visitor's hand. "So, you're the man we've been hearing so much about."

After a round of introductions, a hardy breakfast, and a fresh pot of coffee, Ezra asked, "How many people reside here?"

"Let me see…" Jim Saunders rubbed his chin. "There are sixty-four dwellings and 125 community members, eighteen of which are children."

"A few less since the Hays family moved to Tucson," Randy Bales interjected.

Travis Dayton parked his elbows on the picnic table. "Sir," he drawled, "we understand that y'all have quite a testimony. We'd be pleased if you'd share it with us."

"That's right, Mr. Hamburg," Pricilla echoed her young husband. "We're dying to hear your story."

"Please everyone, call me Ezra." He paused for a moment. "I'll begin with my background. I was born in Jerusalem and raised to be a devout Zionist.

"Like the Apostle Paul when he was known as Saul, I was a religious and political zealot bound by a ridged code of ethics and nationalism. Anyone whose belief challenged mine was an enemy to be persecuted, especially Christians. But, like Paul on the road to Damascus, I was struck down by the hand of God."

Ezra stared down at his disfigured hands. When he looked up again, tears streamed down his scarred cheeks. He quickly composed himself and continued, "One day, I was on my way to a Zionist meeting. I recall being filled with self-righteous anger, and my soul was bent on revenge for a recent terrorist attack on a Hebrew school.

"Up ahead, the traffic slowed and then came to a stop. This was not unusual during the morning rush, so I thought nothing of it. A young boy approached my car with a bucket and a rag in hand and offered to clean my window for pocket change. I was annoyed by this child and told him to go away." Ezra drew a breath. "That's when I noticed the grenade in his hand."

Beneath the shade of the pavilion, no one moved.

"I can still see the fear in that boy's eyes when he pulled that hand grenade pin." Ezra paused. "After that, I only recall the sound and the burning heat. I then remember feeling the sensation that I was floating above the chaos, looking down with a kind of surreal detachment. I recall watching the response teams working to extract my body from the mangled wreckage.

"Suddenly, a blinding light engulfed me, and I heard someone calling my name, saying 'Ezra, Ezra, why do you persecute me?'" He paused again. "During the painful months of rehabilitation that followed, I grieved for that poor boy who lost his life that day and wondered why I had been spared. That's when the dreams began. If I share them, you might think my brain was scrambled by the explosion."

"According to the Bible, we're all peculiar people," Jim said. "Please, go on."

"Very well. The first dream begins with a knock at my door. I opened it to find an old friend of mine. 'What's for dinner?' he asks. After entering, my friend walks to the table and unfolds a map of Arizona. Then, he points to this region and says, 'There will be a big family reunion soon, and they'll all be hungry for some Hamburger Helper.'"

Ezra looking around at their faces. "I had never heard of this American food product. After the dream, I looked it up online."

"Have you received an interpretation?" Bonnie Saunders asked.

Mr. Hamburg nodded. "Yes, and it came in a very unexpected way. While I was still at the rehabilitation center, my regular physical therapist called in sick. His replacement was a talkative woman. She spoke constantly of her grandkids, her knitting circle, and her pets. I was beginning to grow tired of listening when something the woman said piqued my interest.

She told me about her latest hobby. 'It's referred to as Ono-mastics, and it is the study of the meaning of names.' She told me 'Ezra' means helper, 'Ham' translates as water meadow, and 'Burg' is a fortified town.

"That night, I had another dream. My old friend returned, but this time, he folded the map and handed it to me. 'It's time to get ready,' he said. 'They'll be coming in droves, and they're all going to be hungry.'"

"I've got it!" Pricilla exclaimed. "The water meadow is Hope Springs, the fortified town is Arroyo Seco, and you've been sent ahead to help with the preparations!"

"That's right, young lady. I believe that God has called us all to this place for the difficult times ahead."

"I don't believe it!" David said.

"I realize that the whole thing sounds utterly incred-ible..."

"No, I mean I can't believe my eyes!" David pointed to an old Rambler station wagon bouncing up the road.

"Glory to God! This is a divine confirmation!" Ezra raised his hands toward Heaven. "Zeke is the old friend I spoke of, the one who came into my dreams!"

⸙

North Dakota
Tuesday, July 24th

Joel dropped a can of brown bread and some dried fruit into a canvas bag. "I've got a surprise for you," he said to Coco.

She raised her eyebrows. "Let me guess… You've installed a shower in our little bomb shelter."

"I wish." Joel kissed his wife's neck. "I've planned a little outing, but that's all I'm going to say."

"How mysterious." Coco smiled.

"After you, my beautiful bride." Joel motioned to the ladder.

"What about Moses?"

"He'll be all right down here for couple of hours," Joel said as he followed Coco to the surface.

"What a gorgeous day." Coco twirled about in the sunshine. "Look how blue the sky is. There's not a cloud in sight."

Joel reached for her hand and led her up the hillside through the meadow grass that waved in the soft summer breeze.

"Where are you taking me?" Coco's golden-brown eyes were wide with curiosity.

He just held a finger to his lips and led her farther up the hill. Over the crest, they started down the shady path that led to the sheepherder wagon.

"Do you remember how our love blossomed here?" Joel asked as he opened the door and helped his bride over the threshold.

"You've cleaned the whole place," Coco said as she stepped inside. "Now, I know why you took Moses on all those long walks." She picked up a vase of purple clover and Black-Eyed-Susan flowers that Joel had placed upon the table.

"You thought of everything!"

"Yes, I even found the bag of clean bedding in the storage compartment." Joel leaned in for a long tender kiss and ran his fingers down the arch of her back…

Later, in the heat of the afternoon, the young couple lay together in a tangle of salty sheets.

"I could stay right here forever." Coco sighed contentedly.

Joel pulled her close and felt her body relax in his embrace.

Outside, a bird was chirping, and a gentle breeze rocked the old sheepherder wagon. At this moment, all was right with the world. His blue eyes grew heavy, and then a sound met his ear. "I hear an engine. Someone is coming!"

Coco rose quickly and threw on her summer dress. "What if the Signature Killer has tracked us down?"

Joel shimmied into his jeans, trying to form a plan of action. Through a crack in the door, he spotted a grey SUV with dark-tinted windows coming down the road. Joel grabbed a knife from the tiny kitchenette and waited for the vehicle to pass.

It continued down the hill.

"Let's go hide behind that stand of sagebrush," Joel said. "We can see what's going on from there." They hunkered down on top of the hill and watched the vehicle as it came to a stop near the ruins.

The driver-side door opened. A scraggly-looking

character stepped out and hollered, "Earthlings, we come in peace!"

A woman emerged and relief washed over Joel. "It's Katrina."

He stood and waved his arms as they hurried down the hillside. "How did you find us?" Joel asked when they reached the bottom.

"It wasn't easy; I'll tell you that!" Katrina said and then introduced the young couple to Gar.

"Nice to finally meet you gnarly outlaws," Gar said. "So, where have you guys been hiding out?"

"Come and see," Coco said and escorted the visitors to their below-ground abode. "Welcome to our humble, little bomb shelter."

"Wow, totally cool!" Gar responded. "This place gives new meaning to the phrase, 'going down the rabbit hole.'"

"So, what brings you here?" Joel asked.

"I have a proposition to make, one that concerns your podcast," Katrina said.

Joel laughed. "Really? I've been de-platformed, defunded, and I haven't posted anything in several months. All my followers have surely moved on by now."

"Are you kidding!" Gar exclaimed. "Man, your name is trending like crazy. Everybody is buzzing about your disappearance. I've heard all kinds of conspiracy theories like the CIA took you out, or maybe you're being tortured in a political prison somewhere." He played with his soul patch and winked. "Some even believe that you were abducted by aliens."

Gar continued, "A growing number of people are waking up to the fact that information is being controlled by political propaganda. What's going on these days is very similar to the methods used by Soviet Russia and Nazi Germany. If history teaches us anything, it's that this isn't going to end well. Joel, we can no longer sit idle."

"Yeah, I hear you, but how can I make a difference?" Joel asked.

"You already have," Katrina replied.

"That's right!" Gar chimed in. "Man, you may not realize it, but you've become the voice of resistance! Dude, why do you think they've been working so hard to muzzle you?"

Katrina told the young couple about the underground organization known as the Shadow Riders. "We are offering you a secure platform that will allow you to provide unadulterated information to thousands of concerned citizens. If you accept, your podcast will become the voice of resistance for our people," Katrina explained. "Every week, your followers will retrieve imbedded information from a secure site instructing them where they can listen to your next podcast."

"How am I going to manage that without Internet service? I've got to walk half a mile just to pick up a cell signal," Joel said. "Besides, Coco is being hunted by a serial killer, and I don't want to flag any government attention."

"Man, don't you realize that Big Bro already has a big

bullseye on your back? As for that psycho dude, if you come to work for us, we'll provide you cover."

"That's right," Katrina said. "You and Coco will be moved to a new secure location ASAP. We will provide anonymous credit cards to cover living expenses, fresh burner phones, and a new laptop with each move." Katrina paused to let all the information sink in. "Joel, I assure you that the locations of your podcasts will be masked by a randomly shifting IP address. It will be safer to come to work for the Shadow Riders than staying down here."

"Yeah, and if you ever find yourself in deep shit, we've got a gnarly secret handshake straight out of an Ayn Rand novel!"

"What Gar is trying to say," Katrina interjected, "is that there may be times when it becomes necessary to interface with another Shadow Rider. In such cases, they will identify themselves by dropping the name John Galt."

Gar chuckled. "How cool is that?"

"I have to admit it's all very intriguing." Joel turned to his bride. "What do you think?"

Coco smiled. "It sounds like a big adventure to me."

———— ✳ ————

Tucson, Arizona
Sunday, July 29th

Behind the stage of the Memorial Interfaith Assembly, Paige waited with her son, who was scheduled to perform. "Are you nervous, Connor?"

The teenager shook his head.

"I've been listening to the song that you've been practicing. It sounds very good."

Connor shrugged. "It's not like it's a hard piece to play or anything like that."

"Maybe not, but the reverend picked a nice celebratory song," Paige replied.

"Yeah, I know, because he wants to make some special announcement this morning."

Paige peeked through an opening in the black silk curtains and watched the congregants fill the sanctuary. She spotted Brody in the front row. As usual, her husband was engrossed in his cell phone.

Am I the only one who is anxious right now? Paige wondered. Trying to calm her nerves, she took a few deep breaths.

Finally, the big screen came to life, casting light across the stage, and the worship team gathered in the queue from their dressing rooms. When the countdown was over, they bound up on the stage and engaged the crowd with energetic praise.

Paige marveled at the worship team's devotion and energy. Each one of these talented musicians could have chosen stardom over service.

She glanced at her son, who was busy reading a text message, "Everyone at Hope Springs says hi."

"I can't believe you brought that thing." Paige confiscated the phone and silenced it as the worship tempo slowed and soon came to a stop.

As the announcements were made, Max Nellaf stepped through a door marked "Private" and waited behind stage for his cue. He looked regal in his red clerical garment with a gold embellished runner. The reverend positioned himself near the curtains while the tithes and offerings were collected. Finally, he made his entrance onto the stage.

"Blessings, blessings, my beloved!" Nellaf said. "Peace on earth, goodwill towards men!" The ebony podium rose magically from the stage floor, and the reverend took his position there.

"Dear hearts," he said when the room finally settled.

"You are each here this morning by divine appointment, for God himself has you here to be his witnesses. Yes, beloved, you are each chosen emissaries of the new spiritual paradigm. Our prayers for global peace and unity are becoming a manifest reality. We are witnessing the creation of a better world. Little children, we are on the cusp of a utopian vision for all mankind." Shouts of praise filled the sanctuary.

The reverend motioned to the plush row of seats in front of the stage. "This morning, we have some very special guests with us." One by one, he introduced an impressive panel of international leaders and dignitaries. "These selfless men and women have laid their lives down in faithful service for the good of humanity." Nellaf paused and fanned his gaze across the sanctuary. "Will you do the same?" The congregation rose to their feet and roared with thunderous affirmation.

He lifted a hand to settle his followers. "These vision-aries and many others across our globe have linked arms and partnered in the revelation that Alistair Dormin is our divinely appointed harbinger of peace! Beloved, I stand before you today in great humility…" The reverend's voice cracked with emotion. "For Alistair Dormin has chosen me to officiate the dedication of the new Temple of World Harmony in Jerusalem. I have been asked to sanctify the very ground that once was the fulcrum of division. I have been chosen to proclaim a new day of ecumenical brotherhood. Beloved, I am deeply honored and humbled by this honor. Let us celebrate this new dawn for humanity with a special musical tribute."

Backstage, Paige squeezed her son's shoulder. "That's your cue."

"I now present our very own Julliard protégé, Connor Hays, who will be performing the jubilant violin solo—Presto from Sonata # 1."

Connor walked slowly onto the stage. He stopped in front of the live microphone and lowered his head. The seconds turned into minutes, and murmurs rippled through the audience.

Is that a tear glistening in the corner of Connor's eye? Paige whispered a prayer.

Slowly, the boy lifted his violin, poised his bow, and began to play. Like a wail of fresh grief, a mournful tune emanated from his instrument. The melody pierced the atmosphere and cast the somber tones of a funeral dirge across the cavernous room.

That isn't the jubilant solo that the reverend asked Connor to play! Paige watched her son immerse himself in song. With eyes closed and tears streaming down his cheeks, Connor played with an intensity that Paige had never seen before.

She looked across the stage and saw Max Nellaf watching the teenager perform. The reverend clasped his hands, and his face appeared relaxed, but there was something about his eyes that made Paige shudder.

PART 2—The Purge

Did we in our own strength confide,
Our striving would be losing,
Were not the right Man on our side,
The Man of God's own choosing;
Dost ask who that may be?
Christ Jesus, it is He!
Lord Sabaoth, His Name,
From age to age the same,
And He must win the battle.
Martin Luther – 1529

Chapter 13

Jerusalem, Israel
Tuesday, August 28th

Katrina considered the strange twist of fate that had brought her to Israel on assignment for the Shadow Riders. Sadness shadowed her as she walked through the Holocaust Memorial Museum in Jerusalem. Katrina lingered to read the graphic displays and wondered, *How could anyone live through such evil without becoming broken and bitter? Babbeh was truly a living testimony to the resilience of the human heart.*

Katrina made her way to an exhibit called the Hall of Names. There, she searched through pages of testimony until she found the one that her grandmother had written. Katrina projected Babbeh's testimony onto a glass screen and settled down to read. She had heard most of these stories before, but her grandmother hardly ever spoke of her younger brother.

When she was young, Katrina had come across an old sepia photograph of the little boy.

"That's my brother, Aaron. He died at the camp," Babbeh said.

The story on the screen gave more insight to the seven-year-old boy after he arrived at Auschwitz. Aaron, a sickly child, was assigned to a special barrack and subjected to a series of cruel and inhumane medical experiments. "They broke his spirit and finally his tiny body," Babbeh wrote in her testimony.

Katrina considered her own painful childhood. *Some things are just too difficult to mention,* she thought.

A few feet away, a poem, written by a man who was murdered at Auschwitz, was displayed on the wall.

"Remember only that I was innocent
And, just like you, mortal on that day.
I, too, had had a face marked by rage,
By pity, and by joy—quite simply,
a human face!"

Katrina soaked in the sad words for a moment and then moved on to the center of the circular hall where a six-meter-high cone pointed upward. Inside the cone were photographs of faces of people, hundreds of souls who had perished under Hitler's regime. *The light of life in their eyes, once so hopeful, had been extinguished by a monster!* she thought.

Katrina gazed into the pool below the cone. It reflected the blurred faces of those who had died. *Is this a metaphor for the passage of time or a warning for mankind not to forget?* she wondered and then muttered to herself, "How could anyone endure such suffering?"

"For the joy that is set before them," a familiar voice behind her replied.

She spun around and was startled to see Zeke standing there. He looked up at the collage of faces and said, "The sufferings of this world aren't worth comparing with the glory to come."

"Zeke, what are you doing here?"

"Is that any way to greet a friend?" The old man pulled a roll of lifesavers from the breast pocket of his oversized Hawaiian shirt and offered one to Katrina.

"No thanks." Katrina pondered his words. "What glory is there in suffering? I don't see anything good in what happened here."

"Good always triumphs over evil, Missy." Zeke popped a cherry candy into his mouth. "Wasn't it at Auschwitz where your grandmother's faith first took root?"

Katrina considered the odds of this chance meeting, and her suspicions were aroused. "Do you know Ayn Rand or John Galt?"

"Don't believe I've ever had the pleasure," the old man said. "Friends of yours?"

"Never mind," Katrina replied tersely. "I still can't believe you're here."

"I know what you mean. Sometimes I need to pinch myself just to make sure it's really me." There was a playful twinkle in his crystal blue eyes. He twirled the tip of his long white beard. "What do ya say we get out of here and act like a couple of tourists? I'd like to wander around the Holy City and see what's new."

"That's a good idea," Katrina said. "Tomorrow a security perimeter will be set up around the old city. Only those invited to the dedication on Friday will be allowed in."

Zeke chuckled. "My invitation must have been lost in the mail."

They made their way to the museum exit and stepped outside.

"Follow me." The gnome-like man led Katrina to a parking lot where a rusty Rambler station wagon was parked. It was pocked with putty, and the bumper was held in place with duct tape. "This looks a lot like the car you drove to Babbeh's funeral."

Zeke opened the door for her. "What can I say? It gets great mileage."

After a short drive, Katrina and Zeke entered the ancient walled city and found a parking space. They strolled along the stone-paved streets between the limestone walls of buildings with green shutters.

The old man stopped to sniff the breeze. "I just love the scent of olive trees, don't you?"

Katrina was deep in thought trying to imagine what this city had been like when Jesus walked around it.

The ominous presence of troops brought her back to the moment. International Peace Keeping soldiers were positioned all around like armed sentinels. Katrina spotted them on walls, rooftops, and courtyards.

"Lady, you like Star of David?" She looked to see a street merchant dogging her steps. "Nice, very nice..." he said. Katrina shook her head, but Zeke lingered to chat with the man in Hebrew. The merchant laughed at some inside joke and then bolted after another prospect.

"You speak Hebrew?"

"Yup," Zeke replied. "Hey, you're in for a real treat, Missy." The old man led her to a fruit stand where he purchased a small bag of figs. "Lucky for us, they still had a few of the first fruits of season. These are gonna make your taste buds explode with joy!"

Katrina sampled the fruit and enjoyed its sweet, berry flavor.

"Some folks believe the fig tree represents the mysteries of Israel's future," Zeke said cryptically. He offered her another, but Katrina turned it down.

They strolled along with the flow of travelers and locals, stopping periodically to admire the quaintness of an ancient building, a hand-hewn archway, or a flowery courtyard.

"We're almost to the Arab quarter," Zeke announced. "Have you ever been to a souk? If not, you're in for an experience."

He wasn't kidding, Katrina thought as they were swept into a fast-moving sensory extravaganza: bright bolts of colored fabrics, clothing, gold jewelry, toys, shoes, leather goods, housewares, and cages of fluttering birds. Sound seemed amplified as it bounced down the narrow passageway of metal store fronts: Arabic voices hawking for a sale, the whirr of a coffee grinder, and the squeal of children playing.

A scooter whizzed past close enough to make Zeke's

beard flutter. "The first time I came here, my eyes were blinking like a frog in a hailstorm," he quipped.

They passed a perfumery where shelves were lined with hundreds of jars of fragrant oils. A few yards away, spice vendors scooped their wares from burlap bags. The blended smell of perfume, spices, and human odors was overwhelming.

Katrina was grateful when they emerged from the souk and stepped into a quieter part of the ancient city. She stopped at a window display to look at some antique jewelry. "Zeke, do you remember the brooch you gave me at Babbeh's funeral?"

"Sure do!" he said. "I bet you haven't figured out how to open it yet?"

"Open it?"

"Yup. It's not just a brooch. It's a locket."

"Really?" Katrina said. "What's inside?"

"You don't want me to be a spoiler, do you, Missy?" Zeke said. The old man's blue eyes twinkled as they entered the Jewish Quarter. "There's a place around the corner that makes a fantastic Falafel sandwich. Wait until you try their fresh baked Pita bread."

Katrina hurried after the strange little man as he darted down a side street and stopped at the door of a delicatessen.

"Looks like we beat the crowd," Zeke said as they entered. He rang a bell that sat atop a glass counter, and a young man emerged from the back room.

When he saw Zeke, he said, "My good friend, how wonderful to see you again!"

"It's mighty good to be seen!" The old man grinned and laid a hand on Katrina's shoulder. "Levi, I'd like you to meet Babysta's granddaughter, Katrina Katz."

"What an honor this is!" Levi rushed around the counter and vigorously shook her hand. "Saba, my grandfather always wondered what became of little Babysta. They met at Auschwitz."

"Was your grandfather a Messianic Jew by any chance?" she asked.

The question seemed to startle the shop owner. "Why, yes, Saba was forever quoting scriptures about Yeshua. I too share his faith." Levi clapped his hands together. "It will be a great honor to treat you both to a meal."

Zeke grinned, "Never turn down a free meal. That's what I always say."

Levi flipped the sign in his window to CLOSED and disappeared into the kitchen.

After a several minutes of banging and clanging, he emerged with a tray of Chickpea falafel sandwiches, blood orange soda, and rice pudding.

Together they offered a prayer of thanks, broke bread, and shared a meal. Katrina listened to their host lamenting about the changes that had come to his homeland.

"The political climate in Israel is very tenuous," he said. "Nationalists and religious factions are both being blamed for the economic sanctions imposed by the World Fortress Institute. Militant groups and modern-day Zealots seem to take pleasure in provoking hostilities. Meanwhile, the drought continues…"

"Nobody said it was going to be easy," Zeke chimed in, "but remember, God is still in control."

"So true, my friend."

Zeke folded his napkin, placed it onto his plate, leaned back in his chair, and patted his belly. "That meal sure took the wrinkles out."

"Yes, it was lovely. Thanks," Katrina said as they rose from the table.

Levi walked them to the door and shook hands with Zeke. "My old friend, seeing you again has renewed my hope." He turned to Katrina. "It was a great honor to meet you. May our paths cross again!" Levi said just before the door closed.

Zeke and Katrina continued along the Western Wall of the Temple Mount complex. It soon widened into a plaza near the Wailing Wall. Katrina stood back to admire the ancient structure. "Wow, this wall must be a hundred-and-fifty-feet high!" she marveled.

"One-hundred-and-eighty-seven-feet tall and eight-feet thick, to be exact," Zeke told her. "Those lower stones date back to Herod's time, and each one is perfectly fitted together. It doesn't take a rocket scientist to figure that kind of wisdom comes from above."

In the courtyard at the base of the wall, Orthodox Jews stood rocking, weeping, and tearing their clothing. A few yards away, protesters waved anti-Israel signs, jeered, and gnashed their teeth at them while calling for world peace and unity. Strangest of all, scantily clad women with tambourines danced about the courtyard in ecstatic celebration.

Zeke twirled the tip of his beard and shook his head. "If we could harness the power of all this emotion, I believe it would fuel a rocket to the moon and back."

"How did you know that Levi's grandfather was at Auschwitz with Babbeh?" Katrina asked.

Suddenly, a blood-curdling wail rose from the courtyard. Heads turned to see a man wearing a Kaftan and Keffiyeh hurling stones at the Jews.

"I think that's our cue to skedaddle." The old man escorted Katrina to safety at a fast clip. They didn't stop until they reached the Via Dolorosa.

"I think that I've seen enough for one day," Katrina said.

"One more quick stop, Missy." The old man's eyes locked on Katrina. "I believe you will find this little detour very interesting." Curiosity compelled her to follow Zeke through the Lions Gate and into the ancient cemetery in the Kidron Valley. "These folks who are buried here are in for a real treat when the Messiah shows up again," Zeke said.

"Do you really believe that?"

"Of course. It's all written down in the Good Book." He pointed up ahead to a group of people gathered near the sealed Golden Gate. "Almost there, Missy."

As they drew near, Katrina could see that the crowd had gathered to listen to two bearded men wearing primitive sackcloth garments and leather sandals. "Is this some kind of Jewish reenactment?"

"Nope, this is the real deal," Zeke said as they stood behind the others.

Katrina didn't understand the words spoken in Hebrew, but something stirred deep within her heart. "What are they saying?"

"The first fellow just finished reciting Matthew 24," Zeke said softly. "Some call it the Olivet Discourse. Now the other one is talking about the man of lawlessness who has come to exalt himself in the temple."

One of the men spotted Zeke first and then Katrina. He bid them to come forth, and the crowd parted to let them pass.

Zeke and his friends embraced, and then the men turned to Katrina and spoke to her in English. "We have been waiting for your arrival."

The moment seemed surreal, like she was standing in some ancient biblical scene. One of the men said, "Daughter of Zion, you have been brought to the kingdom for such a time as this."

Zeke jabbed Katrina with his elbow and grinned. "Told you it would be interesting."

Jerusalem, Israel
Friday, August 31st

Katrina woke with a start. She felt disoriented. It took her a moment to remember that she was in a tiny rental apartment in Jerusalem. The faint glow of dawn shining through the sheer curtains made her realize that she had slept until the cusp of the morning.

She lay in bed for several minutes and then rolled over and turned on her bedside lamp. Her phone indicated that it was barely 6:00 a.m.

I need coffee. Katrina rose, grabbed her robe, and walked into the tiny kitchen to brew a cup. As morning light spilled across the small wooden table, she remembered the meeting yesterday at the Golden Gate near the Kidron Valley and pondered, *Could these two mysterious men be the prophets whom some believe to be responsible for the worldwide drought?* The strangers had caught her off guard. A reverent provenance about them had humbled Katrina and left her speechless. The words that the two witnesses spoke still burned in her heart. They had given no names, but Zeke seemed to know them personally. Before she had a chance to ask him, he had vanished again.

Anxious about the challenging assignment ahead, Katrina checked the time. She laid out her clothes for the Dedication of the Temple: an expensive linen suit that fit her like a bag and a pair of outdated leather pumps. Katrina double-checked the false ID that the Shadow Riders had given her along with a VIP Invitation supplied by a fellow comrade. *I hope I can pull this off,* she worried. Katrina studied the image of her new identity and committed the details to memory. *I'm Mara Abernathy, a single, forty-six-year-old heiress from Los Angeles.*

At the vanity, Katrina pulled her hair back into a tight

bun and carefully painted streaks of grey near her temples. Next, she slipped on a pair of fake glasses and some dental veneers that were engineered to widen her cheeks. She stared at her reflection and barely recognized herself in the mirror. *What if I'm flagged as an imposter?* she thought. *What if I'm turned away at a security check or worse?*

Katrina did her best to push her fears aside as she waited for the taxi. "God, if you're real, I could sure use a little help right now."

When the cab arrived, she instructed the driver to take her to the Damascus Gate. All the other entrances to the old city of Jerusalem had been closed for the Dedication Ceremony. As they neared the destination, she tried to focus on her breathing. *I'm Mara Abernathy from Los Angeles,* she reminded herself as the cab pulled into the queue.

Just outside the Damascus Gate, Katrina fell in line with dignitaries from all over the world. She tried to act nonchalant as she handed the guard her VIP invitation, but her palms were sweaty.

He studied her photo and then her face. "Mara Abernathy?"

Katrina's heart was pounding. "Yes, that's correct." Relief washed over her when he waved her on to board a waiting tour bus.

Soon, the bus began to move through the old streets past troops of armed guards. The passengers disembarked near the northeast corner of the Temple Mount wall where the guests funneled through another security check. This one included bomb-sniffing canines and metal detectors.

Maybe I'm not cut out for all this cloak-and-dagger business, Katrina thought as she stepped closer to the entrance of the Gate of Tribes. Once cleared, Katrina walked beneath the semi-circular arch of the gate and moved along with the other guests.

Inside the Temple Mount, the group was escorted around the limestone wall of the new temple and then into the Inner Courts. Bleachers had been erected for the event, and the guests were directed to their assigned seats.

The size and grandeur of the temple took Katrina's breath away. Constructed of massive blocks of Jerusalem limestone and finished in white and gold, the geometric lines of the building were austere, yet stunning. The gated walls surrounding the site had watchtowers. *An architectural marvel!* she thought. Directly in front was an area known as Solomon's Court. Katrina gazed past Solomon's Court to the Brazen Altar. Just beyond that, up some marble steps, was the chamber that was once known as the Holy of Holies. Above the door to that sacred place was a large-screen monitor showing the World Fortress Institute emblem: an inverted cross with the face of a leopard, a lion, and a bear paw.

On the Temple Mount, to the left of the new complex, sat the Dome of the Rock with its golden dome seated atop an octagon-shaped building. The Islamic shrine was richly decorated with marble and mosaics, but Katrina thought it seemed out of place beside the simple lines of the new temple.

The media presence for the event was huge! Katrina

counted thirteen camera crews, most of them international. They were strategically positioned on the temple walls to record the historic event from every possible angle.

Soon the stands filled with guests dressed in finery. Ethereal music began to play from a hidden sound system, and the atmosphere was ripe with anticipation. The dignitaries were the last guests to arrive. Excitement rippled through the stands as a host of world leaders were escorted to velvet-clad chairs in the newly renamed Court of Nations, formerly known as the Court of Women.

The music stopped.

Three men and three women, all wearing black and red capes, converged from gateways on either side of the temple. They lined up facing the Brazen Altar. After a moment of silence, they each lifted a ram horn to their lips, and the wail of the shofars pierced the atmosphere like a battle cry. The jumbotron screen came to life to give a full view of Gate of Honor of the Prophets. Throwing white flower petals as they went, barefoot children danced through the gate in flowing silk gowns.

The arrival of the Reverend Max Nellaf was announced next, and the guests were instructed to rise for the holy man. He made a grand entrance through the gate wearing a mitre fit for the Pontiff. He wore a fine golden brocade, and in his hand was a scepter with red stones. A man seated beside Katrina said, "It's strange that they chose that entrance because it was once known as the Gate of Darkness."

The reverend advanced slowly, turned right at

Solomon's Court, and made his way to the Brazen Altar.

The large screen now featured a close-up of Nellaf's pleasant face. "Welcome, Beloved! You have all been divinely chosen to witness this moment in time. Dear ones, this day marks the dawning of a bright new world." Nellaf looked straight at the camera, "I am not just addressing the privileged few who are assembled in this holy place, but all who have hoped, prayed, and labored for peace. Behold, I bring you tidings of great joy!"

While Reverend Nellaf swept his scepter in all directions, he said, "To the east, to the west, to the north, and to the south—I proclaim that the healing balm of unity covers the earth." He raised his scepter skyward. "In the name of my god, I command the turbulent waters of tribal discord and religious divisions be stilled!" The people clapped to show their approval. When they settled, Nellaf continued, "It is a privilege to dedicate this temple as the sacred ground of brotherly love. By the authority given to me, I now consecrate this holy ground as the new hub of secular and ecumenical unity!"

He dipped the tip of his scepter into a vat of oil that had been placed upon the altar and flicked it about. "Beloved, I now present the new Temple of World Harmony! May peace arise, and all enemies be scattered!"

Nellaf turned to the Holy of Holies and bowed his head toward the Paraclete curtain that covered the entrance. "Ladies and gentlemen, our man of peace, the man of God's own choosing!"

The thick veil of scarlet, blue, and purple opened slowly to reveal Chairman Alistair Dormin seated on a gold throne. Someone nearby gasped out loud as the crowd launched to their feet in adulation.

Dormin rose slowly from his gilded seat. He stood like a giant in his stately black suit, white shirt, and red tie. The camera zoomed in close enough to see his sable hair rippling in the breeze. The Chairman's steel-grey eyes fanned across his adoring crowd.

A moment passed before Alistair Dormin beckoned the people to settle. "Ladies and gentlemen, old things have passed away, and the new religious and global order has come! I AM, that I AM," he shouted over the roar of adoration.

Suddenly, a loud crack echoed through the temple. Before the horrified eyes of the world, the Chairman's hands cupped his face. Blood began to gush between his fingers. Alistair Dormin dropped to his knees, and then he pitched forward. On the steps that led to the holy place, a crimson stain grew.

Screams pierced the temple, and the guests scrambled to their feet in mass panic.

The security team launched into action while a stunned world watched on live feed as Alistair Dormin, the Chairman of the World Reserve Bank and the newly proclaimed I Am, lay lifeless.

Nellaf rushed to the Dormin's side. He knelt and gently rolled him over to examine his wounds. "We need a doctor!"

the reverend screamed. "Is there a doctor present?"

The main media feed to the big screen monitor went dark, but a few of the cameras were still fixed on the fallen Chairman.

Katrina, who had risen to her feet, was frozen in place as she watched the events unfold.

She could see the flow of blood that pulsed out of the wound in Dormin's eye. It grew weaker and then stopped as several physicians rushed forward.

"He's not breathing!" someone said.

The sound of a siren wailing drew closer while the doctors did their best to revive Dormin. A team of first responders rushed into the temple, and for nearly twenty minutes, they worked feverishly. Finally, they loaded Dormin's lifeless body onto a gurney. Solemn looks were exchanged among the members of the medical team.

I have just witnessed the assassination of Alistair Dormin, Katrina thought.

"Wait," the reverend yelled. Nellaf laid his blood-covered hands upon the fallen leader, "In the name of my god, I command you to live!" he bellowed.

Then, to the amazement of the watching world, Dormin's finger moved.

The cameras zoomed in for a closer view as the Chairman squeezed Nellaf's hand. His uninjured eye opened, and Alistair Dormin uttered two words. "I am."

"He is risen!" Nellaf proclaimed. "Rejoice, he is risen!"

Chapter 14

Arroyo Seco, Arizona
September 1st

David stood watching the television that was anchored above the General Store lunch counter. Every news station in the country was playing and replaying the images of the Chairman's assassination and miraculous healing, and each reporter put their spin on the story.

"It was a mortal wound," a world-renowned brain surgeon from Johns Hopkins said. "Dormin's recovery defies modern medicine, for there is no indication of impairment."

From ivory-tower scholars to political pundits, everyone agreed that Dormin's "resurrection" had been nothing short of a miracle.

"Can we please change the channel?" Elita asked as she slipped on her apron.

"It's playing on all the stations," David replied. "Probably will be for days to come."

Elita grabbed the remote and switched off the television. "It disturbs me that people are comparing Alistair Dormin to Jesus."

"We should be focusing our attention on what's happening around here. We're almost out of canned soup and beans," David lamented. "Things are flying off the shelves faster than I can reorder."

Almost overnight, the dying town of Arroyo Seco had become a thriving community filled with foreign strangers. With the assassination of Alistair Dormin and his miraculous healing, the media barely had time to mention that Jewish nationals were fleeing Israel by the thousands ever since the World Fortress Institute had seized control of the temple and put a stop to Jewish rituals.

Southern Arizona had become a huge refugee camp. Overnight, the ghost town of Arroyo Seco became a boom town. The first wave of refugees arrived a few weeks ago. Many came with fists full of money. Some spoke English, other's broken English, but most only spoke Hebrew or Yiddish.

The main street now had a pharmacy, a clothing store, a barter bank, and the old Roadkill Café had been reopened as the Kosher Café. Every day brought something new. In the nearby desert, more warehouses had gone up. A rolling convoy of trucks arrived daily carrying supplies and temporary housing.

"Did you notice the solar farm they're putting up outside of town?" David asked.

Elita stared out the window. "Another charter bus is pulling up in front of the store. No, wait, three buses, and they are all full!"

David watched the newest Israeli refugees pouring onto the street. "Looks like I'm going to have to increase the supply order."

Ezra Hamburg was there to welcome each traveler with open arms.

"Where are they all going to stay?" Elita wondered aloud. "The motel is full, and most of the houses in Arroyo Seco are occupied."

"We've got our own worries," David said as a crowd of newcomers headed their way.

The group flooded into the old store and grabbed items from the shelves.

Within minutes, David was ringing up cash sales while Elita was busy loading the griddle with burgers and slapping sandwiches together. Around three o'clock, David locked the door behind a customer and switched the window sign to CLOSED.

He found Elita standing behind the lunch counter staring at a stack of dirty dishes in the sink as water dribbled from the faucet.

"Look at this," she said. "I can't even wash the dishes."

David put his arm around his wife and could feel her trembling. "Have you eaten anything today?" She shook her head. "I want you to go upstairs, fix yourself a meal, and then get some rest."

"Who's going to pick up Joy from school?" Elita's eyes brimmed with tears.

"I'll drive over to Hope Springs and get her." David grabbed a set of keys from the General Store front desk. "When I get back, I want you to be resting."

David drove the old pickup down the highway around patches of crumbling asphalt. *Things can't go on like this much longer,* he thought. By the time David turned down the rutted dirt road that led to Hope Springs, he had made up his mind to hire help at the General Store.

Up ahead, several tractor-trailers parked near the pavilion, and people were unloading crates and boxes. He pulled into a parking space and walked over to see what was going on.

Jim Saunders was standing in the pavilion. He spotted his friend and waved him over.

"What's going on?" David asked.

"Insulated desert yurts, a couple hundred of them. Ezra says there's a bunch headed your way too." Jim ran a hand over his grey flat top. "They're going to be delivering a couple of commercial, solar-powered generators too."

David asked, "Can Hope Springs handle all this?"

Jim shook his head. "We barely have enough water to go around as it is."

"I know what you mean," David said. "We barely have enough water pressure to fill a sink or take a shower."

"There's got to be a solution." Jim rubbed his chin. "God wouldn't have brought all these people here if there wasn't."

"Look." David pointed to a large group of people moving through the desert. "I hope they're not heading here."

"Mexicans migrants," Jim explained. "They are making their way back across the border. With the new government in place, Mexico has become the land of new opportunity."

David was reminded of the swift military coup and the puppet government seated there by the World Fortress Institute. *On the surface, nobody can disagree with cleaning up corruption and ending oppression,* he thought, *but there is something very disturbing about Alistair Dormin and his unbridled power.*

⸺⦉⦊⸺

Tucson, Arizona
Sunday, September 9th

Feeling a sense of dread, Paige sat up in bed. Brody was not beside her, and it took her a moment to recall that he was out of town for a weekend retreat with the church elders.

She turned on her lamp and picked up her Bible. It fell open to the Book of Revelation, and Paige began to read Chapter 13, "Then I saw a beast rising up out of the sea. It had seven heads and ten horns, with ten crowns on its horns. And written on each head were names that blasphemed God. This beast looked like a leopard, but it had the feet of a bear and the mouth of a lion! And the dragon gave the beast his own power and throne and great authority." Paige shuddered when she read the third verse. "I saw that one of the heads of the beast seemed wounded beyond recovery, but the fatal wound was healed! The whole world marveled at this miracle and gave allegiance to the beast."

She reread the text in the light of the recent assassination of Alistair Dormin and his miraculous recovery. *It's just a coincidence, that's all,* Paige told herself. The final book of the Bible—its imagery and its meaning—had always been a mystery to her.

A sound caught her ear. She cocked her head to listen and heard a muffled cry. Maternal instinct launched her from bed. Paige threw on her robe and hurried down the hallway to her son's room. In the shadow cast by moonlight, she could make out Connor's silhouette near the window. "Honey, what's wrong?"

Paige switched on the bedroom light and hurried to his side.

"I had another bad dream," Connor said.

She put her arm around her thirteen-year-old son. "Was it like the one before?" she asked cautiously.

"You mean was it a dream from God?" Connor replied. "Yes, Mom, it was." He wiped tears from his cheek and flashed an apologetic smile. "I didn't mean to wake you up."

"Do you want to talk about it?"

He shook his head. "Do I have to go to church today?"

"You used to love attending church! Besides, your dad will be back in town today. He would be very disappointed if we weren't there."

Conner reached for his tattered Bible and clutched it to his chest. "Mom, can I be homeschooled?"

Paige's heart sank. "Are Bella and the other kids at school still giving you a hard time? Maybe I should have a word with the principal."

"Mom, no! Don't do that, okay?"

Paige had witnessed Bella and her little cabal of mean kids in action. An image of Jolene flashed in her mind. *Like mother, like daughter,* she thought.

"I just think it would be cool to learn at home, that's all." Connor kicked at a throw rug.

"You know how your dad feels about homeschooling." Paige could see the disappointment on her son's face.

She changed the subject. "It's going to be a beautiful sunrise." Paige pointed out the window, and they watched as the colors grew brilliant and then faded.

"I feel like making blueberry pancakes for breakfast!" Paige headed for the kitchen.

After Connor arrived, she did her best to lighten the mood, but her son was preoccupied with his journal. Paige filled some plates and joined her son at the breakfast counter. "What are you doing?"

"I'm writing down the dream before I forget."

"When you want to talk about it, I'm here."

"Thanks Mom."

Paige glanced at the wall clock and said, "We'd better get ready for church!"

"Can't I just stay home and read my Bible?"

Paige shook her head. "Like I said…"

Connor trudged off to his bedroom, "I know. Dad expects me to be there."

Paige didn't like her son's tone, but lately, she also felt the same trepidation about attending the Memorial Interfaith Assembly.

By 10:00 a.m., they were on their way to church and listening to praise and worship music as they went. They crested the plateau and fell in behind a long line of cars inching toward the white monolithic building. "Wow! The place is packed already. I didn't think it was possible to have more visitors than last week," Paige said.

Throngs from all over the country had been making a pilgrimage to the Memorial Interfaith Assembly. They were packed in droves beneath a series of large tents that housed outdoor monitors. It didn't matter that the Sunday services were now broadcast globally, people just wanted to be near the man who had raised Alistair Dormin from the dead.

Paige drove around the left side of the building into a private parking garage that was designated for church staff, elders, and their families. She pulled into their reserved spot near the church limousine. "I see that your dad and the other elders are back in town." She glanced at her son. He seemed lost in thought.

They made their way to the church sanctuary and settled into their usual seats. Once he was seated, Connor opened his sketch pad and began to draw.

If only he could make new friends like the ones he left behind at Hope Springs, Paige thought. "Honey, are you sure you don't want to try Youth Church again? There are probably a lot of new kids attending."

"All they do is play a bunch of silly games."

Paige sighed and then checked her phone for any messages from Brody. A syrupy voice interrupted her. "Good morning!"

"Hello, Jolene."

The woman tossed her blonde locks, tussled Connor's hair with manicured claws, and said, "I would just die to have your stunning red hair!"

Jolene flashed a smile at Paige. "I bet you're brimming with excitement! Aren't you absolutely thrilled about Brody's fabulous news? I know I was!" Jolene wiggled in her tight sheath dress and cooed, "I get goosebumps thinking about it!" Her eyes were fixed on Paige. They widened with feigned innocence. "Oh darling, you don't know yet, do you? When Brody told me, I just assumed…"

The elders trickled into the sanctuary, and Brody spotted his wife. He gave her a nod and paused to visit with a few of the church super tithers.

The worship team bounded onto the stage and began a rousing and energetic song of praise. "Everybody! Clap your hands to the Lord! Rejoice and be glad!"

Brody settled beside his wife and son. He seemed unusually energized.

As the congregation sang along to the words on the monitor proclaiming Heaven on Earth, Paige leaned over to her husband and whispered, "What's going on, Brody?"

"I'll tell you later," he replied.

Finally, the rhythmic melodies gave way to church announcements.

After a brief interlude, an assistant pastor walked onto the stage. "Beloved, the eyes of the nations witnessed a miracle when Alistair Dormin was resurrected by the faith of one man." He paused. "Saints, please rise and welcome the Grand Apostle Maxim Nellaf, a new title recently bestowed upon him by the Global Religious Council!"

The assistant pastor stepped aside and bowed his head as the curtains parted, and the Grand Apostle Nellaf made his entrance. Dressed in his clerical finery, Nellaf smiled for the live-stream cameras. He walked about the stage, basked in the adoring praises of his followers, and made his way to the podium.

"Sons and daughters, it is with deep humility that I have accepted this God-ordained office of Grand Apostle. It is a great privilege to take our global family under the covering of my fatherly wings. The dawning of ethereal peace has come, beloved. Throw open the doors of your hearts! Hesitancy is faithlessness. The moment is now to receive this new and powerful anointing. Heaven has come to earth!"

The congregation went wild with emotion. They shrieked and moaned. Some fell to their knees weeping; others danced in ecstatic celebration or joyous laughter.

After a few moments, the Grand Apostle lifted his hands and said, "Be still!"

Silence settled over the room, and the atmosphere

seemed to shimmer with anticipation as Nellaf stood looking down upon the congregation. "Blessed are you, for your eyes have seen the risen son of the new Jerusalem. Dear ones, you have each been given a holy commission to faithfully serve Chairman Alistair Dormin, our blessed hope and the man of peace who will lead us into our glorious future!"

The large sanctuary thundered with shouts and applause.

Again, the reverend silenced the throngs. This time, he looked somberly across the sanctuary and said, "The battle is not over, dear children. There are enemies in the camp who are troubling the advance of this heavenly kingdom. Beware of the heresy hunters who spew religious rhetoric and point a finger of scorn at God's anointed! Some blasphemers are saying that Alistair Dormin is the Antichrist, and the new equitable monetary system is the Mark of the Beast. Utter nonsense!"

A chorus of laughter and boos issued from the audience.

"Biblical scholars agree that Emperor Nero was the Antichrist, and those who believe otherwise are nothing but ignorant reprobates. They are to be pitied above all creatures, the Devil's spawn sent to demoralize you with empty and deplorable words of woe!"

"That's a lie!" Connor screamed.

Brody launched to his feet, took the boy in hand, and briskly ushered him from the sanctuary. Feeling sick to her stomach, Paige followed close behind. Once inside the elevator, Brody blew up at his son. "What is wrong with you? How could you embarrass me like that?"

Connor lowered his head and kicked at the floor.

"Answer me!" Brody yelled as the door slid open to the parking garage.

"I wasn't trying to embarrass you, Dad," the boy mumbled.

As he marched his son to the car, Brody cast an exasperated look at his wife. "Connor, your behavior was rude, and I insist that you apologize to Apostle Nellaf."

"He's not an apostle, Dad, and he wasn't speaking the truth."

"I don't want to hear it!" Brody bellowed as his son climbed into the back seat of the Mercedes. "Until you apologize, you're grounded, and I'm confiscating that Bible you're always carrying around!" Brody's jaw clenched and unclenched as he jammed his foot on the throttle and sped away from the parking garage.

Paige leaned toward her husband and quietly said, "Honey, maybe you shouldn't take his Bible away. It's all he's got right now."

"Whose fault is that? You've coddled that boy long enough! It's time that Connor learns how things are done in the real world." The family rode the rest of the way home in prickly silence.

As Paige's husband pulled up beneath the carport of their southwest-style home, he snapped at his son, "Connor, go straight to your room!"

Once inside, Paige turned to her husband. "I understand that you have some good news to share with me."

Brody gave her a quizzical look. "You heard?"

"Jolene was bursting at the seams to tell me."

"I wanted to visit with you before the church service started, but there was some business..." Brody's face brightened. "I have been tapped to work with Alistair Dormin and the World Fortress Institute economic team to streamline the rollout of the Vita Signum project."

Paige was stunned. "I thought that you didn't trust Alistair Dormin and the World Fortress Institute. Have you forgotten what happened in New York?"

"As far as I'm concerned, that's water under the bridge," Brody replied. "My eyes have been opened, and I've come to see Dormin in a different light. The man is an economic genius. His brilliant polices testify to that. Of course, this means that I'll be doing a lot of traveling, but that's a sacrifice I'm willing to make." He squeezed Paige's hand so hard her fingers hurt. "Honey, think of this opportunity as a ministry for the good of mankind. Alistair Dormin is on the side of angels."

The hair on the back of her neck stood up, and Paige suddenly felt cold. *What kind of angels?* she silently wondered.

Cedar Key, Florida
Monday, September 17th

From the screened-in porch of the cottage, Joel surveyed their new base of operations provided by the Shadow Riders. He watched a pelican land upon a carved wooden sculpture. The gangly bird fluffed his wings and settled in for a rest atop the brightly painted totem.

An eclectic mix of yard art cluttered the sandy backyard: an orange bicycle that held flowerpots, a giant metal rooster, a purple framed door that opened to nowhere, and an assortment of colorful parrots that hung from the low-hanging branches of an old live oak.

A breeze from the estuary kicked in, sending a metal whirligig spinning. The tide was up, and the sun cast its golden rays across the waters of the estuary, giving promise to another brilliant sunset. Joel watched until the colors faded to grey before he went inside and turned on the TV. From the recliner, Joel watched the talking heads prattling on about the new monetary system and the nano implant, referred to formally as the Vita Signum ID, being applied in the hand or along the hairline—user's choice.

According to the World Fortress Institute, the mandatory rollout of Vita Signum was just around the corner. Big box retailers, service and health care providers, and restaurants were all expected to have their new scanning systems in place. Financial institutions were busy converting accounts and exchanging cash and coins for electronic currency. Before long, cash transactions would become obsolete.

Months of public service announcements had been looping continuously through the media, marketing the ease and benefits of the Vita Signum global system. Joel had heard the messages so many times that he could recite them in his sleep: *The way of the future; ecologically sustainable; an end to poverty, crime, and social injustice....* Social media sites were flooded with banners that read, "I received my Vita Signum!" and banks passed out "I love my Vita Signum!" buttons.

Feeling frustrated, he switched off the television. *Can't people see they are being seduced by elitist propaganda?* Joel checked the time and closed his eyes for a quick nap.

A sloppy tongue roused Joel from his slumber. "Knock it off, Moses. Oh crap, I'm late! I need to go fetch your favorite human." Joel dashed out the door and jumped into his golf cart. He drove past the Low Key Hideaway. It was packed with RVs, and judging from the sounds of revelry, the Tiki Bar was also hopping.

Joel continued down the long narrow key, past the clam cannery, and into the old part of Cedar Key, which was buttoned up for the night. Second Street was quiet, unlike the touristy areas over by the pier. He parked the golf cart in front of a two-story, shiplap building with a wrap-around porch. He went inside the Island Hotel & Restaurant expecting to find Coco waiting impatiently in the tiny lobby.

"Coco shouldn't be too long," the desk clerk told Joel. "Her last table just left a few minutes ago. We thought they were going to stay all night."

"Thanks, Bev." Joel took a seat, thumbed through an East Coast Magazine, and scanned an article about the dramatic rise in fatal shark attacks.

The clerk headed for the back of the hotel and poked her head into the bar. "It's closing time Ollie."

Looking a bit unsteady on his feet, the crusty regular emerged from the hotel bar. "If yer gonna holler at me, marry me!" Ollie quipped.

"Hello, Mr. Purvis," Joel said.

The man paused, lifted a burly eyebrow, and tipped his smelly cannery cap as he stumbled out the door.

Bev was tidying up the front desk when Coco finally appeared. "You certainly earned your tips tonight." The clerk followed the young couple to the door, said, "See you tomorrow," and threw the deadbolt behind them.

"I don't need to ask how your evening was," Joel said as they climbed into the golf cart. "Bev filled me in on the details."

"Good," Coco said, "because I'm exhausted. Have you heard from Katrina yet?"

Joel shook his head. "I'll check again when we get home." His mind wandered as they moved slowly up Highway 24. The only cars on the road were a few patrons leaving the Tiki Bar.

Back at the cottage, Moses tried to impress Coco with his usual tricks. She tossed the ugly mutt a Milk Bone, turned to Joel, and yawned. "I'm going to bed."

"Ah, here's the encrypted email I've been expecting." Joel settled down at the kitchen table to decipher the information that Katrina had gathered. "Civil unrest continues to erupt across the country, and there is an ominous coalition of World Fortress Institute-aligned troops amassing around Israel. Nationals are fleeing their homeland by the thousands!" the email said.

He kept on reading. "Drought conditions continue across the globe. The water levels of the Nile and Euphrates rivers are dangerously low. In the United States, reservoirs are slowly being depleted, and in some areas, the ground water levels are dropping rapidly. Americans have been placed under strict water-rationing mandates, and wheat, corn, and other food crops are deeply impacted.

"Churches are now required to use the Vita Signum system for tithe collections, and legislation is being advanced to outlaw homeschooling." *My gosh, can it get any worse?* Joel worried.

Joel downloaded the material for his podcast and placed his phone on the charger. In the quiet of the night, his thoughts turned to his biological father, the late President Thomas Atwood. *How,* Joel wondered, *would his father respond to the politics of today?*

Chapter 15

New York City
Saturday, October 6th

Back in New York from her recent trip to Israel, Katrina was still reeling from the voicemail left by her doctor. "You have a genetic disorder called Gaucher's Disease. I'd like you to schedule an appointment so we can discuss treatment options."

"Shake it off," Katrina told herself as she stepped from her car parked beneath a maple tree. It was a beautiful fall day with the sun highlighting the fall colors. She turned up the collar of her coat and strolled toward the Bazaar on a carpet of leaves. *There are bigger problems than my health right now.*

The Vita Signum mandate was looming large on the political horizon. Everything was now in place for a smooth transition to making it a mandatory requirement for all global citizens. Even the leaders of Israel had caved into international and internal pressures. Now, only China stood alone in defiance.

How can people not see that their freedoms are on the line? she wondered. The collective mindset had been primed by repetitive feel-good propaganda, lulling the populous into a kind of apathetic euphoria. According to Katrina's mole at the World Fortress Institute, even natural disasters were being used as an opportunity to garner favor for the Vita Signum through humanitarian aid.

Katrina thought about Alistair Dormin. His physical changes since the assassination and miraculous healing were startling. His damaged eye was hidden behind a silver patch, and his sable-colored hair had turned white almost overnight. He looked more formidable than before, and the cadence of his forceful words made his speech hypnotic. Katrina shuddered at the historical parallels to Hitler's charisma and the cult of personality that he created. *Alistair Dormin, like all dictators before him, is a collector of souls,* she thought.

The Gourmet Food Truck Festival was well underway, and the Bazaar grounds teamed with people. As usual, Katrina had no idea who was going to make the Shadow Rider information drop, or even how it would be done.

Trying to blend in, she moved casually among the masses. Between the rows of gourmet food trucks, Katrina skirted lines of foodies waiting to sample delicacies such as gourmet pizza, crepes, confections, and stuffed French toast. Most of the trucks ran generators, and as the fumes mingled with the food smells, Katrina became nauseous. *I hope this doesn't take long.*

She spotted a dark-skinned man serpentine his way through the crowd with a tower of cotton candy in his hand. He approached Katrina and offered her one.

"No thanks."

"Compliments of John Galt." The man smiled and thrust a paper cone into Katrina's hand and quickly moved on through the crowd. *Clever information drop,* she thought. Katrina could feel a thumb drive in the tip of the paper cone.

On her way back, Katrina removed the tiny thumb drive, discarded the cotton candy in a garbage bin, and picked up her pace. Near the sidewalk, Katrina noticed someone leaning against her car. *It's that woman!* She boldly walked up and confronted the stranger. "Excuse me ma'am, are you following me?"

"What's the matter, Trina? Don't you recognize your own mother?"

The woman pushed her sunglasses atop a tangled mop of grey hair. Her face was bloated and blotchy, but those familiar dark eyes stopped Katrina cold. Suddenly, she felt like a vulnerable child. "What do you want?"

The woman's mouth formed a pout. "I brought you into this world, Trina baby."

"Don't call me that!"

"Would you prefer to be called Kitten?" The woman sniffed. "You always were a daddy's girl."

Katrina struggled to regain her composure. "What happened that day, Mother?"

"Water under the bridge as far as I'm concerned. Besides, that was a long time ago." Katrina's hands began to shake as the image of her beloved father lying in a pool of blood flashed through her mind. "Look baby, I may not deserve a Mother of the Year Award, but now that you're all grown up, I was hoping…"

Katrina fished her car keys from her satchel. "You've wasted your time." She climbed into her car, locked the door, and watched the subject of her childhood nightmares casually stroll down the sidewalk.

Suddenly screams emanated from the Bazaar. Katrina turned to see hundreds of seabirds as they fluttered over the food trucks and dive-bombed the customers. *Even the birds have gone crazy,* Katrina thought as a gull shattered her windshield.

Tucson, Arizona
Wednesday, October 17th

Paige opened her oven, and the scent of her gourmet dinner filled the kitchen. The quail was browning nicely on a bed of pancetta, peas, and white wine. Her stuffed Portobello mushrooms and Greek lemon potatoes were in the warming oven. Paige arranged the curried Waldorf Salad on crystal salad plates and placed them in the fridge next to her famous Raspberry Charlotte dessert.

When Brody called earlier, all he said was, "I'm bringing home a special guest for dinner tonight, someone I knew from my Whitehouse days. Adults only, okay?" he added.

After a quick walk-through of the dining room to double-check the place settings of silverware and bone china, Paige retrieved the pizza she'd baked for her son and went to deliver it.

Connor was sitting in a bean-bag chair staring out the bedroom window at the desert.

"I brought you dinner," Paige said cheerfully. "Have you picked out a movie to watch?"

"Mom, when can I have my Bible back?"

"Soon, I hope." Paige laid a hand on her teenage son's shoulder. "I'll talk to Dad again."

"Why does he hate me?"

"Sweetheart, your father doesn't hate you! He's just under a lot of stress lately." Paige kissed her son's cheek and slipped into the hallway to wipe tears from her eyes.

Back in the kitchen, Paige uncorked a couple of bottles of expensive red wine and glanced at the kitchen clock. It was nearly six o'clock, and Brody and their guest would be arriving any minute.

The alarm system alerted her phone, and the security camera captured Brody's Mercedes, followed closely behind by a black limousine, coming down their long driveway. The limo pulled up under the tiled portico, and the driver opened the door for a familiar little man with dark hair. Paige's husband visited with his guest for a few seconds before ushering him inside.

"Paige, I'd like you to meet Jean Pierre of the World Fortress Institute."

"Welcome to our home," she replied.

Jean Pierre took her hand. "Au Chante, mademoiselle," he gushed. "You are even lovelier that I imagined and most gracious to have me as your guest."

Paige served Brody and Jean Pierre a glass of wine and left them in the formal living room to discuss matters of pressing business.

Dinner was soon announced, and the men came into the dining room where they settled into their chairs to enjoy the meal set before them.

"Most delicious," Jean Pierre said as he finished his Waldorf salad.

Brody offered more wine from a decanter, while Paige cleared plates and slipped back into the kitchen to retrieve the main course. Their guest savored every bite of his braised Quail and potatoes. "Most excellent, mademoiselle. Your husband did not exaggerate your gastronomic skills."

Paige thanked him, but there was something smarmy about Jean Pierre and his obsequious flattery. By the time she served the dessert, Paige remembered why their guest seemed so familiar. According to Katrina Katz, Jean Pierre and Alistair Dormin were both responsible for trying to ruin Brody's career when they were in Manhattan!

"You should be very proud of your husband," Pierre told her. "He possesses a brilliant economic mind. He has been most valuable to our organization."

"Thanks for your kind words, Jean Pierre," Brody cut in, "but I'm just part of an excellent team."

"Your humility is refreshing, mon ami."

"Shall we retire to the living room for a nightcap to discuss business?" Brody turned to his wife. "Paige, would you bring out the Grand Marnier?"

In the kitchen, Paige retrieved her best Waterford crystal glasses from the china cabinet and placed them on a silver tray along with the bottle of the French brandy liquor.

When she entered the living room, the conversation came to an abrupt stop.

"Thank you, darling," Brody said after she placed the tray on the coffee table. The men made small talk until she left the room. Something stopped Paige just outside the arched doorway. She lingered, knowing it was wrong to eavesdrop, but her curiosity and a strange sense of foreboding, kept her there.

Jean Pierre began to speak. "We live in fascinating times, don't you agree? Never in the history of mankind have there been so many options available for managing the populous."

"Can you elaborate?" Brody said.

"Brute force was once necessary to control people as history will attest. Mao Tse Tung wrote in his Little Red Book that 'Political power begins from the barrel of a gun.'"

"That's right," Brody interjected. "Joseph Stalin and Hitler wiped out millions of their dissenters."

"This is true, but Hitler also taught us the importance of the use of propaganda to encourage political compliance. Today, technological advances have opened vast opportunities to spread our political message, but we must also recognize mankind's spiritual needs." Jean Pierre paused. "If we are to achieve our vision of a docile utopian society, then politics and religion must be fused under one common umbrella."

"That's easier said than done!" Brody balked.

"Yes, my friend, but it is possible. In the third century, Constantine legalized Christianity and began to address their issues. Many groups were factious and fighting back then, much like denominations of today. Yet, through doctrinal deliberations, Constantine was able to hammer out a unified belief system, one that was also politically committed to him."

"You're talking about a universal church."

"Precisely, mon ami," Pierre replied. "I believe that Karl Marx saw religion as a two-edged sword. An enemy that could foster critical thinking and free thought or as an opiate used to subdue the masses. Our goal is to achieve global religious syncretism."

"I see," Brody said. "Jesus said it two thousand years ago, and I guess it's still true today—people are like sheep."

Jean Pierre laughed. "He was a wise philosopher, mon ami."

Suddenly, the ground beneath Paige's feet began to rumble, and she quietly hurried back to her post in the kitchen. Pots and pans began swinging on the rack and a crystal glass toppled from the countertop and shattered on the floor. *It's an Earthquake!*

She dashed down the hallway to Connor's bedroom and threw open the door. "Are you okay, Sweetheart?"

"Mom, it's all happening just like God said it would," Connor cried out, "and there's nothing we can do to stop it!"

*

Arroyo Seco, Arizona

Thursday, October 18th

The sun had barely risen above the horizon when Jim Saunders pulled up to the General Store where David and Ezra waited.

"Did you feel the ground shaking last night?" David said as he hopped into the front seat of Jim's SUV, and Ezra climbed in back. "Elita said her great, great grandfather talked about the Sonoran Earthquake of 1887."

As he pulled away from the curb, Jim Saunders seemed unusually pensive.

"Do you think the town well was damaged by last night's earthquake?" David asked their resident hydraulic engineer.

Jim turned toward the edge of town. "I'm hoping it didn't. That porous aquifer we tapped into was barely yielding enough to meet the needs of this town. If the tremors shifted things in the wrong direction, we could have a serious problem on our hands."

From the back seat, Ezra spoke up. "David, do you remember what Zeke talked about when he visited a few months back?"

"Refresh my memory."

"Zeke told us about the first time you went to Hope Springs, and how you worried about the desert heat and dehydration."

"That's right, and then he struck the ground with an iron rod, and water bubbled up and pooled in the rocks."

David remembered how they had splashed like children in the sandstone basin.

"Have faith," Ezra said.

The men arrived at the first well site, and Jim Saunders hopped from the SUV to check for damage. David and Ezra watched as he opened the valve, and water gushed out with a mighty force.

"Well, I'll be darned. It's a miracle!" Jim bellowed. "That earthquake must have opened a fissure to a major carbonate rock aquifer!"

"Hallelujah!" Ezra exclaimed. "God provides!"

The men found the same result at each of the other wells.

What are the chances of that? David thought. He looked skyward beyond the clouds that glowed with rays of morning light, and he whispered, "God, nothing is too difficult for You."

Chapter 16

Tucson, Arizona

Tuesday, November 13th

Paige settled into her favorite living room chair and gazed through the window. Even the desert landscape looked stressed from the drought. The once subtle shades of green now looked brown and brittle, and the cacti hung limp from thirst.

She sighed and then reached for her Bible. It wasn't where she had left it. Paige had a pretty good idea where it was. She headed straight for her son's room and found him reading it. "Aha! Caught you red-handed!" she teased.

"Sorry, Mom. I should have asked to borrow it."

Paige sat on the edge of Connor's bed. "Why don't you read to me?"

Connor began to read from the book of Matthew. "'Don't let anyone mislead you,' Jesus warned, 'for many will come in my name, claiming, I am the Messiah. They will deceive many.'"

While Connor read on, Paige's mind wandered to a recent sermon she had heard at the MIA church. "Didn't Jesus tell us that we would do greater works than he did? He showed us how to appropriate the spirit of Messiah," Nellaf had said. "We can become like God!" A shiver had snaked down Paige's spine, and she had wondered, *isn't that the same lie spoken by the serpent in the Garden of Eden?*

Another faint aftershock rumbled underfoot as Connor kept reading, "There will be famines and earthquakes in many parts of the world. But all this is only the first of the birth pains, with more to come."

He closed the Bible and looked earnestly at his mother. "I had another dream last night. I'm ready to tell you about it."

Paige nodded. "I'm listening."

"The dreams all begin the same way," Connor told her. "You and I are in this little stone hut, but Dad isn't there. I am standing at the window watching a really big storm building. You know—lightning, thunder, and swirling wind. Then I notice this red horse coming toward us. Its rider is all dressed in green. They come closer, and I realize that the horse and rider are chasing a kid that I know from school." Connor paused to explain. "Mom, I always felt sorry for this boy because he never ate at the cafeteria or had a sack lunch, so I often shared mine with him. Sometimes I would give him all of it."

"You should have said something. I would have packed extra." Paige smiled at her son. "But it blesses me to hear about your kindness."

He shrugged. "Anyway, Mom, about the dream. I see this horse and rider chasing that kid, and there is nothing I can do to help him. Suddenly, a stone in the bottom corner of the hut begins to glow. It gets whiter and whiter, so bright that its light fills the room like the sun, but it doesn't hurt my eyes."

"What happens then?"

Connor chewed his lip. He looked pleadingly at his mother with an intensity that shook her. "Please, Mom, don't take the Vita Signum chip. Promise me that you won't!"

"Okay, Son," Paige said. "I promise."

<hr>

Cedar Key, Florida
Monday, November 19th

A pelican landed on the end of the pier, and Moses hit the end of his leash, barking until it flapped away.

"Easy boy," Joel said and then turned his attention to Coco, who was looking across the gulf waters to the island that once housed an old pencil factory.

"I'd love to rent some kayaks and go explore that island one day," she said. "We could take a picnic lunch."

"That would be nice." Joel gazed at his Amerasian beauty, her golden skin and silky black hair blowing in the coastal breeze. Peaceful afternoons like this made it easy to forget that they were hiding from a madman and running from a hostile government.

Coco reached for her husband's hand. "I love our life together."

Joel smiled. "It's certainly not a conventional one."

"That's true, but you can't say it's boring either." She laughed.

Hand in hand, they strolled back to the old part of town.

At the Island Hotel and Restaurant, Joel gave his wife a kiss and said, "I'll pick you up after work." He watched her go inside and then headed back to the cottage.

When Joel arrived home, he found the screen door ajar and propped inside was a plain envelope.

He hurried inside to examine the contents: two leather ID bracelets with metal plates—one inscribed with "J" and the other "C." An attached note read, "Counterfeit Vita Signum chip inside. Wear always."

Someone in town is obviously working for the Shadow Riders, Joel thought as he burned the note with a Bic lighter. Joel washed burnt paper down the kitchen sink and tried on his newest survival gear. *Totally inconspicuous,* Joel mused. *I'll take Coco to Steamers on her night off, and we can test it out.* He settled into his chair, booted up his laptop, and put some finishing touches on the script for his next podcast.

Joel turned on the TV to kill time and was just getting into a movie when it was interrupted by "Breaking News." "An assassination attempt has been made on China's President, Chiang Zuolin."

Joel's cell phone rang, and he answered, expecting to hear Katrina's voice on the other end.

"Is Coco okay?" It was Bev, the Island Hotel Desk Clerk.

Joel pitched forward in his seat. "Why do you ask?"

"I'm just worried that she's sick or something. It's not like Coco to leave right in the middle of serving a table full of customers."

"Did she say anything?" Joel asked with growing alarm.

"No, about fifteen minutes ago, her customers started complaining about the service. That's when I noticed she was gone."

"Call the police. I'm on my way!"

Joel raced toward town, muttering, "Please God, let Coco be okay."

He skidded to a stop outside the old hotel, did a quick check inside the hotel, and then bolted outside calling Coco's name. Joel's worst fear came to mind, *The Signature Killer! This can't be happening!* Sickened by the thought, he frantically searched the dark streets.

A faint noise met his ear. Joel stilled himself to listen. Yes, the sound was coming from the two-story, weathered ruins on the other side of B Street.

Joel circled the dilapidated structure, and near the back, he heard a loud thud. He squeezed between some rotten boards and strained to see in the dark space.

"She's back over there and pretty shook up," a familiar voice said. Someone lit a match, and in the dim light, Joel recognized the face of Mr. Purvis, a frequent flyer at the Island Hotel Bar.

Joel launched himself across piles of fallen debris and

grabbed the old man by the collar. "You SOB! What have you done to my wife?"

"Ollie didn't hurt me," Coco cried out.

"That's right, young fella. Don't get yer shorts in a wad."

Coco ran into her husband's arms. "If it wasn't for Ollie…" She began to sob.

"I was having a smoke outside when I seen this fella comin' out the back door of the hotel with yer wife," Mr. Purvis explained. "He had a knife to her ribs, so it didn't take no rocket scientist to figure he was up to no good."

Joel clenched his fists. "Where is he?"

"That belly crawler ain't gonna be bothering this little gal no more." Mr. Purvis pointed to a body lying in a crumpled heap at his feet. "That stupid sod run himself headlong into a four-by-four I was holding." Ollie chuckled.

In the slivers of moonlight that shined through cracks, Joel reached for the old fisherman's leathery hand. "I don't know how to thank you, Sir."

The old man winked. "Buy me a couple rounds sometime, and we'll lift a toast to John Galt."

They heard a siren, and Ollie ambled out to visit with one of the Cedar Key Police officers.

Joel took Coco in his arms. "Are you hurt?"

Coco shook her head. "No, but I thought he was going to kill me."

A lawman appeared on the scene and followed Mr.

Purvis to the spot where the body lay. He searched the dead man's pockets for identification. "Is the name Theron Hunt familiar to anyone?"

"I believe this man is the Signature Killer," Joel replied. "He was stalking my wife."

"I'll need to take statements," the officer said as the state police arrived.

While Coco was being interviewed, Joel punched out a text message to Katrina. "Signature Killer is dead, but our cover may be compromised. We will need to move to a new location ASAP."

⊸∞∞⊷

East Harlem, New York
Friday, November 23rd

It was chilly outside when Katrina entered her new apartment. She laid some boxes on the flimsy coffee table, stopped to adjust her thermostat, and collapsed onto the couch. Fighting exhaustion, she kicked off her shoes, laid her head back, and closed her eyes. *Just a few minutes...,* she thought. Katrina drifted off to the smell of old wood and mildew.

Gar walked through the door with boxes in hand. "These were stacked outside your door. I assume you want them inside." He placed them in the corner and said, "You look like crap."

"Thanks a lot."

"You got anything to eat in this little, fitted kitchen?" Gar rifled through the fridge and grabbed an apple.

"I appreciate all of your help." Katrina raked her fingers through her tangle of hair.

"That's what friends are for." Gar took a bite and looked around the apartment. "Looks like you'll have to rub elbows with the rest of us peons now."

Katrina tried to muster a smile, but the events of the last year had taken their toll. *She missed her beloved grandmother, the career that she had worked so hard to build, and now her health...*

Gar clapped his hands together. "Snap out of it, Kat! Let's celebrate your new digs."

"I'm too tired," Katrina said still sprawled across the couch.

"I noticed a Japanese steakhouse next door. How about some takeout? My treat."

Katrina looked at Gar's eager face and didn't have the heart to say "No."

"I'll be back in a flash with a meal fit for an emperor!" he said as he dashed out the door.

Alone in the apartment, Katrina sat listening to the city sounds outside her single-pane window. She reached for the backpack and began to unpack her most treasured items. She placed Babbeh's Bible and journals on the coffee table along with the family photo album. She picked up the book of memories and lingered over photographs of her grandparents in their younger days. Their happy faces gave no hint of the horrors they had known during the Holocaust.

Katrina once asked Babbeh, "How can you trust in a God who allowed such suffering?"

"The answers are written down in the good book, Kitten," her grandmother had replied.

Katrina glanced over black and white images of picnics, family meals, and group gatherings, but the next few pages were filled with color snapshots of her father. The images progressed from Cub Scouts to graduation pictures.

She turned the page to the photograph that always brought tears to her eyes. The painful memory of her eleventh birthday was something that Katrina would rather forget. She was sitting behind a birthday cake, and her smiling dad was helping her blow out the candles. *If only I had known what was going to happen next, maybe I could have stopped it.* Katrina's stomach ached when she looked at that little girl, totally unaware that her life was about to change forever.

According to Babbeh, this photograph had arrived in the mail one day with no return address. A scribbled note was included, informing Babbeh of her son's tragic death.

"We lost contact with your father after he married your mother," Babbeh had explained to Katrina. "Until this photograph came, I didn't even know that I had a granddaughter."

"Room service!" Gar announced, when he returned from the Japanese Steakhouse. He walked past Katrina leaving a trail of smells in his wake. "The restaurant had their TV playing. Vita Signum PSAs running in a tight loop. It was totally obnoxious." He placed an assortment of takeout boxes on the center of a card table.

"Let me guess," Katrina said, "Deadlines are fast approaching for the new monetary implants that will put an end to fraud and crime, facilitate fast emergency response, streamline healthcare, and banking."

"Yup, and cures fits, farts, and freckles too!" Gar quipped.

Katrina laughed out loud and realized how much she needed that release.

Gar placed flimsy paper plates and a couple sets of chop sticks on the table. "Got any glasses? I picked us up a bottle of Saki."

Katrina rifled her cupboard and found several plastic tumblers.

At the table, Gar pulled out a folding chair and said, "After you, madam."

The first course of onion soup went down easy.

Gar motored through his greens and said, "Man, I really dig this ginger dressing. By the way, I got you some extra yum-yum sauce and chips in case you get the munchies later."

"Thanks," Katrina said as he opened the paper cartons and dished up helpings of Beef Sukiyaki, Tempura Shrimp, and Miso Glazed Scallops.

"I won't be able to eat all this," Katrina complained.

"You need to put some meat on those skinny bones." Gar gave her a concerned look. "So, what did the doctor say about the Gaucher's Disease thing?"

"He recommends Enzyme Replacement Therapy, but I said no."

"What! Why?"

"It's very time-consuming and each treatment costs over twenty-thousand dollars. I can't take a chance on my counterfeit chip being flagged." Katrina poked at a scallop with her chopsticks.

"Your health is worth the risk," Gar scolded.

"That's my call," Katrina snapped. "Besides, there's medication I can take to manage the symptoms."

Gar poured more Saki and lifted his tumbler, "Here's to your health and your new digs."

Katrina ate what she could and pushed her plate aside. "This has been a really nice evening, Gar."

"Sounds like you're trying to run me off, but I just poured myself some more Saki." Gar offered some to Katrina.

"No thanks," she said as Gar joined her on the couch.

"What's this?" He picked up the family photo album and began to thumb through its pages. "This has got to be your father—same eyes and coloring. Where's a pic of your mom?"

Katrina considered telling Gar about her recent strange encounter with her mother. "She left when I was a child."

"Bummer!" He tossed the album onto the coffee table, and a photograph fell out. "Hello! What's this?"

Katrina tried to retrieve the snapshot, but Gar held it out of her reach.

"This girl looks a lot like you, except she's smiling." He grinned and tapped the photo with his index finger. "But who's that curly-haired dude holding your hand?"

"His name is Benjamin. We attended Cornell together," Katrina said impatiently. "Look Gar, I don't want to be rude, but I really am exhausted."

"Okay, okay, I can take a hint."

"Thanks for the dinner." Katrina walked him to the door.

"My pleasure. Better lock up behind me," he added on the way out, "because you're not in Kansas anymore."

In the quiet of her apartment, Katrina held the photograph of her and Benjamin and tried to recall the happiness they had once shared.

Sadness settled over Katrina as she slipped on her nightgown and turned off the lights. She got into bed, but she lay awake, trying to will herself to sleep. When the dreams finally came, they troubled her…

The turbulent waters were cold. "Come on in!" she called out to Benjamin, who was standing on a rock near the shore. Katrina watched him shimmy from his jeans and join her. They splashed like kids in the waters below Ithaca Falls.

"Bet you can't catch me?" Katrina heard herself say. She dove under and then felt her lover's arms around her. They rose to the surface and joined for a tender kiss.

"My turn," Benjamin pushed her away and dove under in the direction of the falls.

"No Benjamin, don't!" Time slowed as she waited for him to surface...

Katrina dove under desperately groping for her lover's hand. The current grabbed her, and she felt her body being slammed to the rocks below. The pressure was unbearable as she struggled, desperate for air.

Then, Katrina, resolved to her fate, gave in. Her body involuntarily drew a breath, and she felt water flooding into her lungs. Katrina could see sunlight through the water. It danced before her eyes and then faded. Just before everything went dark, she sensed someone tugging on her arm.

Coughing and gasping for air, Katrina felt disoriented when she opened her eyes. There was an elderly man kneeling over her, speaking words of comfort. She remembered his pale, blue eyes and water dripping from his long white beard.

The paramedics arrived. They took her vitals and asked questions that she couldn't answer.

A few feet away, a rescue team launched an inflatable boat into the water, and then the fog in her mind began to clear.

Screaming Benjamin's name, Katrina woke herself up. The memories of that tragic day were as clear as if it happened yesterday, but there was something else, something in the back of her mind. Then, in a flash, it came to her. *That old man who pulled me from the water was Zeke!*

⸎

Arroyo Seco, Arizona

Friday, November 30th

The utility vehicle wound its way up the Eagle Pass switchbacks. "There's a pullout on top," David said as they neared the crest.

Ezra parked near a historic marker that chronicled Arizona gold rush days. "I believe these electric utility cars will suit our needs well." Ezra looked to the vehicle roof and added, "The solar panels that are mounted on the roof will recover lost energy, but it's God who provides the abundant sunlight."

David climbed out and stretched. "How many of these were delivered last week?"

"One hundred and fifty," Ezra replied. "Of course, that is not many for a community of thousands, so we must work out an equitable system for their use. Something based on need, I suppose."

David looked out across the desert panorama and tried to recall how it looked the first time he drove up here on his Triumph Rocket 3 motorcycle. The landscape was now eclipsed by a white city of desert yurts and punctuated by carefully placed water towers, composting toilets, and solar bath houses.

I've witnessed some strange events over the years. David thought back to the odd ramblings of an old rancher named Rupert Sims, the arrival of Zeke, and the strange birth of Hope Springs, but nothing had prepared him for what he was seeing now.

His gaze shifted to the Mexican border and the clusters of nationals, who were waiting to re-enter their homeland. Eight miles north of the border sat Arroyo Seco. Once a dusty ghost town, it had blossomed into a bustling burg. The storefronts on main street had been revived by fresh coats of paint and clean glass, but one old building still looked the same.

"Our suppliers have all transitioned to the new monetary system," David said. "As soon as we run out of stock, the General Store will be closing."

Ezra smiled and shook his head. "That won't be necessary." He pointed to the stockyards, poultry farms, and the massive warehouses that had recently been built where the old Civic Border Guard compound once stood. "Distribution centers are being set up across our region as we speak. The General Store is central to your district. If you and Elita are willing to serve the community, we will supply the necessary rations for weekly allocation."

David pondered the proposal. He gazed down below where the roads, which once etched the landscape like veins, had been compromised by convoys of tractor-trailers loaded with supplies and building materials. Among the desert yurts that dotted the landscape, David could see people moving about like industrious ants preparing for a long cold winter. "God, it's really happening," he whispered. For as far as his eye could see, the vision of Rupert Sims had become manifest.

"Let me talk to Elita and get back to you," David finally answered.

Chapter 17

Angel's Camp, California
Tuesday, December 4th

It started to rain harder, and Joel quickly finished dumping slop buckets into the pig trough. He stopped to zip his hooded rain jacket, gathered the empty pails, and went to help Coco with her chores.

He found his wife standing in the middle of a brood of cackling hens and strutting roosters. Coco's cheeks flushed, her black hair was slick from the rain, and Joel was overcome by her natural beauty. She spotted her husband and waved him over. They stood for a few moments watching the frenzied birds pecking at the pellets.

"I love it here," Coco said. "The Shadow Riders never fail to surprise! This time, I hope we can stay awhile."

Joel put his arm around her and felt her shivering. "You're soaked. Why don't you go inside and dry off? I'll do the rest of your chores."

"There's no need because I already fed the goats." She smiled and added, "But thanks for the offer."

They walked back, stomped through puddles in their

wellies, and laughed like children as they went to their bungalow.

Joel hung his raincoat on a peg and stoked the fire in the wood-burning stove while Coco went to the bedroom to slip into some dry clothes.

She emerged wearing her kimono and stood by the window as she dried her hair with a towel. Coco pointed to the vineyard in the valley below and said, "Have you ever noticed how the colors grow richer and more vibrant when it rains?"

Joel joined his bride to gaze beyond the sheets of rain rolling down the glass. He placed his hand upon the small of her back that was now warmed by the fire. "Do you know how much I love you?" She responded with a kiss that ignited Joel's passion. He lifted his tiny bride and carried her into the bedroom.

Later, as the sun sank low on the horizon, Coco scrambled some eggs for dinner while Joel toasted some slices of sourdough bread that their host family had provided. They shared their meal in quiet contentment as the setting sun cast an alpine glow across the landscape. In that moment, all seemed right with the world.

Joel had just finished drying the dishes, when he spotted the Gator headlights bouncing up the road. "We've got company."

"Mrs. Delacroix said she might stop by this evening," Coco said. "I'll put the tea kettle on."

A few minutes later, the plump, pleasant-faced woman was at their door with a basket in her hand. "I won't stay long.

I just thought you kids might enjoy some home-cured bacon and another loaf of bread. I threw in a couple of jars of my homemade jam too."

Coco gave the woman a hug. "Thank you, Mrs. Delacroix. Please won't you stay for a cup of tea?"

"Well, maybe just one, but please call me Nellie." She settled her pudgy frame onto a kitchen chair and smoothed the braided bun that sat atop her head. "You kids have been such a Godsend to me and Clive. With my husband's back troubles and my old knees, the farm chores have become a burden."

Coco set cups and tea bags on the table and poured steaming water from a pot. "You have both been so kind. I was just telling Joel that I hope we can stay here for a while."

Nellie's cheeks flushed with emotion. "For as long as you want."

There was something about the woman's sweet lack of pretense that reminded Joel of Nora, his birth mother. "So, what's Clive up to?" he said.

"Oh, he's been fiddling with the satellite receiver," Nellie replied. "When I left, he was still trying to pick up a free news channel."

Joel thought about the fast-approaching mandates. "Citizens across the globe will soon be required to receive the Vita Signum ID," he said. "According to the constant stream of PSAs, there will be stiff penalties for non-compliance. Things are going to get rough for a lot of people."

"At least you and Clive have this farm to fall back on," Coco said and then offered some sugar and creamer.

Nellie sighed. "I'm afraid it will soon take more than eggs and goat milk to sustain us. Our next installment of property tax is due in the spring. After January 1, the State requires Vita Signum for transactions."

"I never thought about taxes!" Coco exclaimed. "What are you going to do?"

"Pray for wisdom and trust in God. That's all we can do." She stirred a couple lumps of sugar into her tea. "The Bible clearly warned us about the times we're facing now, but I never really thought that I would live to see them happen."

"Like the people who were there when the Red Sea parted, or the walls of Jericho fell, we are witnessing these events that are actually foretold in the Bible," Coco interjected. "It's kind of exciting when you think about it."

Nellie smiled. "How can one so young have such faith?" She glanced at the kitchen clock. "My goodness, is that really the time?" The old woman hoisted herself from the table and made her way to the door. "Clive and I would be honored if you two would join us for dinner on Christmas Eve. I usually roast a big turkey. We can't eat it all by ourselves, and you guys are like family."

"We would be delighted!" Coco said without hesitation.

Tucson, Arizona
Sunday, December 16th

Paige drove into the Memorial Interfaith Assembly private parking garage and pulled into the space reserved for the Hays family.

She glanced at Brody in the passenger seat. He was busy flipping through papers in his briefcase.

"When did you say you'll be returning from Paris?"

Brody replied without looking up. "I sent a calendar invitation to your iPhone. I'm the Keynote Speaker at the Global Economic Conference this Tuesday, but I'll be in Paris for a week and then on to Munich to conduct an economic workshop."

"So, you won't be home until after Christmas?" Paige asked.

"It can't be helped," Brody replied. "Try to understand the importance of what we are doing here."

"Yes, of course." Paige could feel the tension between them. "Honey, won't you let me drive you to the airport after the service?"

Brody retrieved his suitcase from the trunk. "That won't be necessary. Besides, the security around the private hangar is tight. They are expecting me to arrive in the church limo right after the service."

They walked to the elevator in the parking garage in strained silence.

"Have you thought more about what I said?" Brody asked as they ascended.

"Honey, it just doesn't feel right. Besides, I promised…"

"That boy needs counseling, not a helicopter mom. You're feeding his delusions!" Brody snapped.

Anger rose inside Paige. "Connor. Your son's name is Connor."

"Look Paige, I'm tired of fighting. Can't you see how it looks? I helped develop this new system, yet my own family acts like I'm a tool of the Devil." Brody's jaw clenched. "When I return, I expect you and Connor to be fully Vita Signum compliant. Do I make myself clear?"

"Very," she replied as the elevator door opened.

In the sanctuary, Paige sat silently fighting the turmoil that raged inside while Brody milled about shaking hands and chatting with church VIPs. Paige stood through the worship mouthing the words. *Brody expects loyalty, but at what cost?* she wondered.

According to the teachings of the MIA church, "Alistair Dormin was resurrected from the dead, just like his forerunner, Jesus. The Chairman is the new chosen man of God, the one who will usher in the age of global peace!" Paige lost count how many times these words had been spoken from the pulpit.

A tutorial on tithing with the new Vita Signum system appeared on the big screens behind the stage:

> **1: Use the QR code to open the tithing app on your phone ***
>
> **2: Enter the amount**
>
> **3: Hold your phone near your Vita Signum chip**

4: "You are successful" will appear on your screen
For those without a phone, an electronic giving plate with a Vita Signum chip reader will be passed to you by an usher

An elder walked onto the stage and waved his hands like he was fanning a flame. "Blessings, blessings upon all generous givers. You are advancing the mighty Kingdom of God on earth. Great shall be your reward!"

The image on the screens shifted to the silk curtains that hung at the back of center stage, and one of the deacons said, "Please rise for the Grand Apostle Nellaf!"

The crowd stood and reverently lifted their hands in worshipful adoration as Max Nellaf made his entrance. He walked back and forth on the stage, and Paige had the feeling that the man was breathing in the praises of his people. Mounted on a platform, a professional camera crew captured a live feed for the international church community. Nellaf finally took his place behind the podium, and with a gentle flick of his hand, he quieted the congregation. "Welcome to your father's house, my little children! You may be seated."

Paige's thoughts shifted to Connor, home alone with his childlike faith. Her eyes brimmed with tears, and she barely heard a word the reverend spoke. "Help me, Jesus. Please, give me wisdom," she prayed under her breath. The Bible on her lap was open, and she began to read from Isaiah 43, where the Lord says, "But forget all that; it is nothing compared to what I am going to do. For I am about to do something new. See, I have already begun! Do you not see it? I will make a pathway through the wilderness. I will create rivers in the dry wasteland.”

A video image of Alistair Dormin appeared on the big screen. His once sable-colored hair had turned white, and he wore a silver patch over the eye that had been pierced.

“A new statue of Alistair Dormin is being erected on the site where our beloved Chairman rose from the dead!” Reverend Nellaf announced. “The date of his divine resurrection is to be honored as a global holiday.”

The congregation applauded the news.

Brody nudged his wife. “Maybe you and I should attend the unveiling.” It was more of a statement than a question.

On stage, Max Nellaf began to shout, “He once was dead, and now he lives!” The words echoed through the cavernous sanctuary. “All glory to the risen Chairman who leads us on in victory!”

Paige’s husband launched to his feet along with most of the congregation, and in that moment, Paige felt as though her whole world was falling apart.

Chapter 18

Arroyo Seco, Arizona

Tuesday, January 1ˢᵗ

Elita nudged her sleeping husband. "Honey, there's someone knocking on the door downstairs."

David sat up in bed and looked at the lighted dial on his bedside clock. "It's almost 3:00 am!" He put on his robe and got into his slippers. "I'll check it out."

"Be careful," Elita whispered as he made his way to the stairs.

David grabbed the baseball bat that he kept behind the General Store cash register, flipped on the porch light, and peered outside. Looking back at him was the face of his teenage nephew. He threw back the deadbolt and said, "Connor! What are you doing here?"

"I have run away, Uncle David. I had to…," the boy blurted.

"How did you get here?"

"A nice Mexican family gave me a ride." Changing the subject, he said, "Everything is so different here. I wasn't even sure this was Arroyo Seco."

David was still trying to process the information as he ushered Connor inside. "You were hitchhiking? Don't you know how dangerous that is?"

"Dad told Mom and me that we had to get the Vita Signum injected before he gets back from Paris. I just can't do it, Uncle David, so I sneaked out while Mom was sleeping." The teenager began to cry. "Dad hates me."

"I'm sure you're mistaken."

"He thinks that the Vita Signum program is going to make the world a better place, but if he would just read the Bible, then he'd know it's wrong."

David considered his nephew's plight. "You must be exhausted. We'll talk more in the morning."

Elita was waiting at the top of the stairs. "I heard," she said, putting her arm around Connor. "I bet you're hungry. Let me fix you a bite to eat, and then I'll make up a bed on the couch."

"I'm going to step outside and make a phone call," David quietly told his wife. "Hopefully, I can get a hold of Paige before she wakes up and finds him gone."

——

East Harlem, New York
Monday, January 7th

Katrina paid for her prescription and then lingered while she read the list of potential side effects. *Some are almost as bad as Gaucher's Disease,* she thought and tossed the bottle of pills into her satchel. As she was heading out the door, her cell phone rang.

"Listen, I'm outside your place. Where are you?" There was an urgency in Gar's voice.

"Just around the corner at the pharmacy," Katrina replied. "What's wrong?"

"I'll explain everything when you get here."

Anxiety needled Katrina as she walked home. She saw Gar's scooter parked behind her car and found him waiting for her at the base of her stairs.

Just inside her apartment, Gar asked her to sit down. There was a somber look on his face as he settled beside her on the couch. Gar cued up a newsreel on his phone and handed it to his friend.

Katrina watched in utter disbelief as the pitiful-looking face of her mother mugged for sympathy. "Trina was always a difficult child." The woman sniffed as she tried, but failed, to coax out a tear. "I tried. The good Lord knows I tried."

The interviewer offered a tissue. "What can you tell us about that day?"

"It was my girl's eleventh birthday. We had a cake and everything. My daughter was upset. Trina didn't get the gift she wanted." The woman turned her sad cow eyes to the camera. "How could I have known what would happen next? I never imagined that she would shoot her poor daddy in cold blood!"

Katrina's throat tightened. "That is not true!" Her words came out like a squeak.

"Where did your daughter get the gun?" the interviewer asked.

"Her father bought it for protection, but I never wanted a gun in our house."

Another lie, Katrina thought as she watched her mother's pathetic trembling lip.

The camera zoomed in for a close-up of the woman. She dabbed a tissue at her dark, tearless eyes. "After it happened, I felt that I had no choice. If anyone knew what she did, her life would be ruined. Don't you see, I had to leave for my little Trina's sake?"

"What a piece of work!" Gar quipped, "Your old lady definitely won't be in line for any parenting awards."

Katrina felt like she was going to be sick. "I did not shoot my dad," she said emphatically.

"Naw, you aren't the killing type, but I can't say the same about that Momster of yours." Gar shook his head. "That woman is getting off on all the media attention."

As a child, Katrina had believed that she was somehow to blame for the woman's cold indifference. Even now, her mother still had the power to inflict pain.

Gar played with his soul patch. "I don't think it's a coincidence that your old lady turns up just to follow you around and twist your crank?"

"What do you mean?"

"I'd be willing to wager that the man behind that gang-stalking thing put your old lady up to this."

Katrina's recalled the look on Alistair Dormin's face the day of the interview. *He won't stop until I'm destroyed,* she thought.

Gar rose from the couch. "Look, we don't have very much time. The police are going to want to talk to you, and we can't risk exposure."

"What are you suggesting?"

"I talked to Mr. Cassidy. He wants you to gather some things and go to the coffee shop to await further instructions." Gar grinned. "It's official. You're a real outlaw now, Sundance!"

⸺ ❧ ⸺

Hope Springs, Arizona
Thursday, January 10th

"I can't go back to Tucson. Please, Mom, I don't want you to go either," Connor pleaded.

"Your father is back from his trip by now, and he's probably worried," Paige said. "Maybe we're making too much of this Vita Signum thing. According to Reverend Nellaf, the new monetary system is a blessing, and there is nothing to fear."

Connor shook his head emphatically. "He's just telling people what they want to hear. Ask anyone here at Hope Springs or at Arroyo Seco. Accepting the Vita Signum chip is like telling God that you choose the world instead of Him."

Paige sighed. "We'll talk more about this later."

The teenager grabbed his jacket. "It's not going to change anything!" he said as he dashed out of the Airstream.

Coming through the door right after Connor's abrupt exit, Bonnie asked, "What was that all about?"

"Come on in, and I'll explain." Paige poured her friend a cup of coffee and settled down at the small dinette.

"I'm here to listen." Bonnie's caring words opened a floodgate of emotion in Paige.

"I just don't know what to do. I'm exhausted from arguing with my son, and I'm worried about how Brody will react."

Bonnie set her mug down. "You still haven't been able to reach him?"

Paige chewed on her lip. "There's something wrong with my cellphone."

"No, it's not your phone. As of today, all Internet and cellphone providers have locked all accounts that don't meet the Vita Signum requirements."

Paige suddenly realized that her hands were trembling. "Everything is happening so fast. How do we live a normal life? What are our options?"

"The choice has become very clear. We can put our trust in God or put it in the worldly system," Bonnie said. "The scriptures warned us that difficult times would come, but just look around. A few months back, there was a water shortage, but God split the rock and provided. This community is a living testimony to His faithfulness."

"Some people are saying that the world is getting better and that Dormin is some kind of savior. How do we know who is right?" Paige said.

"When the Devil tempted Jesus in the desert, he mixed some truth with a little bit of error. Unfortunately, that's still going on today." Bonnie pointed to a Bible that was lying on the table. "We prideful humans aren't the arbiters of truth. God's word is our plumb line."

"You have a way of making complex biblical principles so simple."

Bonnie joined hands with Paige and prayed for God's supernatural peace, the peace that passes all understanding.

"I just thought of something," Bonnie said. "Mr. Mike has been working on some kind of communication bypass."

"Do you think he can help me reach Brody?"

"It's worth a try." Bonnie rose from the table. "Let's stroll over to his place and ask him." Paige grabbed her sweater, and they walked up the dirt road that ran between RVs and other make-shift dwellings.

The women stopped along the way to visit with neighbors and friends before turning up the path that led over a small sandstone outcropping. Mr. Mike's school bus conversion came into view when they reached the top.

Paige took a moment to soak in the broader view. The once stark landscape was covered with white desert yurts and the people abiding there. An electric cart was moving between them to distribute supplies. "I just can't get over how much things have changed around here," she muttered.

They picked their way through a boneyard of old electronic parts, and Bonnie knocked on the door of the old school bus. The door opened, and Mr. Mike poked his head out. "Is something wrong?" His eyes blinked behind thick lenses.

Bonnie laughed. "You don't get many visitors, do you?"

"What's up?"

"I know you're busy, Mr. Mike," Paige began, "but I was hoping that you could help me with a problem."

He invited the women inside. "Just shove some stuff aside and make yourselves comfortable."

Paige repositioned a spool of wire, brushed some metal shavings from the bench, and sat down. "I was hoping you could help me call my husband in Tucson."

Mr. Mike rubbed some stubble on his chin. "It can be very difficult to patch into a cellphone. Got a landline?"

"Yes, but we seldom use it."

"Great, it's relatively easy to patch into a landline, if you know how. What's the number?"

With information in hand, Mr. Mike hurried over to a cluttered bench and fired up his Ham radio. Paige watched him—hunched over his electronic devices—move dials, flip switches, and toss his uncombed hair. *He looks like a caricature of a mad scientist,* she thought.

Moments later, Mr. Mike got a dial tone and motioned to Paige. The phone began to ring and ring. Just when she was expecting the answering machine to kick in, someone answered. "Hello."

The sing-song voice on the other end made Paige cringe. "Jolene? What are you doing there?"

"Well, darling, I came over last night to console your husband. Poor man was just beside himself with worry when he realized you'd run off again."

"I need to speak to Brody!"

"He's in the shower right now," Jolene cooed. "Do you want to leave a message?"

Paige felt herself go numb. "Just tell him that Connor and I are at Hope Springs, and we won't be coming back."

Chapter 19

Arroyo Seco, Arizona

Monday, February 4th

The line of people began on the porch of the old General Store, ran all the way down the main street of Arroyo Seco and ended somewhere just out of sight.

Joy set up a thriving lemonade stand, while David, Elita, and an elderly Jewish couple named Chasha and Uri doled out paper bags loaded with weekly rations of crackers, dried fruit, and canned meat. Tickets for incidentals like toothpaste, composting toilet paper, and castile soap were included in the bags to be redeemed at the pharmacy down the street.

Many of the refugees spoke only Hebrew or Yiddish, but the old Brillo-haired woman named Chasha spoke both, and she was more than happy to fill the community in on the latest gossip.

"You could kibitz all day, but these good people have things to do," her husband complained.

"Nonsense! I'm always learning what is going on around here by listening," Chasha retorted. "Did you know that a shipment of carts and horses will soon be delivered, and that the Schwartz family is hoarding? And you know Sarah, the one whose family fled to an encampment in Egypt, well, her daughter Maya is expecting," Chasha whispered, "and no one knows who the father is."

"Oy Vey, such a font of knowledge!" Uri slapped his forehead. "Enough already babushka, take me home."

"Not just yet," she said as a black suburban pulled up out front.

They all watched as two official-looking men in suits climbed from the vehicle and made their way up to the porch.

"We're looking for David Fillmore," one of the men said.

"That's me. How can I help you?"

They introduced themselves as agents from Homeland Security. "We are here to give notice of an upcoming visa check. On the fifteenth of March, we are requiring all immigrants to be present along with their papers."

"They are political refugees," David replied. "What about asylum?"

"That's not applicable in this case, Sir. Temporary visas are only good for 180 days. Any resident in possession of expired documents will be detained and deported."

Chasha shrieked something in Yiddish and then scurried from the porch and down the street.

"In a few minutes, everybody in the whole community will hear the news," Uri said as he watched the men drive away.

"We need to call a meeting ASAP," David said. "I'll ride

over to Hope Springs and get Paige to help. Between the two of us, maybe we can find a legal loophole."

⁂

Angel's Camp, California
Friday, February 15th

At the Java Junkie, the most popular coffee house in Angel's Camp, Coco placed a cappuccino beside her husband and watched Joel open the package that they had just picked up at the post office.

"A new burner phone," he said as he scrolled through it until he found the latest encrypted message from Katrina.

"So, what's new?" Coco settled into the trendy chair beside him.

"The situation for people like us is getting pretty dicey," Joel said softly as a group flooded through the door. Soon the coffee shop was filled with chatter and the noise of the Barista frothing milk.

Joel slipped the phone into his pocket and decided against spoiling his wife's happy mood. "I'll fill you in later."

Back at the farm, Coco busied herself with her latest sewing project, and Joel turned his attentions back to Katrina's message. "As you know, since the first of the year, cash has become obsolete and officially a thing of the past," she wrote. "Now, a new fraud-detection system has been developed to identify counterfeit Vita Signum activity. Those found to be non-compliant are being detained, and it's rumored they are being sent to reeducation facilities across the country. Citizen spies are offered digital cash incentives to turn in resistant neighbors, friends, and even family members.

"Legislation has been introduced to make homeschooling illegal, and public-school curriculums are heavily laced with World Fortress Institute propaganda. Books that challenge the current views are being banned, and a new global anthem has replaced the Star Bangled Banner."

With a heavy heart, Joel punched out his podcast text and sent it off into the ethos. He thought about the Constitutional freedoms that his late father had fought so hard to preserve. It was obvious that Alistair Dormin had no intention of returning sovereignty to the nations that had ceded control, yet the masses didn't seem to care.

"Are you ready to go?" Joel asked.

"You're finished? That was quick!" Coco rolled up the skirt she was working on and gathered her needle and thread. "Don't forget I told Nellie that we'd pick up a few items at the grocery store."

Joel drove Clive's farm truck back into town to the Save Mart on South Main. He was feeling some trepidation about running their counterfeit chip. "I'll go in too," he said.

Coco gave her husband a quizzical look. "What's going on?"

"They've developed a Vita Signum fraud-detection system. Let's just hope the Save Mart doesn't have one yet."

Inside the store, Coco threw some whole-wheat flour, yeast cakes, and a box of Honey Nut Cheerios into the cart. On the way to the checkout, she tossed in a bag of potato chips. "Impulse buy," she said with a smile. Relief washed over Joel when the transaction went through without any problems.

With groceries in hand, the young couple returned to the parking lot. A few yards from the farm truck a crowd had gathered. It only took a few seconds to realize what was going on. "You should be ashamed of yourself!" a tall red-headed woman snarled. "What kind of mother are you?"

Joel and Coco pushed past some locals to see a young woman in tears.

"Please," she cried out, shifting her toddler to her other hip. "I'm only asking for a little help for my baby. Anything you could spare…"

"If you really cared about that child's welfare, you would go out and get yourself the Vita Signum chip, just like the rest of us!"

A farmer wearing overalls bobbed his head in agreement. "That's right, lady! As far as I'm concerned people like you don't deserve to have kids."

The toddler began to wail.

"Leave her alone!" Joel took the box of cereal from their bag and gave it to the young mother. "What's wrong with you people?"

The man with the overalls eyeballed Joel suspiciously and said, "Aren't you that new kid working over at the Delacroix Farm?"

⌘

Hoboken, New Jersey
*Thursday, February 21*st

Katrina woke up disoriented and shivering. It took her a few moments to recall that she had been relocated by the Shadow Riders to a tiny basement apartment in Hoboken, New Jersey. She slipped from between her covers and stood barefoot on the cold cement floor. Katrina turned up the thermostat on the small electric baseboard and waited for it to rattle to life.

Through the ceiling, she could hear the landlady's muffled TV, which played at all hours of the day and night.

In the bathroom, Katrina splashed water on her face and then burst into tears. Maybe she cried because of the state of the world, or maybe it was the fact that she felt tired and weak.

She raked a brush through her messy hair and scraped it into a hair clip. Katrina stared at the gaunt woman in the mirror and hardly recognized herself.

Katrina threw on her favorite pair of jeans, which now hung loosely on her scarecrow-like frame. Feeling numb and alone in the tiny living room, she sank into the couch. On the floor beside a chair was the backpack that contained some photos and other mementos. From it, Katrina retrieved Babbeh's worn Bible. For a few minutes, she held the leather-bound book in her hands, tracing the gold embossed words on the cover. Finally, Katrina opened the Bible and thumbed through its dog-eared pages. Babbeh had written notes in the margins.

She thought about the spiritual wisdom that her grandmother had tried so hard to impart. "I could use a little now," Katrina muttered to herself and then tossed the Bible aside. Something between its pages caught her eye, and she pulled out a sealed envelope. "Kitten" was written on the front in Babbeh's spidery cursive.

Katrina tore it open and began to read, "My sweet Kitten, you are not alone. The Lord will be with you wherever you go. He has commanded you to be strong and courageous! Don't be afraid, for the Lion of Judah will go before you, and He will be your rear guard. You have been called to God's kingdom for such a time as this."

Katrina was stunned. These were some of the same words spoken to her by the two prophets in Jerusalem!

She read on, "There is only one thing you must do, my precious one." Babbeh had written a scripture reference, Romans 10:9. Katrina was just about to look it up when someone knocked on her door.

"Who is it?"

"Billy the Kid!" replied the familiar voice.

Katrina rose, opened the door, and saw Gar standing there with a duffle bag. "It's official," he said with a big grin on his face. "I'm an outlaw too!"

Chapter 20

Arroyo Seco, Arizona

Wednesday, March 6th

The lunch counter at the General Store was littered with documents and law books. David and his sister, Paige, had been up all night long trying to help the refugees avoid the threat of deportation.

When Elita came downstairs, she took one look at them and said, "I can tell by your faces that you haven't come up with a legal solution."

"We're one pot of coffee away from finding a loophole," David said wearily.

"Sanctuary Community status may be our best option, but getting the Arizona Governor to sign off on it would be a long shot," Paige added.

David rubbed the day-old growth on his face and yawned. "Where is Joy?"

"Still sleeping." Elita fastened an apron around her waist. "What you two need is some brain food—eggs, toast, and some stout coffee."

Paige followed with a sympathetic yawn. "What we really need is a miracle."

Elita dropped butter into a skillet. "There are folks over at the old Watering Hole praying for just that!" She cracked eggs into a bowl and added a little milk. "They've been taking shifts all night long."

There was a gentle knock on the door of the General Store.

"Who could that be at this time of the morning?" David slid from his stool at the counter. "The sun hasn't even begun to rise," he said, making his way across the store to peer through the window. "It's Ezra, and he's not alone."

Elita said, "I'll throw in a few more eggs."

"Greetings, I bring you good tidings!" Ezra announced.

"We could use some," Paige said as she cleared the legal clutter from the counter.

"Everyone, I'd like you all to meet Saul Bernstein."

"I'm one of the Jewish American expats," Saul said. "I moved to Israel a few years back to be close to my heritage. Bad timing, eh?"

"So, what are these good tidings?" David pressed.

"What about a Sanctuary Community?" Ezra said. "Brilliant idea, don't you think?"

Paige and her brother exchanged a look of frustration. "We've been looking into that, but it's a very complicated pro-cess," she began. "First, we would need the Arizona Governor to sign off on the idea, but with politics the way they are…"

Saul settled down at the counter as Elita served plates of steaming hot eggs and toast. "This looks delicious, young lady," Saul said. He bowed his head to pray, and the others joined in.

David noted the grin on Ezra's face. "What are we missing here?"

"It just so happens that the governor and I are brothers," Saul said. He broke some bread and took a bite.

"Wait, your last name is Bernstein, and our governor is Michael Burns," David said.

Saul laughed. "Burns is the Americanized version of Bernstein. My brother always had political ambitions, and he thought this would help his career."

"Do you think he will help us?" Paige asked.

A massive grin spread across the man's face. "I've already spoken to my brother," Saul said. "He's just waiting for the paperwork."

⚬⚬⚬

Angel's Camp, California
Monday, March 18th

Joel sat down at the little farm table with a cup of coffee. It was quiet, except for the sound of Moses crunching his dog food.

Outside, the sun was just beginning to rise over California farm country. It was 6:00 a.m., fifteen minutes since the last time he checked his phone. It was mid-morning on the East Coast, but he still hadn't heard from Katrina. Lately, communications had been thin and sporadic, and the advent of radio silence was an ominous sign.

On the wall above the table hung the little plaque that Zeke had given to the couple. "Buckle up, it's going to be a bumpy ride!" it read. *How odd that an old movie line would foreshadow what is fast becoming reality,* Joel thought.

In the next room, he could hear Coco moving about in the bathroom. When she turned on the shower, Joel thought about joining her, but his iPhone signaled a message from Katrina. "Will the real Joel Sutherland please stand up?" it said.

As Joel continued reading, the strange message became clear. "You have been cloned by an AI version of Joel Sutherland. All previous podcasts from Joel, the voice of resistance, have been taken down. The new AI Joel has experienced a remarkable social transformation! Apparently, your doppelganger has become the voice of peace, love, and social compliance."

"No way!" Joel said aloud.

Katrina's encrypted message continued with a report on tightening political mandates and policies. "The new global curriculum is being taught from elementary schools to universities. The thought police are hard at work," she wrote. "Elitist youth clubs are springing up to train and encourage a generation of citizen spies. People are disappearing, sometimes whole families." The message ended with a warning. "Trust no one, Joel. There are rumors that our organization has been compromised."

"Good morning, my love!" Coco emerged from the bedroom wearing a flowy spring dress. Her damp hair fell softly around her shoulders. "What are your plans today?"

Joel smiled at his young bride. He didn't have the heart to tell her about the tone and tenor of Katrina's message. "I'm helping repair the pig pens and then going with Clive to walk and mark the boundaries of the property that he is bartering with his neighbor."

"Oh right, the one who will pay the property taxes on the farm in exchange for land. I really hope things work out for Nellie and Clive. They are such sweet people." Coco sighed and looked out the window as the morning sun fell softly across the dew-covered farmland. "I pray for them every day."

Joel draped his arms around his bride. "What are you going to do this morning?"

"Nellie is teaching me how to bake bread. If we have any dough left over, then we're going to make some cinnamon rolls too."

"Well, don't bring any home," Joel teased. "If I eat another loaf of Nellie's bread, I'll need to buy new jeans." The young couple walked to the door and collected their jackets. As Clive arrived, Joel slid on a pair of Wellies, and they went outside together.

"Want a lift to the main house, young lady?"

"No thanks, Mr. Delacroix," Coco replied. "I'd rather walk on this beautiful spring morning,"

Joel climbed into the passenger seat of the Gator.

Clive threw it in gear, rocked over some ruts, and drove them down into the little valley. With a tool belt fastened around his waist, he led Joel to the pen and pointed out a speckled pig. "That old sow over there is a real feisty one. She's always the first one at the trough, fussing and pushing her weight around." Clive chuckled. "Ain't that right, Hortense?" he said to the pig. The old farmer lifted his John Deere cap, scratched his shiny bald head, and said, "I forgot the slop buckets. They're in the Gator."

"I'll get them," Joel said. He retrieved the loaded pails and returned to the trough.

"You fetched their meal, so you can feed 'em." Clive drew Joel's attention to a small black boar that was squealing, biting, and pushing his way to the trough. "I call that bad boy Franco, cuz like the famous Pittsburgh Steeler's running back, Franco Harris, there's no stopping him, and he always leaves carnage in his wake." The old farmer chuckled. "An old friend once said that we could learn a thing or two about human nature from these pigs. I guess that's why the good book tells us not to throw our pearls to the swine."

Sounds like something Zeke would say, Joel thought.

"Daylight's burning. We'd better get to work."

Clive made his way over to a pile of scrap lumber, picked out some pieces, and went to repair the damaged fence. "Hortense has been cribbing. That old sow will eat anything."

When they finished the repairs, Clive said, "Good day's work." He looked at his watch, and said, "Cripes! Where did the time go? Dale Krimper is probably waiting for us." They jumped into the Gator and bounced over the rough terrain.

"How long have you known Mr. Krimper?" Joel asked

as they approached the meeting place. The man was already waiting there.

"He bought that vineyard about fifteen years ago." Clive slowed to a stop.

"Morning, Krimper!" Clive called out as he walked over to his neighbor.

"You're late, Delacroix."

"Sorry about that. We lost track of the time while doing chores. You know how it is."

Krimper was visibly annoyed. "Yes. I should be back at the winery tending to my own chores."

"I'd like you to meet Joel. He's a good hand," Clive said.

"I believe we've met," Krimper replied. "You were enabling that deadbeat mother who was begging over at the Save Mart parking lot."

"It seemed like the right thing to do," Joel replied.

"Shall we get down to business? I don't have all day," Krimper snapped.

It took them nearly twenty minutes to pace the ten acres of land that abutted the vineyard. After reading the purchase agreement, Krimper signed it, and said, "I'll get my surveyor out to mark the property line. It's a pleasure doing business with you, Delacroix."

Clive was unusually quiet as they drove back to the farm. "My dad is probably turning over in his grave about now."

Nellie was sitting on the porch of the main house when they arrived. She took one look at her husband, and said, "Remember Honey, it's only a little piece of land. Nothing on this earth truly belongs to us."

"I've got a few chores to finish," the old farmer said and then ambled off toward the shed.

Nellie sighed. "Clive goes there when he's trying to pretend that he's not upset."

"Where is Coco?"

"She's in the kitchen slicing bread. Your little bride is a natural-born baker!" Nellie rose from the porch rocker and followed Joel inside. "How does a roast beef sandwich sound?"

"Hard to turn down." In the kitchen, Joel was hit with the scent of hot bread and cinnamon. His stomach growled loud enough to make the women giggle.

"There's a cure for that." Nellie retrieved the roast beef from the fridge and went to work building sandwiches. She placed lunch on the table and said, "You kids go ahead and eat. I'm going to take a sandwich out to Clive."

A few minutes later, Nellie raced back inside, gasping for air. Her face was as white as a sheet.

Coco stood so fast that her chair fell over. "What's wrong?"

"It's Clive. I don't think he's breathing!" Nellie cried out, "Call an ambulance!"

Hoboken, New Jersey
Friday, March 29th

The grey sky was spitting rain as Katrina and Gar walked the last several blocks to Carlo's Bake Shop. Katrina clutched her backpack to her chest and stifled a shiver.

Rubbing his hands together, Gar said, "Dang, wish I had some gloves. This whole meeting thing is so cloak and dagger. Didn't Butch give you any hints about why he wants to meet with us?"

Katrina shook her head. "Mr. Cassidy just said that we're to be at Carlo's Bake Shop at 8:00 a.m."

When they turned down Washington Street, Gar pointed ahead to the maroon storefront of the bakery. "Well, at least, I'll finally be able to say that I've tasted one of Carlo's famous pastries."

In the minutes before the store opened for business, Gar and Katrina took refuge under a striped awning as the rain turned to sloppy sleet.

When the door finally opened, they settled down at one of the tables to wait for their boss to arrive. A line of people had formed at the counter by the time Butch Cassidy showed up. *He looks like he's aged five years,* Katrina thought as he approached their table. "Good morning, Boss," she said.

"Wish I could say the same," Cassidy said as he settled into a chair. "I came to warn you both that the Shadow Riders headquarters and the Happy Trails Coffee Shop have been raided. Many of our people have been arrested and charged with sedition. We all know what that means." Butch's face was etched with concern.

"Have we been named as operatives?" Katrina asked.

"I have no way of knowing, but I suspect it's only a matter of time," Cassidy replied.

"Well, if we're going to have a last meal, it might as well be one of Carlo's pastries." Gar rose from the table and said, "I'm buying."

"I don't think it's wise to run your chip right now, especially with the posse on your trail." Cassidy stood. "Be careful and good luck to you both."

On the way back to the apartment, Gar said, "This explains why I've been feeling a bit paranoid lately. I've been getting some weird vibes from your landlady."

Katrina switched her backpack to her other shoulder. "Yes, me too." As they rounded the corner, she grabbed Gar by his jacket and pulled him into the recessed doorway of a building.

"Not the most romantic move," Gar grinned, "but, hey, if your thing is spontaneity, then count me in."

Katrina held a finger to her lips and pointed in the direction of her apartment building.

Gar peeked around the corner. "Oh crap. She's turned us into the authorities!"

"What are we going to do now?" Katrina could feel her heart pounding in her chest.

"My scooter is chained to a hydrant on the side street.

If it hasn't been spotted yet, I'll be back around to pick you up." Gar disappeared around the corner, and the minutes ticked away.

The door behind her opened, and a woman with a little dog stepped out. "Awful drizzly day isn't it, Dear?" she said.

"Yes, very," Katrina replied as the woman buttoned her raincoat. "I hope you don't mind me taking shelter here."

"Not at all, Dear," the lady said and then hurried off.

The sound of Gar's scooter was music to Katrina's ears. He slowed to a crawl, she jumped on board, and they sped away.

Chapter 21

Arroyo Seco, Arizona
Tuesday, April 2nd

Mr. Mike was fiddling with the battery pack on the satellite feed at the old Watering Hole when Paige walked through the door.

David took one look at his sister and said, "What's wrong?"

She pulled some papers from her purse and held them up. "I've been served with divorce papers."

"What are you going to do?" David said.

"What can I do? I can't go back to Tucson, so if Brody wants a divorce, I'm not going to contest it." The sadness in Paige's eyes was evident. "I only wish that I'd done something good with my trust money when I had the chance. Now, it doesn't really matter. Brody can have it all."

Ezra laid his scarred hand on Paige's shoulder and said, "I'm so sorry to hear this."

"I fixed it!" Mr. Mike announced as the television screens came on.

The group listened as a stern-faced commentator announced, "Governor Burns is standing by his March 14th decision to declare Sanctuary Community status for a gathering of Israeli and Christian refugees located in southern Arizona. Declaring a Sanctuary Community is tantamount to harboring criminals and social reprobates!"

The media talking heads chimed in, attacking the Governor's actions, hurling verbal indictments and predicting the end of his political career. A long-legged blonde said, "Steps are being taken to recall Governor Burns. Some groups are calling for his immediate removal from office." The footage of angry protesters hurling anti-Semitic slurs filled the screen.

"Nothing new under the sun," Ezra said.

Mr. Mike rubbed his thick eyeglass lenses on his dirty overalls. "We ain't getting the whole story on the national news," he said. "I've been tapping into a few social media sites, and there's a whole lot of chatter about mob killings, land seizures, and persecutions. You don't hear those media folks talkin' about any of that."

"Some of these crazies are probably heading our way right now," David said. "How are we going to defend ourselves?"

"The Lord warned us about these perilous times," Ezra replied. "We must trust in Yeshua regardless of the cost."

The view on the television shifted to a blonde with her long legs crossed. A breaking news story interrupted the talking heads, and the stern-faced anchor announced that a coup had just taken place in Israel!

They watched footage of tanks rolling through the city of Tel Aviv, soldiers searching dwellings with automatic weapons at the ready, and cabinet members and dignitaries being cuffed and loaded into vans.

Suddenly the imagery switched to the newly installed Israeli Prime Minister. "Conflict and political contention will no longer be tolerated in this nation," he said. "I am offering a short window of mercy to the non-compliant citizens of Israel. Join with all peace-loving peoples of the world and receive the Vita Signum—the mark of life."

Ezra groaned aloud and began to pray. "God help all of our brothers and sisters to stand firm under such oppression."

⸙

Michigan
Saturday, April 6th

Traveling had grown complicated and dangerous since Katrina's counterfeit Vita Signum chip was flagged at a gas station last week. Gar knew of an abandoned property in the Upper Peninsula that was once owned by a relative. They tossed their chip-reader bracelets into a dumpster and hitched a ride.

In Michigan, a kind-hearted man stopped for the transients and offered to take them as far as Detroit.

Traveling in the bed of the truck beneath the camper shell, Gar had been singing an old Simon and Garfunkel tune in a loop. "Michigan seems like a dream to me now… We've all come to look for America…" Finally, the singing turned to snoring.

Katrina envied his ability to sleep. Her mind was

hypervigilant, and she was fighting a tension headache. *By now, the flagged counterfeit chips have been registered with the international compliance police. Authorities are probably reviewing surveillance footage from the quick stop and facial recognition software will soon identify us as enemy combatants,* she worried.

It was cold in the covered bed of the pickup. A chill racked Katrina's body, and she was emotionally exhausted. She closed her eyes and tried to steady her breathing. A voice roused her from her slumber, and Katrina saw the smiling face of the good Samaritan.

"I'm afraid this is the end of the line for you kids," he said as the tail gate dropped open.

Gar scrambled out and offered a hand to his friend. "Thank you for the ride, man."

"Yes, we really appreciate it," Katrina echoed and then looked around. "Where are we?"

"Just outside of downtown Detroit."

"Wish I could take you in for the night, but I've got a house full as it is." The man handed them an apple and some jerky from his lunchbox and pointed down a side street. "There's a Salvation Army a few blocks over that away. There is a bin around the back where you can get some warm clothing. You're gonna need it 'cause it gets cold 'round here at night. You kids take care."

They thanked the stranger again for his kindness and watched him drive away.

"Look at this place," Katrina said as they strolled

through the decaying neighborhood with tight rows of tiny, unpainted, shuttered houses, sagging, splintered porches, and yards filled with refuse. "Those houses have been peppered with bullet holes," she whispered. "Looks like some kind of third-world country."

"The politically correct term is 'Developing Nation,'" Gar said with a grin. "Get it right, Ducky!"

"Oh, right. How silly of me." Katrina spotted the Salvation Army store up ahead, and they made their way around to the back of the building. The bin in the alley was loaded with clothes destined for the shredder. Gar climbed inside and began to sift through the pile. Holding up a hoodie, he asked, "What size are you?"

"Size 4," Katrina replied, and he tossed it to her.

"Bonus round!" Gar's rummaging produced gloves and a threadbare wool jacket. He even found a worn pair of lace-up boots that just happened to fit Katrina.

"This boutique has great prices!" Gar hopped from the bin with an armload of flannel shirts and a cap, which he pulled over his unruly hair.

"Aren't you worried about head lice?"

"I'm more worried about getting frost-bit ears."

Katrina slipped on her tattered jacket as a stiff breeze kicked up. "It's going to be dark soon. I think we should try to find some kind of shelter."

The sun sank below the building tops casting eerie shadows, and in the distance somewhere, music pulsed though car speakers. As they made their way past shuttered windows,

Katrina felt like they were being watched.

A few blocks later, the travelers came upon an area that once had been a thriving downtown. Many of the buildings now sat empty and were crumbling. Broken glass covered the sidewalk, and some of the windows were boarded up. Walking carefully, they tried to stay close to the graffiti-clad buildings.

As nightfall approached, Katrina's sense of dread grew. The sliver of moonlight was swallowed up by thick clouds, and the streetlights didn't work. The darkness was total. They could hear whoops and yelps nearby like the sounds of war cries. Somewhere in the distance, they heard a spray of gunfire.

Gar tugged on Katrina's coat sleeve and led her beneath an old theater marquee around to the boarded-up ticket window. "It's not much of a place to hole up, but we'll be out of the weather here."

Katrina hunkered down on the cold cement and huddled close to Gar for warmth. As the sound of voices drew close, he whispered, "Listen."

Out on the street, they could hear laughter and taunts, "Renounce your stupid God or be prepared to die you Jesus Fish!"

The crack of a gunshot rang through the streets and then another.

Straining to hear, Katrina sat motionless. Her heart thumped like a kettledrum inside her chest. Finally, after what seemed like an eternity, the voices faded into the distance.

In the quiet, Katrina began to shiver. The sensation of

wet warmth trickled down her chin. "Oh no—another nose-bleed."

"Here." Gar handed her one of his flannel shirts to use as a rag. "Lay your head on my shoulder. I'll take care of you."

The sound of sub-woofers could be heard a few blocks away, and suddenly overcome with exhaustion, Katrina began to weep like a frightened child. She opened her mouth to speak, but Gar held a finger to her lips.

On the sidewalk, just a few yards away, they heard footsteps crunching on broken glass. Then, suddenly in the shadows of the old marquee, two dark forms appeared. One tall and the other petite. Gar squeezed Katrina's fingers.

"Look, someone is hiding over there," a woman's voice said. "Are you in need of help? Don't be afraid. You're among friends."

"Who are you?" Katrina asked.

"We're sojourners like you." The woman tapped lightly on the ticket counter, and a moment later, the theater door swung open.

"Quickly, follow me," the tall man said as he ushered them inside and through a doorway covered by heavy velvet curtains. People were gathered inside the old theater. Katrina estimated that there were nearly fifty of them.

"You'll be safe now," the petite, middle-aged woman said. "I'm Abigail, and this is James." She turned to the others and said, "We found these two survivors huddled outside our door." She smiled kindly at the newcomers. "It is like they were led here by angels."

Bathed in dim lantern light, people made their way over to welcome them. "You must be hungry and thirsty." Someone handed Katrina a bottle of water, and she drank it down.

"Where are Betty and Ray?" a heavyset black man asked.

"I'm afraid they didn't make it," Abigail replied.

Katrina recalled the gunshots and shouts of revelry that she had heard earlier and felt a rush of sadness. To her surprise, these peculiar people all began to praise God.

Abigail seemed to sense her confusion. "We are rejoicing because Betty and Ray's work on Earth has ended. They are safe with our Lord now."

Gar took a swig of water, leaned close to Katrina, and muttered. "This is definitely the strangest wake I've ever attended."

⸻ ❦ ⸻

On the Road

Monday, April 29th

In the early morning hours, Pastor Joe had stopped by the farm to warn Nellie that the word was out and that the compliance police would soon be paying her a visit.

With haste, Joel, Coco, and the old woman threw supplies into Nellie's old minivan and fled the community. The lack of loyalty from Nellie's friends and neighbors after the sudden death of her husband weighed heavy on the woman's grieving heart, but she had mustered the strength to come up with a plan. "I have a brother in Wyoming. He will give us shelter."

Joel drove the back roads to avoid being seen. Finally, they hooked up with I-80 and clipped along with the other travelers. He looked in the rearview mirror. He saw Nellie weeping quietly while Moses licked the salty tears from her face. Finally, she cried herself to sleep.

"Poor thing," Coco whispered. "I still can't believe they treated her like that. What's wrong with people?"

Joel nodded, but his eye was on the gas gauge as they traveled across some dry lake beds that were between mountain ranges. "We'll need to gas up in Winnemucca."

By the time they rolled into town, the sun was sinking low on the horizon.

"There's a station." Coco pointed to a big-name service center.

Joel rolled on past. "We need to look for a small, independent station. Some businesses haven't upgraded their system yet." On the far side of Winnemucca, they located Marty's Garage and Petrol. A thin man with coveralls rolled out from beneath a car, and hollered, "Need some help?"

"No thanks. I've got it." Joel swiped his bracelet over the chip reader and relief washed over him when the transaction went through. He filled the minivan's tank along with two gas cans that were strapped to a small rack on the back of the van.

He climbed behind the wheel of the minivan and said, "That was lucky."

"No such thing as luck." Coco fingered the amber cross

on her necklace. "God heard our prayers."

"That's right," Nellie echoed from the back seat.

Looking in the rearview mirror, Joel asked, "Did you have a nice nap?"

Nellie smiled back. "How about a little sustenance?" She handed Joel and Coco a slice of her homemade bread and then passed around the water jug.

Outside of Winnemucca, Joel turned north on US 95 and traveled along a valley toward a plateau that was softly backlit by the light of a half-moon.

"We should stop somewhere and try to get some rest," Coco said.

"I'd like to press on to Idaho," Joel replied. "Really, I'm fine."

The next four hours passed slowly. No one was in the mood to talk, least of all Nellie.

On the far side of Boise, Joel pulled into a Rest Area to close his eyes for a few minutes. The next thing he remembered was the morning sun beating through the windshield of the minivan. He looked around for Coco and Nellie, and then he followed Moses' intense gaze to the restroom door. The women emerged and returned to the van.

Coco opened the door and kissed her husband's cheek. "Good morning, sleepy head. We washed up a bit. If you want to do the same, I'll take Moses to the dog run."

"What time is it?" Joel asked as Nellie settled into the back seat.

"Almost 8:00 a.m.," Nellie said, "but we're in no hurry."

Fifteen minutes later, they were back on the road and traveling east across the high desert plains.

Joel turned on the car radio and found some news: "Epidemiologists are racing to identify the toxic bacterium strain that is affecting water supplies across the planet. Millions have fallen ill, and many of them are dying."

The newscast continued. "Nations that previously refused Dormin's mandates have now addressed the suffering and starvation of their people by embracing the Vita Signum monetary system. Despite military threats, China remains defiant, turning a blind eye to the staggering death toll on their citizens. Some speculate that a half-billion Chinese may have perished."

The announcer droned on from one story to the next. "An earthquake in the Italian alps claims thousands… Environmentalists are addressing man-caused increases in geothermal and seismic activity in Yellowstone... Strange wild animal behavior has resulted in fatal human attacks… Dormin and the World Fortress Institute are being honored by the international community for saving the planet and reshaping the bonds of global brotherhood…"

Joel switched off the radio in disgust. "Let's get real. The world is a better place with Dormin at the helm, right?" he said sarcastically.

"Look!" Coco pointed to the north. "I see the Rocky Mountains in the distance!"

Wait until you see the Craters of the Moon up ahead," Nellie said. "They're otherworldly."

As they neared the grey ethereal sea of volcanic lava flows with islands of cinder cones and fissures, the phrase '*Scorched Earth*' came to Joel's mind.

"It makes you shudder when you consider the violent volcanic event that took place here." Nellie shook her head. "They say it can happen again someday."

"I think it looks like a nuclear bomb exploded here," Joel retorted.

"Nope, it was all done by the hand of God," Nellie explained, "but there is a ghost town somewhere around here called Atomic City. It was the home of America's first nuclear reactor. That was definitely all manmade."

Past Rexburg, Joel turned east on ID 33, and they traveled in silence, each lost in the views of snowcapped mountains and Teton Pass. On the other side of Jackson Hole, they drove over Togwotee Pass and the Continental Divide. From there, time passed quickly.

On the outskirts of Dubois, Wyoming, Moses began to whimper, so Joel found a pullout. They women took the dog for a much-needed walk while Joel emptied one of the gas cans into the minivan's tank. Back on the road again, Nellie handed out more snacks and said, "We're coming up on the Wind River Canyon. Some folks call it a geological marvel."

"Wow," Joel replied as they entered the towering gorge with a rolling river running through it. "Do you want to stop and read one of the signs?"

"No. I can tell you what they say." Nellie began her narrative. "See those colored layers in the cliffs? They're made by a complex seismic upheaval of dolomite, limestone, and Precambrian rock. If you cross that river, you'll be on the Wind River Indian Reservation that is occupied by the Shoshone and Arapaho Tribes."

A small village named Thermopolis was on the other side of the canyon. "Tell me a little about your brother," Joel said as he drove through the small town.

"Wayne used to be an LA cop. Clive thought that he had a breakdown, but I think that job just took a toll on him. Anyway, Wayne quit his job, bought some property in Clark, Wyoming, and invited some of his retired cop buddies to relocate to the area. We used to come for visits, but Clive couldn't stand that bunch. He used to say, 'Their elevators don't go all the way to the top.' You know the sort, conspiracy theories and all that. Clive always said, 'Clark is more of a state of mind than a place.'"

Coco gave her husband an anxious look. "I just wish they knew we're coming. What if they turn Joel and me away?"

"Don't worry. I'm sure you'll be welcomed." Nellie leaned back and closed her eyes as they motored past the sagebrush hills and intermittent badlands.

In Cody, Joel followed the directions that Nellie had given him. "At the south edge of the town, turn left off of WY 120 onto US 14, 16, and 20. Proceed into town and down the

Greybull Hill. At the bottom and around a corner, take a right off Sheridan Avenue onto US 14A towards the Chief Joseph Scenic Byway and then left onto the Belfry Highway, WY 120."

About eight miles north of town, the gas tank pinged as they started up Skull Creek Pass.

In the back seat, Nellie stirred. "My goodness, don't tell me that I slept through Meeteetse and Cody! I must have really been tired."

"We're low on gas," Joel said.

"It's not far," Nellie reassured him.

Coco was engrossed in the sagebrush-covered hills and escarpments. "It's really beautiful here in a stark sort of way."

Nellie pointed to the junction with the Chief Joseph Scenic Byway and said, "That will take you over Dead Indian Pass and into the Sunlight Basin. Most breathtaking views I've ever seen and one of the best-kept local secrets."

"Who was Chief Joseph?" Joel asked.

"He was Chief of the Nez Perce Indian Tribe," Nellie began. "They were fleeing from the US Cavalry and trying to get to safety in Canada. They came through here on the way."

"Weird," Coco interjected, "They were running from the government just like we are. What happened?"

Nellie shook her head. "You don't want to know."

The landscape began to flatten out, and Joel searched for the County Road 1AB sign. "The turn is just up ahead on the left," Nellie said. After a few minutes, she instructed Joel to turn down a long dirt road. In the distance, he could see a cluster of buildings: some Quonset huts, sheds, two long buildings, and an old RV.

The road grew rough and rocky, but that was the least of Joel's worries. Up ahead, he saw a tall, curly-haired man awaiting their approach with a rifle in his hand.

Another man emerged from a Quonset hut, followed by a pudgy kid wearing his ball cap backwards. They stood in the middle of the road, each bearing arms.

"Maybe this isn't a good idea," Coco cried out.

"Don't worry, Honey," Nellie reassured her. "Just let me do the talking."

About forty yards shy of being stopped, the minivan sputtered and died. *Great time to run out of gas,* Joel thought as a gust of wind rocked the van.

The first man leveled his gun and yelled, "State your business!" Nellie emerged slowly, and he barked, "Let me see your hands!"

"I'm Wayne's sister. Is he here?"

"Got any ID?"

The others kept their eyes on Joel and Coco in the van.

"For heaven's sake. Just let me get my purse." Nellie retrieved her oversized handbag from the van and fished out her wallet.

"I'm scared," Coco whispered.

"It'll be okay," Joel said, hoping that he was right.

After checking Nellie's driver's license, the curly-haired

man said something to the pudgy kid who ran away. He soon returned with a gangly woman with big glasses and flaming red hair.

"Nellie!" The woman threw her arms around her. "It's been a long time."

"It's good to see you, Jinx. Is my brother here?"

"Wayne went for supplies with Lyle and Lonnie, but they should be back soon." The woman's gaze shifted to Joel and Coco sitting in the minivan. "Where is Clive?"

"We buried him last week."

"Oh, I'm so sorry, Hon." Jinx looked again at the young couple. "Not sure how Wayne will feel about those strangers you brought here, though."

The curly-haired man cocked his head towards the kid. "Trip, go unlock the shed. Rawley, I want you to check those two for devices."

Joel and Coco were ordered to step out. With hands raised, they were frisked. Joel's cell phone was confiscated and held up like a trophy.

Bruce spit on the ground and said, "Boys, I think we've got ourselves some spies."

"Take it easy, Bruce!" Jinx pleaded. "They're Nellie's friends."

The kid waited at the shed with padlock in hand. A gust of wind sent his ball cap tumbling, but he stood like a soldier while the young couple was escorted inside.

Just before the door closed, Joel looked back at Nellie's

apologetic face. Joel pulled his wife close and could feel her trembling. The wind pounded on the metal building making it creak and rattle. "It's going to be okay," he whispered again.

"Yes, but I really think we need to pray," Coco replied.

Chapter 22

Clark, Wyoming

Wednesday, May 1st

Joel and Coco sat near the head of the long pine table that was set with mismatched dinner plates. From his captain's chair, Wayne offered a toast to the young couple. He hoisted a can of cheap beer and said, "Here's to our newest comrades in arms!"

The folks at the table raised their drinks and said, "Here, here!"

The elder man looked earnestly at Joel. "No hard feelings, right? I'm sure you, of all people, can understand the need for caution, right?" Joel nodded and stared at the plate of greasy pork, applesauce, and baked beans. "Boys, I still can't believe we've got Joel Sutherland sitting right here at our table. You're like a celebrity in our neck of the woods! Right boys?"

The group echoed the sentiment, downed more beer, and Jinx hurried into the kitchen to retrieve another six-pack.

Across from Joel, the cook, Maxine, sat noshing on her dinner. She slapped another helping of beans onto her plate and said, "You boys can party all night if you want, but I ain't cleaning up after you!" Maxine shifted her huge body, and the chair creaked under her weight. "I spent all afternoon cookin' this meal, and my damn feet hurt."

"We got a surprise for you kids." Wayne wiped a dribble of grease from his chin. "Lyle and Lonnie over there spent all day clearing junk out of that old Winnebago motor home that we were using for storage. Now, you two lovebirds can have a place of your own."

"Yup, found a couple rodent nests too, but it's all cleaned up now," Lyle added.

Lonnie elbowed his brother and flashed a creepy toothless grin at Coco. "Even put clean sheets on the bed."

Joel reached for his wife's hand under the table. "That's very nice. Thank you."

"That camper is our gift to you, especially since we treated you so harsh when you first got here." Wayne glanced at his sister Nellie. "That was a real good idea you had there, Sis."

After the meal, Joel and Coco volunteered to help with the cleanup.

"Jinx and I have got this covered," Nellie said. She handed them the keys to the motorhome, gave Joel and Coco each a hug, and said, "See you both in the morning for breakfast."

With their bags in hand, the young couple made their way to the Winnebago. "I wonder if this thing still runs?" Joel said as he unlocked the door. "I'd carry you over the threshold, but we're being watched."

Coco glanced over her shoulder to see Lyle and Lonnie standing outside gawking. "They give me the creeps."

Joel silently agreed. Once inside, he closed the door and pulled Coco close. "I know this isn't an ideal situation," he whispered, "but for now, it's our only option."

After they climbed in bed together, Coco said, "Hold me." He kissed her neck, but she pulled away. "I just want you to hold me."

Joel pulled her close enough to feel the rhythm of her breathing, and they drifted off to sleep as one.

⸰⸰⸰

Arroyo Seco, Arizona
Monday, May 13th

From the porch of the General Store, David could hear a drone buzzing overhead. The harassment had been steadily increasing since the Sanctuary Community had come under the media radar. Networks across the nation were all incensed over the failure of Governor Burns recall election. "Why should those Jews live in our country and openly flout the mandates instituted by Chairman Dormin and the World Fortress Institute? They should be deported or, at least, locked in reeducation camps like the rest of the non-compliant!" the sycophants said.

Joy pushed through the screen door with a sketch pad and a bucket of crayons in hand. Elita followed close behind and settled next to her husband on the bench. They watched as a drone buzzed down the main street of Arroyo Seco and spun around to capture the view. "I wish they would just leave us alone. We're not hurting anyone," Elita said.

David's thoughts turned to the recent chatter picked up by Mr. Mike. There were rumors of organized protesters gathering near the boundary of the Sanctuary Community.

Paige pulled up in one of the solar-powered utility vehicles. She parked in front of the General Store, and she and Connor hopped out and joined the Fillmore family on the porch. "I just heard the good news about Governor Burns recall election," Paige said. "Praise God! We are still a Sanctuary Community!"

"At least, for now," David said.

"Don't be such a pessimist," Elita told her husband. "Have a little faith."

"What are you coloring?" Connor asked his cousin.

"A picture of Jesus in the sky." Joy selected a blue crayon.

"Speaking of that," Elita interjected, "there's something supernatural going on around here. Chasha told me that the Messianic revival tents have been so packed lately that there's standing room only. She also said that most of the Hebrew Bible translations have been snatched up."

"Chasha said?" David raised a skeptical brow to his wife.

"I know, she's a kibitzer, but this is all true."

"Some of the refugees have been showing up at Hope Springs asking us about the Gospels," Paige said. "I understand it's causing some friction. The zealots are saying that their religion is being corrupted here, and some are even talking about receiving the Vita Signum and returning to Israel."

David couldn't believe his ears. "I haven't heard about any of this."

Elita smiled. "That's because you don't listen to Chasha."

Connor was busy drawing a picture of a jet going down in flames. "They shouldn't go," he quietly said. "I had another dream…"

⁂

Detroit, Michigan
Friday, May 17th

Katrina thought back to that frightening night when Abigail and James had found her and Gar huddled in the corner beneath the marquee. A swell of gratitude washed over her as she studied these strange people. Dozens of questions swirled through her mind.

"How do you all survive in here?" the journalist in Katrina asked.

"God provides," James said patiently. He pointed at a gangly man. "Adrian here used to work for the City of Detroit, and he knew how to rig our water supply. Our food is mined from the grocery store dumpsters in the early morning hours before the garbage trucks roll through. You wouldn't believe the expired goods those stores throw away."

The more Katrina observed these peculiar people the more they confused her. She politely thanked James for the information and retreated to her make-shift bedroll made from discarded clothing. There she tried to process all that she had learned. Nightly, these people ventured out on the mean streets of Detroit, risking their lives to bring back supplies and preach the Gospel.

Such selfless love reminded her of Babbeh, who despite the injustice of her past, carried a peace that puzzled Katrina. *How can anyone find joy in the face of persecution?* she had often wondered.

Across the room, someone began to strum a guitar, and the people sang an old hymn.

Feeling a bit annoyed, Katrina slipped quietly into the back room for some solitude. She settled her frame against the door. A sliver of sunlight shone down on the dusty, concrete floor, and a spider scurried beneath a potted plant that someone had been tending. Sometimes, Katrina would just sit in this place and watch that light slowly travel along the wall until it faded away along with the dusky light outside.

How quickly things are changing, she thought. It seemed like only yesterday when she could jog through Central Park. Katrina closed her eyes and tried to imagine the feeling of a cool, spring breeze and the warm sunlight on her skin.

Katrina rose and returned to the theater and the kind people she dwelt among. Beneath the light of a single LED that sat on the stage, she watched them praising God and ministering to one another.

A few yards away, Abigail said, "A penny for your thoughts, Dear? Come over here and sit with me."

Katrina settled beside the elderly woman. "Pennies aren't worth anything," she quipped cynically. "Cash and coins are a thing of the past, remember?"

Abigail smiled sweetly and patted Katrina's shoulder. "Whatever is troubling you, I'm here to listen."

"You really have to ask?" Katrina waved her hand around the old theater and said, "No offense, but it feels like I'm in the Twilight Zone or something. Just look at Harold over there praising God when his wife was murdered on the street last week. Or Mr. and Mrs. Smith who haven't seen their children since the authorities took them away." Katrina pointed at Reverend Holliday. "And what about the preacher over there? He's still praising God even though his only son turned him in to the compliance police. Either everyone here is in denial, or they're suffering from some kind of cognitive dissonance. They've lost everything!"

Abigail sighed. "We don't see it that way. No one can ever take away our hope. I believe that there is a deeply rooted hunger for God planted in the hearts of all humanity, but people try to fill that void with politics, science, drugs, alcohol, or whatever because to trust God requires vulnerability." The older woman smiled. "Maybe that hunger for the truth is the reason you refused to take the Vita Signum implant."

Across the room, Gar was sitting with a cluster of people. He seemed engrossed in conversation, and then to

Katrina's surprise, he joined hands with the group and bowed his head to pray.

Darius, an African American gentleman, came up to Abigail and Katrina. "You ladies are lookin' mighty serious. Mind if I join you?" He plopped onto one of the theater seats.

"Say, that's an interesting piece you're wearing young lady." Darius pointed to Katrina's brooch. "I used to deal in estate jewelry. Mind if I take a look?"

Katrina unfastened the pin and handed it over.

Darius slipped a penlight from his pocket and studied its details. "Russian cloisonné, I believe. Can I peek inside the locket?"

"Help yourself," Katrina said. "It's a photograph of my grandmother when she was a little girl."

"Nice. Who's the old white guy standing behind the bench?" Darius asked as he handed the brooch back.

Katrina stared at the photo. "May I borrow your penlight for a minute?" *It can't be! That's impossible!* Katrina stared in disbelief at the old man standing behind her grandmother. He was the spitting image of Zeke!

"Young lady, you've got yourself a nosebleed." Darius said and then hollered for the others to come.

"I'll be fine." Katrina pressed a rag to her nose while the people gathered around to pray. A peaceful sensation enveloped her as she listened to their heartfelt petitions.

"Look—the bleeding stopped," Gar said. "It's a miracle!"

Placebo effect, Katrina told herself, but she could not deny the tingling warmth that radiated through her aching bones.

Darius stood in front of her and said, "The Lord just gave me a word for you."

"A word?" Katrina said.

"There's something that He wants you to do."

"Like what?"

"I have absolutely no idea." The black man flashed a toothy smile. "But God will let you know when the time is right."

Chapter 23

Detroit, Michigan

Sunday, June 1st

In her dream, *Katrina huddled inside a cave watching drops of water drip from a rock overhead. Outside, she could hear wails and cries for help. Katrina crawled from the cave and peered over the edge of a steep cliff. Fire fell like rain from the red tumultuous sky. As far as her eye could see, the landscape was set ablaze.*

"Help me!" someone cried out.

Katrina looked over the edge to see the faces of desperate people clawing up the steep granite face. Some lost their grip and plunged into the inferno below.

Suddenly, a figure wearing a white robe appeared. His hair was snow white, and his face shone like the sun. He looked at her with eyes that blazed with love. The figure spoke, "Have faith, Katrina, for you will be a witness in Jerusalem. You have been called to the kingdom for such a time as this."

The sound of singing roused Katrina from her slumber. She lay upon the heap of old clothing and listened to the words:

"Blessed assurance, Jesus is mine!

Oh, what a foretaste of glory divine!
Heir of salvation, purchase of God,
Born of his Spirit, washed in his blood.
This is my story—this is my song—
Praising my savior all the day long..."

"I have something for you."

Katrina was surprised to see Abigail hold out a tiny bouquet of purple flowers. "What's this?"

"Spikenard," Abigail replied.

"It's lovely. Where did you get them?" Katrina climbed to her feet.

"I've been growing some in our back storage room."

Katrina was puzzled. "But how? The windows are all boarded up. Don't plants need sunshine?"

"A bit of morning light shines through a crack in the boards. Besides, Spikenard thrives in the shade."

A sweet, woodsy fragrance filled the air as Katrina took the flowers in hand.

"Did you know that we grow best in God's shadow?" Abigail said with a smile. "We thrive in His presence, and it's there that our prayers rise to Heaven like the scent of Spikenard." The elderly woman paused for a moment. "Katrina, the Lord longs to nurture and care for you like a young tender plant. You may not realize it yet, but you are his delight."

Katrina waited until Abigail was gone and then fell into a reflective silence. She reached for her grandmother's Bible and reread the note that Babbeh had tucked between the pages. "Don't be afraid, my little kitten, be strong and be courageous. For God will be with you wherever you go. You have been brought to the Kingdom for such a time as this."

Three times now, the same message was given to Katrina. It was written in her grandmother's note, spoken to her by the two witnesses in Jerusalem, and now, in her dream last night. *What are the odds of that?* she wondered.

Katrina noticed a scripture reference that she had overlooked. Scribbled on the bottom of the card was a reference to the Book of Esther. Katrina thumbed through the pages of the Bible and was stunned to read that these very same words had been given to a woman called by God to facilitate the deliverance of His people.

No way—not me! Katrina told herself. *Dormin and the World Fortress Institute are in control, and with the current Vita Signum fraud-detection software, the whole notion of returning to Jerusalem is ridiculous."*

"With God all things are possible!" The preacher had bellowed the phrase from the other side of the theater. "I don't know why," he added, "but the Holy Spirit told me to shout those words out loud!"

⸛

Arroyo Seco, Arizona

Thursday, June 20th

In the apartment above the General Store, David sat in front of an open window hoping for a breeze. He had tossed and turned all night. Finally, he gave up on sleeping. Outside, the hot dry air had not cooled after the sun set the evening before, and the heat was oppressive. An unusually intense heat wave had blanketed the nation, making the effects of the global drought worse.

From the darkness, David heard mournful wails and petitions rising and falling like the sound of the eastern Cicadas. The refugees in Arroyo Seco and the surrounding community had not ceased praying since they received word about the atrocities that had been inflicted on their people.

Under the tight-fisted control of the World Fortress Institute, non-compliant Jews were cut off from the temple, and now they were being slaughtered in the streets! The Holy Land was being "sanitized and purged" in preparation for the upcoming dedication of the statue of Dormin.

How can the media gush over peace efforts in the middle east, David wondered, *while turning a blind eye to the human suffering there?*

He pondered a Bible passage from John 16:2 that Ezra recently quoted. "…the time is coming when those who kill you will think they are doing a holy service for God."

David thought about his sleeping wife and daughter. *Is this really happening?* A lump formed in his throat, and David fell to his knees beside the chair and prayed from the depths of his heart, "God help us!"

Clark, Wyoming
Tuesday, June 25th

After the breakfast dishes were cleared from the table, Nellie made the rounds with the coffee pot, and Joel gladly took a second cup. He watched steam curling from the stout brew and then turned his gaze to the window. Outside, the morning sun rose softly over the Pryor Mountains as a rooster crowed.

Nellie sat down beside him and said, "When the cock crowed three times, Peter was reminded of his betrayal of Jesus."

"Yeah?" her brother Wayne interjected. "If anyone ever screwed me over like that, they'd get what's coming to them." Wayne pointed his finger like a gun and said, "Pow, right in the forehead!"

Nellie sighed and gave her brother a disapproving look.

Wayne downed the rest of his coffee, hoisted his heavy frame from the table, and walked over to Joel. "Young fella, I think you've proven your loyalty, so I've decided to take you on a special tour of our facilities."

Across the table, Lyle and Lonnie bobbed their heads in agreement. "Welcome to the fold bro," one of them said.

Wayne clapped his hands together. "Let's get a move on, boys! Daylight's burnin'."

At the door, Joel glanced back at his wife, who stood

near the kitchen door. She looked troubled.

Bruce strode on ahead to fiddle with the padlock on one of the Quonset huts. He threw open the door as Wayne and Joel approached, and the smell of sweet hay filled the air. "Get to work, Trip," Bruce ordered, and the kid hurried over to a stack of hay bales and began to toss them aside.

The farm boy brushed aside straw and located a ring on the floor. He opened the hatch and hurried down the ladder to switch on a lantern. The boy hollered, "All clear," and the others descended after him.

Joel found himself standing in an earthen dugout with crudely built shelves loaded with all kinds of munitions, including boxes of grenades. The other side of the bunker housed racks of military-style weaponry and even a mortar launcher.

Bruce watched Joel through the slits of his eyes while Wayne strutted about and perused his arsenal with pride. "When was the last time these guns were cleaned and oiled?"

"It's been a few months, boss," Lyle volunteered. "We will get right on it."

Next, Joel was escorted to the horse barn, where more weaponry was stored. Some of them were medieval. Finally, he was shown another cache that was hidden behind some bunkhouse shelves. When the tour was over, Wayne said, "None of what you've seen is registered or traceable. What do you think?"

"Impressive," Joel replied carefully. "You've stockpiled enough weaponry for a small army."

"Damn right, soldier!" Wayne punched Joel's arm. "It's war man, but we're prepared. Most of us here are former military or retired cops. Everyone here knows how to handle a gun, even the women."

Coco was seated on a Molesworth-style couch and reading from her Bible when they returned. Joel immediately detected tension in her face.

"Next week, right after the Fourth of July, I want you and that little gal of yours to do some target practice over at our rifle range. We'll start you off with a Glock pistol and then work our way up to some of our semi-auto rifles before trying out some fully automatic weapons." Wayne flashed a yellow grin. "We'll see what yer made of!"

He wrapped his knuckles on the kitchen door and hollered for Maxine.

The door flew open with a bang, and the cook's body filled the doorway. She waved her wooden spoon in the air and squawked, "You must think I'm just sitting on my duff in here! What's so damned important?"

"We're celebrating, that's what!" Wayne retorted.

"We've got ourselves some new recruits, so why don't ya whip up one of yer famous German Chocolate Cake and start thawing some steaks."

Maxine stood with her big arms crossed.

"What are you waitin' for, woman?" Wayne barked.

"A 'please and thank you' would be nice."

Wayne softened. "Those kids will never be the same

after they taste your culinary masterpiece."

"Well, I'll see what I can do, but it's short notice, mind you," she replied.

Nellie made her way over to where Joel and Coco stood. She leaned close to the young couple and whispered, "I'm so sorry I brought you here."

Wayne cracked open a beer and said, "Welcome to the fold."

"It's really nice of you to throw us a party," Coco said as she squeezed her husband's hand.

"Maybe we should go back to the camper and change out of our work clothes," Joel added.

Lonnie snickered out loud and gave his brother a shove.

Wayne slapped Joel on the back and said, "We'll save you some cold ones. Don't be too long now, ya hear?"

The wind pummeled the young couple as they made their way back to the motorhome. A gust nearly took the door off as they climbed inside. Joel pulled his wife close to his chest and held her close. "We have to find some way out of here."

"I've got an idea," Coco said, "but we're going to need Nellie's help."

Chapter 24

Cody, Wyoming

Thursday, July 4th

By the time Joel and Coco made it to Cody, the main road through town had been cordoned off for the Fourth of July Parade. Looking for a place to park, Joel drove the Winnebago down a side street. They finally found RV parking a block off the main drag that wasn't completely full.

"What if Wayne and the boys find out that we aren't camping in Sunlight Basin?" Coco said as she gathered their things.

"Nellie was very convincing when she told them it was our wedding anniversary," Joel replied. "They've got no reason to think that we've skipped out on them."

"But what if they decide to come to Cody?"

"That antisocial bunch?" Joel shook his head. "I'm more concerned that someone here will recognize our faces from the news."

"Oh, yeah, I almost forgot that we are wanted for sedition."

Joel slipped on a ball cap and waited for his bride to tie a bandana around her head as Moses raced to the motorhome door. Coco grabbed a leash, donned her big sunglasses, and they all went off to the parade.

"What a beautiful day," Coco said as they strolled toward the festivities in the gentle breeze.

As Joel and Coco neared Sheridan Avenue, Cody's main thoroughfare, they were joined by clusters of lawn-chair-toting tourists and locals. They passed the barricade and wound their way through the crowded sidewalk among the balloons and children with dripping snow cones.

Joel and Coco finally settled in front of a gift store that sold cheap Western items, t-shirts, and beaded jewelry.

"They start the parade up there," a nearby man said as he pointed out the Buffalo Bill Scout Statue at the end of Sheridan Avenue.

The monument-sized bronze statue by Gertrude Vanderbilt Whitney had been strategically placed at the west end of the main street with Cedar and Rattlesnake Mountains as the backdrop. *An eclectic mix of eastern money and western bravado,* Joel thought.

A high-school band began to play. Heads turned in anticipation, and soon the parade was underway. Shriners driving mini cars and throwing candy for the children, baton twirlers, and cloggers all passed by escorted by cowboy outriders on every showy horse from miles around.

A dude rancher led his string of white pack mules up the parade route. Behind them, a trailer carried rafts from a local river float company, and the guides lobbed water balloons at the crowd.

"Look at that!" Coco pointed to a vintage, horse-drawn surrey that carried handwaving dignitaries.

Moses woofed when a woman wearing period-style clothes and carrying a parasol strolled up the street with a pink miniature poodle on a leash. More floats than they could count rolled past. One had dancing saloon girls, another had singing barber-shop bells, and still another that carried a massive Winchester rifle.

Finally, the Elks Club Band Wagon full of aging musicians made yet another trip down the parade route—either their second or third time. The parade was over except for the cleanup crew, who scooped horse droppings from the main street.

"That was really awesome!" Coco said as the crowd dissipated.

Joel nodded, but his thoughts turned to their next move. "Did you bring your water bottle?"

"It's in my pack, but there isn't much left."

"There's an old hotel and restaurant over there. Maybe we can find a place to fill it up."

The young couple crossed the street and headed for the Irma Hotel. They walked past a long porch and went inside the restaurant. At the cashier counter, Coco grabbed a pamphlet of free tourist information and looked around. "Wow, this place was named for Buffalo Bill's daughter, and that cherry-wood bar behind the lunch counter was a gift from Queen Victoria."

A restaurant hostess appeared. "How many?"

"We're just looking for a bathroom," Joel explained.

"Oh," she sniffed. "You must be here for the gun-fighters." The hostess motioned to an open doorway just beyond some booths. "You'll find one through there."

Joel waited for Coco outside the restroom in the tiny hotel lobby. She emerged with a full bottle of water and said, "Let's stick around for the Gunfight Show. It might be fun."

On the porch of the Irma Hotel, they settled at a picnic table to wait for the show to begin. The reenactors, men and women dressed in period-style garb, strolled around the porch talking to tourists.

"We've got to come up with some kind of a plan," Joel said.

"Someplace far away," Coco replied. "I don't even want to think about what's going to happen when that Clark crowd realizes we've gone. I have been praying that God will direct our steps."

More people began arriving for the show, and soon, all the picnic tables were full.

A group of tourists shared the table with Joel and Coco and initiated small talk. "So, where are you two from?" one said.

"There's something familiar about you," another man said to Joel.

It was a relief when the gunfighters gathered on the street, and all eyes turned their way. There was a sheriff in a white hat and a group of shaggy-looking outlaws who looked like they had just stepped from the screen of an old-time western. A predictably loud mock gunfight involving the sheriff and an assortment of bad guys played out before the delighted audience.

Finally, the sheriff had the rustlers in tow, and the shooting stopped.

The man across the table jabbed his friend and quipped, "They should send a group of real gunslingers to deal with those Jews who are camped out in the Arizona desert. Sanctuary Community, my ass!"

Joel waited until the people left. He turned to his bride and smiled. "Coco, I believe that God just answered your prayers, but it'll take nothing short of a miracle for us to get all the way to Arizona on one tank of gas."

⚬⚬⚬

Hope Springs, Arizona
Wednesday, July 10th

Along with David and his family, Paige and Connor joined the community beneath the pavilion. The atmosphere there was heavy as the sun sank low on the horizon.

Alarming reports continued to trickle in from Israel. Non-compliant Christians and Jews were rounded up and shot or caged in neighborhoods reminiscent of the ghettos of Warsaw, Poland. Some of the lucky ones had escaped to the mountains.

In Arizona, Governor Burns received death threats for helping the refugees, and increasing numbers of protesters gathered to harass the Sanctuary Community.

Tonight, the people had gathered to pray.

Connor opened the Bible in his hand and began to read from the Gospel of John. "The time is coming when those who kill you will think they are doing a holy service for God. This is because they have never known the Father or Me. Yes, I'm telling you these things now, so that when they happen, you will remember my warning."

Light flickered across the roof of the pavilion, and the people turned to see a car approaching. As it drew closer, it became evident by the lights on top that it was law enforcement. The Crown Vic parked near the pavilion, and a uniformed man wearing a cowboy hat climbed from behind the wheel and lumbered over to the gathering. "I'm looking for Paige Hays."

"Over here."

He identified himself as Sheriff Hodges. "Mrs. Hays, a complaint has been filed. I'm here to investigate allegations of child neglect regarding your minor son, Connor Hays."

"That's ridiculous!" Paige cried out. "My son has never been neglected."

"Ma'am, I understand that Connor has not received the Vita Signum. Is this true?"

"Yes."

"Then I'm afraid your boy is being denied proper medical care and access to education."

"Connor is home-schooled, and there is a free clinic in Arroyo Seco," Paige replied.

"Maybe you haven't heard, Mrs. Hays, but home schooling is no longer recognized by the state, and unless that's a board-certified physician you folks got over there…"

"Brody is trying to build a case for full custody, isn't he?"

"I don't know about that, Ma'am." Sherriff Hodges looked weary. "I'm only here to investigate the charges. Where is your son? I'd like to speak with him."

Paige looked for him, but Connor had vanished into the night.

Detroit, Michigan
Wednesday, July 31st

In the abandoned theater, the people gathered to pray. Sick with worry, Katrina paced anxiously around the room.

Fear gripped Katrina's soul at the sound of gunfire on the streets outside. In the last few weeks, eleven believers had been killed, and the streets were stained with blood. Yet, despite these facts, Gar had just volunteered to go on a night mission with Abigail and the preacher.

Someone began to sing on the other side of the room. Others soon joined in.

"God is my refuge and God is my strength,
A very present help in trouble…
Therefore, I will not fear,
Though the earth be removed and
Though the mountains be tossed into the midst of the sea…"

When Gar and the preacher walked through the door, Katrina felt a rush of relief quickly followed by panic. "Where is Abigail?"

"She's safe in the arms of the Lord," the preacher replied. "Her work here is done."

"What if she's lying out there wounded?" Katrina looked at the serene faces of the believers, and anger arose within her. "I don't understand you people!"

Gar placed a hand on her shoulder, but she shrugged him off. "You've changed," she barked.

"Yes, that's true," he admitted. "For the first time in my life, I've come to realize that there is something bigger than me. It's a relief to know that God is in control."

Katrina was just about to respond when there was a soft rap on the front door. "Abigail!" she cried out and followed Darius to the lobby.

The big man held a finger to his lips and peeked through a crack in the boards on the ticket-teller window. "I swear this dude looks just like the guy in your granny's brooch."

She peered outside and was stunned to see Zeke's smiling face. They opened the door and ushered him inside. "I can't believe you're here."

"We've got to work on that unbelief of yours, Missy," the old man replied. "God's been laying out a lot of breadcrumbs for you, but you're not picking them up. What's holding you back?"

Katrina bristled at the question. "Just look around at the

state of the world." When Zeke chuckled, she said, "You find that funny?"

"No, Missy, I'm just amazed that ol' slew foot is still peddling that same tired soundbite." Zeke twirled the tip of his long white beard and asked, "Have you ever walked down the soap aisle at Walmart? Even with all that soap, there's still a lot of dirty people in this world."

"You're obfuscating," Katrina said.

"I'm making a point, Missy. Just like soap, faith must be personally applied if it's going to make a difference in our lives."

"What makes Christianity so special?" Katrina challenged.

"There are a whole lot of 'isms' out there, that's for sure. They teach you how to work your way to some kind of heaven, nirvana, or enlightenment, but Christianity is the only religion that tells us that we can't do it, that only God can. Jesus took our guilt and nailed it to the cross so that mankind can receive the gift of salvation. Think about it Missy. You can't earn a free gift."

"It's true," Gar said. His voice was choked with emotion. "Jesus paid the penalty for all my screw-ups. All I had to do was confess that Jesus is Lord and believe that he died for my sins."

Something stirred deep within Katrina. Zeke took her hand in his. "God knew you before you were even born, Missy. He's just been waiting for you to trust Him."

A lifetime of stoic pride began to crumble around Katrina. Suddenly, she felt as though the Lord himself was standing before her with outstretched arms. The preacher led Katrina in the prayer of salvation. "The Bible says, 'For it is by believing in your heart that you are made right with God, and it is by openly declaring your faith that you are saved.'"

As she spoke the words aloud, a feeling of joy entered Katrina's heart, and she felt like a heavy burden was lifted from her soul.

"Okay, Missy," Zeke said, "you've got a plane to catch. A redeye to Tel-Aviv."

"I don't see how that's possible."

"Didn't God part the Red Sea?" The old man smiled. "He is a way maker. You'll see."

Katrina grabbed her backpack and said her goodbyes to the people she had grown to love. "I'll be praying for you, my friend," Gar said as she went out the door.

Outside, Katrina was alarmed to see Zeke's Rambler station wagon parked in front of the theater. She spotted street gangs lumbering up the street whooping and hollering over Abigail's crumpled corpse. "I'm afraid," she said.

The old man, clad in his trademark Hawaiian shirt and Bermuda shorts, just grinned and opened the car door. "Be strong and be courageous, Missy. The good Lord will be with you wherever you go."

She kept her eye on the hoodlums as Zeke climbed behind the wheel of his car and fired up the engine. To her amazement, they didn't even seem to notice the rusty Rambler puttering right past them. *It's like we're invisible,* Katrina thought.

Beside her, Zeke whistled a carefree tune as he meandered through the streets and then merged onto an Interstate.

She clutched her backpack, felt the outlines of her grandmother's Bible, and for the first time, she had a hunger for the words inside it.

"You just passed the exit to the airport," Katrina said.

Zeke gave her a sideways glance. "We just have one little stop to make first," he said and then took the next exit.

"I don't have an airline ticket. How am I going to get past security without a Vita Signum chip?"

"Have a little faith, Missy," Zeke said as he turned down an alleyway. "You'll see." He drove up a cement ramp, stopped at a garage door, and tooted his horn. In the light of the Rambler headlights, a garage door slowly opened. Zeke drove inside and parked between a limousine and a silver hearse.

"What's going on? Is this a mortuary?" Katrina asked as a young man stepped up to greet them.

The old man hopped from the Rambler and introduced Katrina. "Matt, this is the little gal I was telling you about earlier. Is everything set for the trip?"

Suddenly, it hit Katrina. "Wait! I hope this doesn't mean what I think it means?"

"God's ways aren't always our ways, Missy," Zeke said with a wink.

"Don't worry," Matt said. "It'll be the most comfortable ride you've ever had. Let me show you." He led them inside the funeral home and to a room with an open casket.

"I lined it with padding, and it's stocked with everything you'll need," Matt said proudly. "It's equipped with an air circulation system, LED lights, and a camel pack with water." A hint of a blush passed across the young man's face. "The only undignified part will be the adult diapers which are highly recommended since it's a twelve-hour flight, maybe longer."

Katrina was too stunned to speak. "You'll be as snug as a bug in a rug," Zeke said with a big grin.

PART 3—The Promise

And though this world, with devils filled,

Should threaten to undo us,

We will not fear,

For God hath willed His truth to triumph!

The Prince of Darkness grim,

We tremble not for him;

His rage we can endure,

For lo, his doom is sure,

One little word shall fell him.

Martin Luther – 1529

Chapter 25

Jerusalem, Israel

Katrina awoke feeling disoriented in the dark and cramped space. Then she heard the wheels of the jet skid on the runway below, and she realized what was happening. *Have I been asleep all the way across the ocean?* The last thing that Katrina remembered, just before the casket lid was closed, was Zeke's warm hand upon her head and his prayers.

The cargo hold creaked as the jet taxied off the runway and finally came to a stop.

A few minutes later, Katrina heard stirring and then movement in the cabin above. The passengers made their way from the plane.

Her mouth was dry. She fumbled for the light switch. Surrounded by golden satin, Katrina's fingers searched for the tube of her camel pack, and finding it, she drank her fill of water.

The cargo hold door opened with a thump. She switched off the light and waited in the darkness. Someone yelled something in Arabic, and Katrina heard luggage being moved.

Finally, she felt the casket shift as it was lifted, placed onto a conveyor, and then loaded onto a runway cart. After several bumps and jarring movements on the tarmac, the casket was placed somewhere quiet. *A storage room,* she surmised.

In the stillness, the satin-lined box began to close in around Katrina. *Breathe,* she told herself as the minutes ticked away. It seemed like an eternity before she felt movement again. This time, the casket was being carried. Katrina felt the casket sliding across some rollers. A motor started, and then there was road noise. The vehicle finally came to a stop, and the casket was again off-loaded.

Someone tapped on the casket's lid and said, "Are you alive in there?"

Very funny, Katarina thought, but she remained quiet.

She was just about to have a panic attack when the lid opened, and two Arab-looking men dressed in long white robes stood looking down at her.

Katrina's heart was pounding hard in her chest, and then one of the men said, "Don't be afraid. You are among friends."

"I know you," Katrina said to one of the men.

"Yes, Zeke brought you to my little deli. We reminisced about our grandparents who met at Auschwitz."

"That's right. You're Levi. Why are you dressed like a Muslim?"

"It's safer this way." He helped Katrina from the casket and introduced her to Dagar. "He is proof that we still have Muslim friends, even among the compliant. My friend, Dagar, is taking a great risk helping us. We must move quickly."

Levi handed Katrina a bag and directed her to a restroom. "Slip these garments on over the clothes you're wearing. Be sure to tuck your hair beneath the scarf."

Katrina emerged wearing a dark burqa dress and a long grey scarf. When she grabbed her backpack from the end of the casket, Dagar said, "No! That will not do. If we are stopped, your American sack will arouse suspicion."

"Maybe you can wear it in front—underneath your burqa," Levi suggested.

When she did as they directed, Dagar nodded his approval. "You look like a pregnant Muslim woman. Now, we must go," he said as he ushered them out the door.

"I encountered no checkpoints on the way here," Levi said as they climbed into a van. "Let us pray that God will be with us as we travel back to Jerusalem."

The sun cast a reddish pall as it rose over the city of Tel Aviv. Low grey clouds seemed to hang in the air over the cityscape. "I smell smoke," Katrina said. "Are the forest fires in Lebanon still burning?"

"Yes, but many Jewish homes and businesses have been looted and set on fire."

"What about your deli?"

"The buildings in old Jerusalem are under the protection of the World Fortress Institute, yet my business has been seized and boarded up by World Fortress Institute troops." Levi glanced at his passenger. "Much has changed since you were last in Israel. Those of us who choose to resist the new mandates are few. To Dormin and the World Fortress Institute, non-compliant Jews and Christians are considered an enemy that must be exterminated."

As the morning sunlight filtered through the haze, Katrina tried to process what she was hearing. With a heavy heart, she looked around at the blackened remains of the smoldering urban landscape. There were bloodstains on the roadside, some fresh. Katrina's thoughts drifted to the friends she'd lost in Detroit.

"Oh no! Please, Yeshua, deliver us!" Levi was staring up the highway at a random military checkpoint. He glanced at Katrina and said, "Do not speak—do not even make eye contact."

A guard approached the vehicle, and Levi spoke to him in Arabic. The man walked around peering through the windows of the van. He lingered for a moment, and Katrina could feel him staring at her, but she kept her head lowered looking only forward.

The guard returned to Levi and slipped a scanner from his belt. He was just about to use it when an old station wagon blew past the check point and sped up the road. The officials all scrambled to their waiting cars and gave chase.

"Glory to Yeshua," Levi said. They traveled without incident the rest of the way.

"Where are we going to stay?" Katrina asked as they parked outside of the walled city.

"My grandfather was a man of vision. God prepared him for these perilous times, and he made provisions as you will soon see."

As they strolled casually through the streets of the old walled city, Levi gave Katrina a quick tutorial on the culture of Islam. "It is forbidden for a woman to speak to an unfamiliar man without cause. You must remember that."

"What if a Muslim woman talks to me?"

"Since you don't speak Arabic, I suggest you pretend to be deaf and mute."

"This is the Jewish Quarter," Katrina said as they walked along the street.

"It was." Levi shook his head. "It is now referred to as the Sector of Nations." He led Katrina down the side street where his Deli was located. The windows of the business were boarded up, and a sign hung on the door warning trespassers that this building was under the authority of the World Fortress Institute.

Levi peered up and down the street, and when it was clear, he motioned Katrina into a narrow alleyway that ran between his building and the next. In the back, there was a rustic wooden shed that leaned against the ancient stone of the adjacent building. Levi stepped beneath its cover and tapped gently on the wall.

Katrina watched him slide a knife between some stones, lift a latch, and open a hidden door made of wood and stone. Levi ushered her inside.

A woman was sitting at a table that held a lantern, some pottery vessels, and a laptop. She rose when they entered the room and said, "Welcome."

"Thank you." Katrina smiled at the petite young woman with big dark eyes.

"This is my sister, Yonah," Levi said. "She has been looking forward to meeting you."

Yonah stepped forward and gave their guest a warm embrace. "I have heard so much about you, Katrina. It's a great honor to finally meet."

"Please, make yourself at home," Levi said.

Katrina pointed to the laptop. "You have electricity?"

"I added it a few years ago," Levi explained, "but we use it sparingly, so the meter won't attract suspicion."

Yonah motioned to a doorway covered by a thick Persian rug. "We will share that room. You will find a bedroll there for you."

"The room to the left is where I sleep," Levi added and handed Katrina the lantern. "You may look around, if you like."

In the main room, there were crates stacked to the ceiling, each of them loaded with canned goods and bottled water. In the opposite corner, hidden behind a privacy screen, there was a porta potty and a porcelain wash basin.

Katrina slipped into the small room that she and Yonah would share, left her backpack near an unused bedroll, and returned to the main room. "I'm very grateful for all you're doing."

"It is our pleasure to serve those who love the Lord." Yonah smiled and said, "You must be hungry and thirsty."

Katrina accepted a bottle of water. She slipped off the head covering and fluffed her damp hair. "How did you know that I was coming?"

"Zeke came to me in a dream and told me when and where to pick you up," Levi replied.

"Are you kidding?"

"Yes, I'm joking." Levi grinned. "Zeke sent me a letter several months ago, which I immediately burned."

"Several months ago? But how did he know?"

"I am surprised that you ask that question. You have met Zeke." Levi paused and added, "God always has a plan, even if we don't know what it is."

The young woman poured some wine and retrieved a loaf of unleavened bread from the pottery container on the table. She handed them each a piece of bread and a glass of wine and said, "Let us give thanks for the plans He has for you."

For the first time in Katrina's life, she took communion and found herself reflecting on the wounds and anger that had once held her back. "How many Christians and Jews are still living here in the Holy City?"

"It's very hard to say, but some of us have formed a small underground network. You shall meet our brothers and sisters in due time," Levi said.

Katrina was just about to say something when they heard a commotion outside.

Levi pressed his ear to the wall. "I hear voices of people

yelling and the sound of hurried footsteps in the street." He turned to the women and said, "Stay here. I am going out to see what's happening."

The muted sounds of the activity continued while Levi was gone, and Katrina fought the journalistic urge to investigate. Nearly an hour had passed as they waited.

When Levi returned, he looked visibly shaken. "What is happening?" Yonah asked.

"The crowd was rushing to the temple shouting that a miracle had happened," Levi explained.

Levi lowered himself onto a chair. "As you know, I am banned from the temple because I have refused the Vita Signum. But the crowds pushed, and they overwhelmed the temple guards. Suddenly, I found myself inside." He shook his head. "If I had not seen it with my own eyes…"

"So, what was the miracle?" Katrina pressed.

"It's best if I show you." Levi booted up his laptop, clicked on breaking news, and turned the computer toward Katrina and Yonah.

Dormin's statue was in the frame, and the camera zoomed in for a close-up view. The Grand Apostle Max Nellaf, all dressed in his priestly garb, was standing at the marble feet of the sculpture. In his hand was a thurible filled with burning incense. He waved the smoking vessel towards the statue and uttered a liturgy of prayers.

Then, to the astonishment of all who watched, the marble sculpture of Dormin became animated and began to speak!

"No way!" Katrina shook her head in disgust. "This is

nothing more than a conjurer's trick! They probably used Artificial Intelligence." She looked earnestly at Levi. "Surely you don't believe this is real?"

"Maybe not, but I do believe in the Holy Scriptures and the prophecies that were given to prepare us for the future."

The look on Levi's face sent a chill down Katrina's spine. "Can you give me an example?

Levi explained, "This event was foretold in the books of Daniel, Revelation, and Matthew. Jesus himself tells of a time when the abomination of desolation, spoken of by the prophet Daniel, shall appear. Our Lord said in the Gospel of Matthew, 'The day is coming when you will see what Daniel the prophet spoke about—the sacrilegious object that causes desecration standing in the Holy Place. (Reader, pay attention!) Then those in Judea must flee to the hills.' Then Jesus added, 'For there will be greater anguish than at any time since the world began.'"

<hr>

Bisbee, Arizona

Somewhere south of Tombstone, Arizona, the Winnebago began to sputter. Joel pulled to the side of Highway 80 just before the motor died. He grabbed a road atlas from the glovebox and pinpointed their approximate location. "I'd say that we're at least twelve miles from Bisbee."

The internal temperature of the RV began to rise quickly turning the place into an oven. Joel, Coco, and Moses were forced outside into the equally sweltering desert heat.

"What are we going to do now?" Coco mopped sweat from her brow with a bandana.

Joel looked up and down the highway, but the only movement he spotted was made by the heatwaves coming off the pavement above the mirages. Even the desert flora seemed to be languishing beneath the searing sun.

Moses panted hard, waddled over to the shadow of the RV undercarriage, and plopped down with a grunt.

"It must be over a hundred degrees in the shade," Coco said.

"We don't have much water left in the camper, but we'll collect every drop we can to take with us," Joel said.

Coco looked worried. "I don't think it's a good idea to walk. What about heat stroke?"

"We'll go slow." Joel tried not to sound concerned. "I'll grab our hats and fill the jugs with water."

The young couple and their dog headed out on the parched desert soil. They followed the highway but avoided the blacktop and its radiant heat. After traveling on foot for several miles, Coco's face began to flush. "I don't feel well. My head hurts."

Joel gave her an extra sip of their rationed water, dampened her bandana, and tied it loosely around her neck. They rested for a few minutes in the paltry shade of a saguaro cactus and then pressed on. After another mile, Coco dropped to her knees and said, "I can't go any farther."

Joel knelt beside his bride and stroked her black silky hair. He was shocked to find it so hot to the touch. He took her pulse and was alarmed by her pounding heart. *Lord help!* he silently prayed, and then to his relief, Joel spotted a yellow school bus coming out of the mirage. It was heaven-sent.

He hurried to the road and frantically waved his arms. The brakes on the old bus squealed as it came to a stop.

The door swung open and a kid with his hair scraped up into a bun on top of his head stepped outside. "Yo man, I assume that is your vintage Winnebeater broke down back up the road."

"Yeah, I'm afraid it finally quit us for good," Joel replied as he helped his wife to her feet. "Can we bum a ride?"

"No problemo, man. Hey, your little gal don't look too good."

Relief washed over Joel when they climbed onto the school bus and felt a rush of cool air. Most of the seats were filled with young people and aging hippies who welcomed the newcomers enthusiastically.

"I bet you two are coming in for the big protest. We're meeting up with some organizers down in Bisbee." Man bun handed Joel and Coco some bottled water and directed them to some empty seats near the back.

"Just take little sips," Joel told his wife as the bus started to roll.

The passengers were all buzzing about some kind of miraculous occurrence at the temple in Jerusalem.

"What happened?" Joel asked the couple sitting in the seat in front of them.

"Where have you been?" One man croaked. "You're

probably the only person on the planet who hasn't heard about the statue of Alistair Dormin. It's all over the news!"

"The radio in our Winnebago is broken," Joel said.

"Grand Apostle Nellaf was in Jerusalem praying over the statue when it began to speak—for real!" A misty-eyed woman seated in the next row explained. "The universe is telling us that we're all a part of something really big."

"What did the statue say?"

"It said something like, 'Dormin is anointed and to wait for instructions.'"

"I'll have to check it out," Joel said, but he was troubled by the blind faith of these people. *Would they march over a cliff for a hunk of marble?* he wondered.

"How many people are expected at the big protest?" Coco asked.

A few seats away, a balding man with a pencil-thin ponytail responded. "About five hundred, I understand. Maybe those Jews will finally get the message and go back where they belong."

Moses settled at the young couple's feet and began to snore.

Coco laid her head on her husband's shoulder. "We don't belong with these people," she whispered.

Joel looked out the window as the bus rolled down Highway 80. They traveled through the Mule Pass Tunnel, and just around the bend, the small, historic-mining town of Bisbee came into view. The bus maneuvered through some narrow streets and came to a stop in a parking area in Brewery Gulch. The group spilled from the school bus and began to mingle with the hundreds of people who were milling about, all kindred souls.

Joel's gaze fell upon the long line of protestors waiting to collect picket signs with slogans like: "Go home Jews!" or "Get a Vita Signum or die!"

More people arrived in cars and buses, and finally, someone with a bullhorn climbed up on a makeshift platform to rally the crowd with collective chants. A few doors down at Saint Elmo's Bar, belligerent partiers downed liquid courage and cheered on the crowds.

The young couple wandered over to a building that was once an old brewery. "How are you feeling?" Joel asked.

"Physically better, but this is very upsetting." Coco's honey-brown eyes betrayed her sadness. "A year ago, these same people were calling for equality, love, and peace. Now, they are spewing out hatred."

"Cause Fever makes people do irrational things," Joel replied. "Let's just play along until we get close enough to walk to that Sanctuary Community."

By 2:00 p.m., they all loaded back onto the bus that was now packed with picket signs. The cramped space rolled along and was filled with angry chants and hateful screeds. By the time they came to a stop near the Sanctuary Community perimeter, the passengers were spoiling for a fight. "Everybody off the bus!" man bun hollered.

Someone with a bullhorn advised the newest group to stay hydrated with water provided in nearby coolers, and then the organized protest began.

Joel was amazed when he saw the vastness of the Sanctuary Community. It looked like a city of white yurts, warehouses, and stockyards. Beyond that, he spotted the buildings of a small town.

The organizer blasted obnoxious music at the refugees, while the protesters thrust their picket signs in the air and screamed obscenities. A car horn cut through the cacophony of rants, and the packed crowd parted and shifted from the highway as a convoy of law enforcement vehicles rolled along the blacktop and crossed the sanctuary perimeter.

Moses barked when a canine passed by in one of the SUVs.

"I think they're all heading for that town," Joel said. "I wonder what's going on?"

Some of the protestors had brought drones and several took flight to buzz and harass the residents of the Sanctuary Community. As the minutes ticked by, the chants and slurs grew more vitriolic. Amid the chaos, Joel and Coco managed to slip away.

They moved stealthily from bush to bush until they were certain that they were out of the line of sight. On the other side of an outcropping, the young couple hunkered down in a cleft in the rock to wait for the protesters to leave.

⸙

Arroyo Seco, Arizona

It was mid-afternoon when David sat at his desk in the storage room and pondered the recent events. The strange occurrence at the temple in Jerusalem had set the whole community on edge. Some said that it was an ominous sign of things to come. Others wailed in grief and ripped their clothing, but David was convinced that the animation of the Dormin statue was just some kind of technological manipulation.

According to Ezra, the world has been primed to believe anything. "Society has turned away from God, and many churches have twisted the truth to make the lies more palatable."

David sighed. Even inside of the General Store, he could hear the protestor's bullhorn bellow, "Go home, Jews!" *They're back again. Why can't they see the hypocrisy of their words and actions?* he thought with disgust and then shrugged it off. "I've got my own family problems to consider," he muttered to himself. It had been almost six weeks since Connor ran away. His nephew's words still echoed in David's mind. "The time is coming when people will think that they are doing God a favor by killing us, but don't be discouraged because the sufferings of this present time are nothing compared to the awesome things that God has prepared for us!"

David had never seen such faith. Connor, though only a teenager, had spoken like a man full of courage and conviction, and then he vanished in the night. It was as if he somehow knew that the authorities would soon arrive to take him into protective custody.

How can Brody accuse Paige of child endangerment? he fumed.

David recalled Chasha telling him that Connor was still living in the community and moving from tent to tent. "They call him, 'Nasi Katan,' which means 'Little Captain' in Hebrew," she had said. "That boy is preaching the Gospel to anyone who will listen!"

Hurried footsteps moved across the wood floor of the General Store. Elita threw back the tapestry curtain that hung on the backroom door and said, "The State Police are back, and this time they've brought dogs!"

Joy was standing on the porch, and her parents joined her there. They watched law enforcement officers unloading blood hounds. Overhead, the sky grew dark as churning clouds rolled in, and a sprinkling of raindrops began to fall.

"Brody is hunting down his own son like a fugitive," David muttered as thunder rumbled overhead. "I can't believe Brody's disdain and anger has come to this."

The dogs ran about sniffing the air and then hit on a scent. The handlers hurried after the baying hounds.

Fat raindrops fell upon the thirsty ground, and a bolt of lightning split the air closely followed by an explosion of thunder. Suddenly, the sky opened, and a deluge of driving rain came down upon the town.

With the rain knocking down any scent, the frustrated dog handlers slogged back to their vehicles and loaded the wet hounds back into their crates. "We'll be back!" one of the handlers yelled.

After they drove away, Joy said, "I'm going to dance in the rain." She jumped from the porch and spun around catching raindrops in her mouth.

Elita smiled at her husband. "Isn't God amazing? You never know what he's going to do next."

Through the tempest, David spotted a young couple walking toward them with an ugly mutt trailing close behind. "True. You never know what's going happen next," he echoed as he welcomed the latest refugees in from the storm.

Chapter 26

Arroyo Seco, Arizona

Paige drove the utility vehicle past a cluster of refugees and parked in front of the General Store. A new thunderhead was building to the west. *There's going to be another afternoon rain shower,* she thought.

Paige grabbed her rain jacket from the back seat and headed inside to help with the distribution of the weekly rations. Her brother and Ezra stood near the lunch counter, talking with the young couple who had recently joined them. For days, Paige had a strong feeling that she knew the young man named Joel Sutherland, but he assured her that they had never met.

Joy clambered down the apartment stairs followed by her mother, who was holding a stack of old clothing in her arms. "Coco is helping us sew outfits!" Joy announced as she twirled around to show off a new gingham and polka-dot dress.

Paige bent down to give her niece a big hug and a kiss. "You look beautiful!"

Elita placed the armful of old clothing on the lunch

counter. "Coco is a gifted seamstress, so we're collecting pieces of material."

"I'm very impressed." Paige smiled at the pretty Asian-looking woman.

Chasha burst through the door and filled the room with her presence. "Hello, campers! Let's get busy, shall we?" The elderly New Yorker clapped her hands to rally the troops, and soon everyone in the room was lined up to work. Several minutes later, they were busy filling bags for the weekly distribution of rations. Outside, as the line of people lengthened, Ezra took his place by the door, and Chasha signaled for him to open it.

Joel and Coco distributed bags from the porch of the General Store until the last rations were delivered.

"Well, that went smoothly," David said. "We finished half an hour earlier than normal."

Paige kept looking at Joel, and suddenly, it came to her. "I know why you look familiar. Your face was all over the Washington Post. You're Thomas Atwood's son," she said. "My husband was working at the White House when the President learned about you."

"What? I don't believe what I'm hearing," Ezra said. "Are you really Atwood's son?"

Joel's face flushed with embarrassment. "The late President was my biological father, that's true, but I was adopted and consider the man who raised me to be my real dad."

"That brings to mind a biblical principle," Ezra said. "Each of us have earthly fathers, but when we receive the free gift of salvation, then we are adopted into God's family." Mr. Hamburg's scarred lips stretched into a smile. "It's an honor to meet you, young man. Thomas Atwood was a great friend to Israel during a time when they had few supporters."

"Fewer still, I hear," Joel said.

"Yes, this is unfortunately true, but in the book of Zechariah, God says that he will make Jerusalem a burdensome stone for all people. History testifies that every nation that sought to control or destroy Jerusalem has fallen into decline."

Just then the screen door banged open, and Mr. Mike rushed inside. He looked at them through his thick lenses and said, "You'd better come see. That statue of Dormin is twitching those cold lips again!" The group hurried after the gangly technology geek, and soon they were gathered in the media center watching the television monitors.

Talking heads had come together for a special report. "Ladies and gentlemen, if you are just joining us, movement of the Alistair Dormin statue has been detected." The anchor spoke with a whispered tone of reverent expectancy. "We believe he is about to speak to us."

The camera crew zoomed in for a closer shot of the marble face of the sculpture.

The eyes appeared to blink, the mouth appeared to open, and then it spoke. "The Chairman's power and authority have come! People of the globe give Alistair Dormin and his image the worship due and live! The rebellious blight upon civilization must be purged!" the statue said.

Suddenly, the monitors all went blank, and the media center lights were cut out.

"What's happened?" David asked.

"Maybe something's gone wrong with the generator and the satellite feed." Mr. Mike grabbed some tools and went to investigate.

As residents of the desert community trickled into the media center, Chasha filled them in on the latest ominous developments in Jerusalem. Word spread quickly throughout the Sanctuary Community. Out on the street, a drone fell from the sky, and the voices of the refugees could be heard lifting their petitions to Heaven.

A half hour later, the lights blinked on, and the news feeds returned, leaving Mr. Mike scratching his scruffy head.

They watched the talking heads chattering in confusion and chaos. They were desperately trying to reach experts to explain the worldwide outage. A scientist weighed in, speculating that the massive global power outage had been caused by some kind of undetectable solar flare. Every media outlet, cell tower, radio, and satellite feed had been rendered silent for thirty minutes.

All electricity sources, including hydro, nuclear, and geothermal power sources, had also shut down. The buzz and speculation worsened as more news began to trickle in. "We have never seen anything like this," experts said. They rolled images of freeway pileups and transit systems sitting idle.

Even wind turbines, solar panels, and coal and gas-powered electric generation plants had ceased to operate. "Ladies and gentlemen, we have just received unconfirmed reports of several major airline crashes!"

Abruptly, Alistair Dormin appeared on the screens. He looked severe with his silver patch over one eye and his stark white hair. He sat in a stoic pose behind his ebony desk. He stared into the camera with his one good eye. "Ladies and gentlemen of the new world do not be alarmed by what you have just witnessed. The silence was sent as a cosmic sign and a confirmation! The time has come for absolute obedience. Those who honor me with their lives shall be richly rewarded, but all who refuse to prostrate themselves to my will, shall perish!"

⦿⦿⦿

Jerusalem, Israel

Katrina followed Levi and his sister along a narrow underground passage. At a fork in the tunnel, Levi pointed his flashlight to the right. They walked silently beneath the old walled city for what seemed like miles. Finally, the narrow passage opened to a larger space.

Three people who were also hiding from the authorities were huddled there praying in Hebrew. When they finished, Levi introduced Katrina to a large man named Boaz, a teenager called Elam, and finally to an elderly woman named Geeta.

Two other men, who were known as Etan and Joseph,

soon joined them. Their demeanor was somber. "We are bearers of sad news," Joseph said. He turned to the teenager and laid a hand upon his shoulder. "Elam, I'm afraid that your parents were detained and executed today."

The stunned high schooler began to weep, and the old woman, Geeta, hurried to his side to offer him comfort.

"I am so sorry for your loss, Elam." Yonah said.

Levi nodded. "You shall come and stay with us."

Anger burned inside Katrina's heart when she thought about the man responsible for all this pain. She had personally seen the evil in Dormin's eyes.

The group began to speak among themselves, and Levi translated. "They are discussing the statue, its wicked decree, and the silence that followed," he explained to Katrina. "The situation is getting much worse. Dormin's allied troops have gathered north of here, and there are rumors of a full-scale invasion. Anyone without the Vita Signum will be shot on sight."

Just as the gathering was breaking up, a middle-aged woman arrived. She fell to her knees and began to wail as she told them what she had just witnessed. "The two prophets have been killed, and their bodies are being paraded through the streets of Old Jerusalem."

"Yeshua, let it not be so!" Yonah cried out.

Levi bowed his head in prayer. "Yeshua, help us through the darker days that lie ahead."

Darker days? Katrina thought. *How can things possibly get any worse?*

Chapter 27

Jerusalem, Israel

Three days had passed since Katrina learned that the two men whom Zeke had introduced to her had been murdered. After receiving the news, she hadn't eaten or slept much.

Katrina rose, splashed water on her face, and slipped on her burqa and head covering. "I have to go see it for myself," she announced.

Elam looked up from the table but said nothing.

"I strongly advise against going out on the streets right now," Levi cautioned. "Troops have mobilized all around the city to crush any opposition. Soldiers are going from home to home conducting searches. I understand that offenders are being tortured."

"Yes, my brother is right," Yonah agreed. Her dark eyes filled with concern. "You could be killed."

"I need to go see for myself," Katrina repeated. "I've met those men you call prophets. They spoke a word to me."

Levi and his sister exchanged surprised looks. "What did they say to you?"

"It doesn't matter right now," Katrina said. "I can't really explain why, but I've got to go pay my respects."

"We shall all be praying for you," Yonah said as Katrina slipped through the door and left the safety of the shelter.

Out on the street, Katrina moved along disguised by her dark burqa dress and a long grey scarf. She kept her head down as she went. The mood on the old streets of Jerusalem was festive. A group of gleeful young men passed by carrying a bloody head impaled on a stake.

Fighting back the urge to be sick, Katrina hurried onward.

In the courtyard of the Wailing Wall, a crowd had gathered to rejoice over the deaths of the two witnesses. Armed guards stood near the bodies to keep the revelers at bay. Someone spoke in English, and said, "Those charlatans got exactly what they deserved for troubling our planet." It was repulsive to see those old men laid out as a spectacle for the world to mock.

A woman selling candied dates approached Katrina, but when she pretended to be deaf and mute, the woman moved on to the next group.

I've seen enough, she thought. Katrina was just about to leave when she spotted a little white-haired man wearing a Hawaiian shirt. From behind, he looked a lot like Zeke. She watched as the old man strolled right past the guards as if he were invisible! Then he knelt down beside the bodies of the two dead prophets.

Katrina looked around, but no one in the crowd seemed to notice what was happening.

Suddenly, one of the dead men sat up and then the other. The old man in the Hawaiian shirt helped them to their feet. Someone shrieked and pointed. Pandemonium erupted in the crowded courtyard. People scurried away in all directions.

The soldiers, who had been guarding the corpses, raised their weapons, and Katrina gasped! "Zeke!" she yelled. Zeke turned, blew softly on the men, and they fell back like they were toppled by a hurricane.

The courtyard was eerily quiet now. Only a media crew remained, and they cowered behind their live-feed cameras. Overhead a thick cloud shadowed the courtyard and thunder rumbled.

Katrina spotted a sliver of white light shining through the cloud, and golden rays shined down upon the two prophets. She stood transfixed and stunned to see the men floating skyward as though weightless! They rose upward until they vanished in the clouds.

Without warning, the ground beneath Katrina's feet began to shake. Abandoning their equipment, the camera crew fled in fear. An ancient stone fell from the wall and crashed into the courtyard as the paving stones began to buckle and heave. *It's an earthquake!* she thought and then cried out, "What's happening, Zeke?"

There was a somberness in the old man's crystal gaze that she had never seen before. "From here on out Missy, there's gonna be a whole lotta shakin' goin' on!"

Katrina heard a crash behind her, turned to look, and when she turned back, Zeke was gone.

❧

Paris, France

In the 16th Arrondissement of Paris, Jean Pierre flashed his ID badge and Vita Signum for the guard and was buzzed through. The quaint-looking gated community was home to Dormin, his servants, and essential World Reserve Bank staff.

Under the watchful eye of security cameras, Pierre walked down the cobblestone sidewalk that led to the Chairman's estate. He climbed the steps and engaged the facial-recognition sensor. The door swung open, and a butler welcomed Jean Pierre into an impressive entryway with marble inlaid floors and an original Rodin statue that stood near a curved staircase.

"This way, sir. The master is expecting you."

Jean Pierre was escorted through an ornate sitting room with gold frescos and ceiling murals of painted clouds and then through a music room with a grand piano. He clicked his tongue in annoyance as they moved past the library, for he knew that Dormin's private elevator was hidden behind a trompe l'oeil bookshelf. *Surely, as the Director of the World Fortress Institute, I should be given special access. After all,* Jean Pierre thought, *I am the one who helped Alistair Dormin rise to his present status.*

The butler led the way through a formal dining room

and then into the La Cornue-equipped kitchen, where a world-renowned chef was preparing a meal. He stopped near the servant's entrance and keyed in the special code. When the doors slid open, Pierre boarded the elevator and reminded himself that only Dormin's most trusted confederates were allowed access to the bottom level.

The elevator descended past the first basement level, which housed a bar, a pool table, and an impressive collection of ancient museum-quality pottery.

The next level down had a tiled sixteen-meter lap pool, a hot tub, a sauna, a massage parlor, and Dormin's personal hair salon. As an elite and trusted friend, Pierre had sometimes been invited to enjoy these privileged services.

At the lowest level, the elevator doors opened to a massive media center with theater seating. The monitors were alive with real time images from around the globe. Interactive maps indicated time zones, allies, and trouble spots. On one end of the room, there was a massive conference table, and on the other side, there was a podium with a backdrop of World Fortress Institute emblems.

There was a mysterious door with a keypad. Only Jean Pierre and a few others knew that behind that vault door was a fully stocked bomb shelter.

Jean Pierre kept an eye on the hallway that led to Dormin's private elevator. With each passing minute his anxiety grew, for the last visit he'd had with the Chairman had been unsettling, to say the least. Alistair Dormin had been more than outraged by the unexplained power outage and collapse of technology. Dormin ranted, "How can the leader of the world be cut off from information? Someone will answer for this!" The chief technology officer was promptly fired.

Pierre secretly suspected that it was really the subsequent resurrection of the so-called two witnesses that had really sent the Chairman over the edge. Not only had that incident alarmed the international community, but it had diminished Dormin's sense of personal victory. Jean Pierre shuddered when he thought about how the Chairman had slammed his fist on the table and screamed, "I am the one they should fear!"

After considerable time had passed, Dormin's private elevator opened.

Pierre stood respectfully when the Chairman entered the room. He looked somber with his white hair and silver eye patch. It was remarkable how much the man had changed since they had first met.

Relief washed over Jean Pierre when Dormin said, "I have called you here to discuss the international relief efforts after the earthquake in Israel."

"Yes, Monsieur Chairman," Pierre replied, "The numbers are still coming in, but I understand that the casualties are in the thousands." He paused to draw a breath. "I'm afraid that your statue was damaged, but repairs are being made."

Alistair Dormin waived his hand dismissively. "The statue has served its purpose, and the casualties don't concern me. The good news is that this natural disaster has shifted the focus from the so-called resurrection of that pair of charlatans. Our Grand Apostle has agreed to put a stop to any ridiculous speculations that God was behind that event." A fleeting micro smile passed across his lips. "In fact, Nellaf believes that it's time to roll out a few signs and wonders of our own."

"Very good, Monsieur Chairman." Jean Pierre tried to summon the courage to tell Dormin about the painful boils that were breaking out on some people who had received the Vita Signum implant. "Sir, there is another matter…"

An urgent call interrupted the moment. The NASA Planetary Defense Director appeared on the teleconference screen. "Mr. Chairman, I have some alarming news. For some time now, our Coordination Office has been tracking a seven-mile-long asteroid named Wormwood. It has not been a concern until now. I'm afraid that Wormwood has collided with another asteroid, and this collision has altered its trajectory. Currently, it appears to be on track to make contact with Earth."

"What time frame are we looking at?" the Chairman asked. "And what are our options?"

"According to our calculations, the impact will be thirty days from now. I assure you that we are carefully monitoring this situation, and our planetary defense missiles are on standby alert."

"Fine, then I expect you to deal with it!" Dormin snapped. "I don't want any of this information leaked. Do I make myself clear?"

Chapter 28

Jerusalem, Israel

Katrina tossed and turned on her bedroll. All night long, she dreamed about Zeke, the two prophets rising into the clouds, and the devastating earthquake that followed.

For several hours, Katrina struggled over fallen debris and traversed crevasses, but she finally found her way back to the hidden dwelling behind the deli. It was a miracle to find it untouched, and her friends were unharmed by the earthquake. *That's all that really matters right now,* Katrina thought as she got up and slipped into her dusty jeans and a t-shirt.

She drew back the rug that hung in her bedroom doorway, and Elam said, "Hey everybody, it's alive!"

"Very funny," Katrina said as she stepped into the lantern light to examine her broken fingernails and bloody fingertips.

"How are you feeling?" Yonah asked.

"Better," Katrina replied.

"You must eat something."

Katrina nibbled on a piece of matzo cracker and washed it down with some water.

"Are you ready to tell us what you witnessed?" Levi asked.

"Yeah," Elam interjected, "since the earthquake, we've got no Internet access, so we can't watch the news."

Katrina told them about Zeke and the incredible resurrection that took place near the Wailing Wall. "You probably think I'm crazy."

"On the contrary." Yonah smiled.

"You needed to see this with your own eyes because the word is not yet written upon your heart," Levi explained. He opened his Bible to the eleventh chapter of the Book of Revelation and handed it to Katrina to read.

She was awestruck by the words that described what she had witnessed. "This was written thousands of years ago, but I saw it happen yesterday."

"Yes Katrina, we serve a powerful and amazing God," Yonah replied. "Revelation was written by the Apostle John about two thousand years ago, and the books of the prophets are even older. Many people believe that prophesies about the end of the age have already been fulfilled, but we are clearly seeing their fulfillment today."

⊗⊗⊗

Tucson, Arizona

At the Memorial Interfaith Assembly, Brody rose along with the rest of the congregation as the worship leader began. "Put your hands together people. Come on! If you love God, show it!"

Brody's heart just wasn't in it this Sunday morning. He cast a sideways glance at Jolene. She seemed to sense it and ran her red-painted fingernails down a gold necklace to her cleavage.

The woman's voracious sexual appetite was exciting at first, but Brody had come to realize that she was incapable of love.

He felt a pang of guilt when he looked at his boss, Jolene's husband. While Gavin Thorne had been in the hospital recovering from a heart attack, Brody had been carrying on with Gavin's wife. *What has happened to me?* Brody wondered, with a sudden pang of conviction. *My priorities have been shallow and worldly. I've lost sight of all that matters—my family and my moral compass.*

As the praise music shifted to soft emotive melodies, Brody noticed the stage lighting shifted from yellow to blue and then to green as the tithes and offerings were taken up. As usual, the Grand Apostle Nellaf made another spectacular entrance on stage and paraded himself in shimmering clerical garb. Finally, he took his place behind the ebony podium that rose like magic from the stage floor.

Nellaf invited the congregation to be seated, and there was a frown on his usually pleasant face. "It has come to my attention that wild speculation and rumors have been circulating among some of you. Beloved, let me put your hearts and minds at ease regarding the events surrounding those two charlatans in Jerusalem. They are not risen prophets as some have suggested. This is unenlightened nonsense! Those imposters are a blight on the planet, hurling baseless curses upon the innocent. Dear ones, I assure you that it was divine intervention that purged them from the earth, and I say good riddance!"

Cheers rippled through the sanctuary as Nellaf's words settled over the minds and hearts of his global followers

"My children, the life and ministry of Jesus foreshadowed the coming of our blessed waymaker!" An image of the Chairman of the World Reserve Bank appeared on the big screen. "Beloved, this is the man of God and the God of men! Alistair Dormin was once dead, but now he lives to lead us forth in victory!"

Ecstatic excitement roared through the cavernous room, while Max Nellaf basked in the glow of adoration and purple light.

Someone in the sanctuary cried out, "I can see!" Heads turned to a woman with a white-tipped cane. She tossed it aside and danced her way up the aisle, saying, "Praise be to Dormin!"

Another person rose up from a wheelchair and bellowed, "Glory! I've been healed!"

The people began to chant, "We will follow you anywhere!"

It's all stage-managed, Brody thought. As an elder, he had justified the use of smoke and mirrors because of the revenues they generated from the congregation, but now all the pretense seemed hypocritical.

Brody's mind wandered to the failures of his marriage

and career. *Everything I touch seems to go wrong.* He looked down at the painful boils on the back of his hand that were now spreading up his arm, an unforeseen side effect of the Vita Signum implant that was now afflicting millions. There was talk of replacing the implant with a digital tattoo, but that would take months. *How could I have known this would happen?*

On stage, the Grand Apostle yammered on with his usual flamboyant zeal, but his preaching rang like a clanging cymbal in Brody's ears, and he wondered, *Have I made a terrible mistake?*

⸺⦿⸺

Arroyo Seco, Arizona

Coco and Joel joined the Fillmore family on the porch of the General Store. They watched hordes of refugees trudging past as they headed north on the main street of Arroyo Seco. "What's going on?" Joel asked.David shrugged. "I don't know." He looked at Elita.

Elita pointed to the crowd of people and waved. "There's Chasha. She'll know."

The village kibitzer hurried over to tell them. "Everyone is going over to Hope Springs because Nasi Katan has a message for the people." The old woman wagged her finger at David. "I thought you, being his uncle, would know all about this."

"Who is Nasi Katan?" Coco asked.

"That's the nickname the refugees have given my

nephew, Connor," David explained. "It means 'Little Captain' in Hebrew."

"Leader, not captain," Chasha corrected. "The good book says a little child shall lead them." She spotted her husband walking on ahead and dashed off yelling, "Uri wait up!"

Joy looked eagerly at her parents. "Can we go listen to Connor?"

"Why don't we all go," Elita said. "It's a beautiful day for a walk in the desert."

"It sounds interesting," Coco said, so they grabbed backpacks and some water and fell in with the others. More people joined in along the way. They strolled across the desert letting Joy alert them to Prickly Pear Cactus, horned toads, and jack rabbit burrows.

Joel looked around at the sea of sojourners and said to Coco, "It feels like we're in that old Charlton Heston movie, The Ten Commandments."

As they walked, a fleet of white pickup trucks came into view, kicking up dust as they approached from a county road. Coco pointed out the oval symbol on the vehicles and read the words out loud. "U.S. Department of the Interior—Bureau of Reclamation."

David shook his head and said, "I wonder what our government is up to now?"

"The Sonoran Dam is located up that road," Elita replied. "They're probably just doing an inspection or maintenance." They walked on, but they kept an eye on the Bureau of Reclamation fleet until it disappeared over the rise.

"Wow," Joel said as they approached Hope Springs and the vast crowd of Jewish refugees who had gathered at the base of a large sandstone outcropping.

"Look! I see Connor!" Joy pointed to the red-headed teenager who was kneeling on a massive rock on top of the outcropping.

The boy they called Nasi Katan stood and began to pray, "O' Lord, our Lord, how excellent is Your name in all the earth. You have set your glory above the heavens! Out of the mouth of babes and nursing infants You have ordained strength…" A hush settled over the crowd. The boy looked towards Heaven as though seeing a vision.

"Prepare the way of the Lord. Make straight in the desert a highway for our God. Every valley shall be exalted, and every mountain and hill brought low; the crooked places shall be made straight and the rough places smooth; The glory of the Lord shall be revealed, and all flesh shall see it together," he cried out. "The Lord loves the gates of Zion. The Lord is strong and mighty in battle! Arise O' Lord, deliver us from our enemies and contend with those who contend with us. Arise O' Lord, do not let man prevail; Let the nations be judged in Your sight. Put them in fear, O' Lord, that the nations may know themselves to be but men."

I see why they call him Nasi Katan, Joel thought as spontaneous worship filled the atmosphere with sweet songs of joyful praise in Hebrew and other tongues. Something deep inside Joel was moved, and he began to reflect upon his life.

Coco seemed to sense a dramatic change in Joel's countenance. "Are you okay?"

"It's like I've been tilting at windmills," he said.

"What do you mean?"

"I used to think that if I exposed political policies that restrict individual freedoms, then people would wake up," Joel began. "I believed that self-determination and reason would change this world, and that religion was a breeding ground for doomsday zealots. I hate to admit it, but judging from world events, maybe some of them were right."

Joel wiped a tear from his eye. "I'm beginning to understand why you love all scripture, even the difficult parts." He looked at his beautiful bride. "I want the faith to believe that God is really in control, and that He—not mankind—will sort it all out in the end."

Coco smiled. "I've been praying for this moment. The Apostle Paul said that, 'If you openly declare that Jesus is Lord and believe in your heart that God raised him from the dead, you will be saved.' It's as simple as that Joel." Coco took her husband's hand, and together they prayed.

Suddenly, a distant loud explosion shattered the peaceful atmosphere.

The crowd turned towards the source of the sound and saw a cloud of dust rising up in the valley where the Bureau of Reclamation trucks had gone earlier.

"The dam!" Elita cried out.

The crowd waited and watched. A white wall of water

appeared in the mouth of the valley between the mountains and then spread out across the flats. It was rushing straight toward the village of Hope Springs and the people who had gathered there.

"Don't be afraid," Nasi Katan yelled. "The Lord is our refuge and strength. He is a very present help in trouble!"

Joel looked around, but there was no place to go, no place to run.

What happened next, only God could explain. As the water roared closer, the ground trembled and then shook violently. A huge fissure opened across the path of the waters, and to everyone's utter amazement, the earth swallowed up the flood.

Chapter 29

Kennedy Space Center, Florida

Jean Pierre and Alistair Dormin arrived at the Kennedy Space Center and were promptly ushered into the Mission Control Room VIP observation booth to await the launch of the Space X Falcon Heavy Missile.

Key personnel from the NASA Planetary Defense Coordination Office were also in attendance, along with representatives from Johns Hopkins Applied Physics Laboratory, the Jet Propulsion Laboratory, the Langley Research facility, and the Goddard and Johnson Space Centers.

"How confident are you that this will work?" The Chairman of World Reserve Bank asked a physicist seated to his left.

"Extremely, Sir," the scientist replied. "Double Asteroid Redirection Tests have already been deployed from Vandenberg Air Force Base in California with astounding results. Several smaller asteroids have had their trajectories altered by DART with amazing mathematical precision. In this instance, we are using the Space X Falcon Heavy so that we can achieve the greatest possible kinetic effect on the asteroid known as Wormwood."

The Kennedy Space Center's Control Room began the countdown: "Ten, nine, eight, seven, six, five, four, three, ignition, one, and lift off." The space engineers prattled on reciting numbers, something about throttling down, and the vehicle reaching supersonic speed. The technical jargon was all nonsense to Jean Pierre whose only concern was mission success.

The view switched to a camera mounted on the craft, and the observers watched it rocketing through space on its way to divert the course of the massive seven-mile-wide asteroid. The Control Room engineer announced that everything looked "nominal" with the Stage One trajectory. A few minutes later he said, "Stage One separation, Stage Two ignition. Everything is still looking nominal."

In the distance, as the transition to Stage Three was completed, the asteroid came into view. There was a sense of excitement in the room as the Space X rocket advanced toward its target.

"How long will it take to hit the mark?" Dormin asked.

"We estimate approximately forty-six hours, Sir," the engineer said. When the rocket reached approximately 25,000 miles per hour, cheers and celebratory congratulations rippled through the Control Room.

"Well done, gentlemen," Alistair Dormin said and then turned to Jean Pierre. "I want you to put together a press release and let my people know that we have just saved the planet from destruction." Without waiting for a response, the Chairman of the World Reserve Bank moved about the room offering vigorous handshakes.

Jean Pierre looked at an Astro Physicist, who was sitting stoically beside him. "Is there a reason that you seem less optimistic than your comrades?"

"Pride and presumption make me uncomfortable," the scientist replied.

"Tell me, what will happen if this mission fails to redirect the asteroid?"

The man turned his somber gaze to the Director of the World Fortress Institute. "Mathematical calculations have been done by the top minds at NASA and the European Space Agency. We all concur with our estimations of the trajectory…"

Jean Pierre stopped the physicist, "What do you mean 'estimations?'"

"Sir, the object is still a great distance away, and there are many variables at play."

"Worst case scenario? Make it quick." Pierre glanced at the Chairman, who was still strutting about the room.

"Sixty-five million years ago, a six-mile-long asteroid struck the Yucatan Peninsula in Mexico. We believe that impact knocked the earth from its axis and plowed billions of tiny particles of rock into the atmosphere. These tiny particles, called spherules, had massive amounts of kinetic energy the equivalent of multiple large hydrogen bombs. About forty minutes after the initial impact of the asteroid, these spherules began their descent back to Earth. As they fell their energy was converted to heat and infrared radiation. For several hours, these tiny incandescent torches pummeled the entire earth, igniting the planet with fire.

"If this mission fails, then the impact of this asteroid will cause a chain reaction of earthquakes, volcanic eruptions, and tsunamis. It will be a mass extinction event of unimaginable proportions. Billions of people will perish." The Astro Physicist paused to gauge Jean Pierre's reaction. "Shall I go on to discuss the enormous catastrophic impact that such an event will have on the climate?"

Keeping his eye on the Chairman, the Frenchman shook his head. Someone had rolled a champagne cart into the Control Room. Alistair Dormin raised his crystal flute for a toast and said, "Here's to the health and wealth of my planet!"

For the first time, Pierre caught a glimpse behind the Chairman's mask, and it sent a shiver down his spine. He genuflected. *That man really believes he is God!*

Jerusalem, Israel

When Levi returned from a meeting with their comrades, the look on his face sent a chill through the room.

"What is happening out there?" Katrina asked.

"World Fortress Institute troops have swarmed the area under the guise of humanitarian aid. The world is being told that they have come to help restore Israel and the old walled city after the earthquake, but it is obvious they have ulterior motives." Levi's dark eyes filled with tears. "The streets are stained with the blood of anyone found without the Vita Signum."

"What about the tunnels and our friends?" she asked.

"They are secure for now." Levi began stuffing some food and supplies into his pockets. "We don't have much time. The troops are conducting a grid search a few blocks from here."

Elam launched to his feet and began to load a burlap sack with food and water.

Levi shook his head. "We must travel light. It will look suspicious if we are carrying bags."

"I'll do the pregnant Muslim woman thing again," Katrina said.

"Good idea," Levi said. Everyone agreed, and they filled her pack with essentials and added a pair of field glasses. Katrina looked full term with the over-stuffed backpack under her burqa. She fastened her head covering, and a few minutes later, the four of them ventured outside.

Some of the rubble had been cleared away since the earthquake, but mounds of broken paving stones and debris still stood in the way.

The group turned north and walked along like they were meant to be there. No one suspected them as they entered the Muslim Quarter, which had been spared much of the earthquake destruction. They traveled past buyers and sellers as they haggled over merchandise.

The women kept their heads lowered as they went by a group of soldiers. From the corner of her eye, Katrina watched as Levi rattled off something in Arabic to Elam, and they all strolled past the soldiers without incident.

Everywhere they looked, World Fortress Institute flags were flying. It seemed ironic to Katrina that this ancient town, which had been the epicenter of a Middle Eastern power struggle for centuries, was now under complete the control of Dormin and the World Fortress Institute. *It's probably going to be a new playground for the elite,* she thought cynically.

They passed the Church of the Holy Sepulcher, a place where some believe that Jesus was buried. Up ahead, the Damascus Gate necked down to a narrow passage that was crowded with Islamic hawkers selling jewelry, handbags, and other wares.

Katrina felt a rush of relief as they moved through to the courtyard outside the wall, but it was short-lived. Several armed guards inspected cars in the parking lot. Her breathing quickened when one of the soldiers approached with a scanner in his hand and asked Levi to show his Vita Signum.

Behind them, a commotion erupted from the Damascus Gate. A merchant was beating a young man with a stick, screaming, "Las, las, las!" A crowd gathered around parroting the angry chant.

Yonah leaned close to Katrina. "This is your chance," she whispered. "You and Elam must go quickly and find a place to hide."

⎯⎯∞⎯⎯

Arroyo Seco, Arizona

David drove the solar-powered utility vehicle with Ezra in the passenger seat. Joel was sitting in the back and felt every bump of the rough desert terrain as they headed out to inspect the fissure that had swallowed the floodwaters.

Jim Saunders, the retired Hydraulic Engineer for Hope Springs, and a couple of other Jewish experts were already at the site when they arrived. "You've got to come see this," Jim said after they parked the vehicle. "Don't worry, we've checked the ground, and it's stable. Mostly solid rock."

The trio walked over to the long fissure that had miraculously swallowed an entire reservoir of water. One of the Jewish engineers shined a beacon of light into the darkness, and they peered inside to see a residual of water pooled in the rock basins below.

David scratched his head. "Where did all that water go?"

"It dropped into the community's aquifer," Jim said. "We could turn this place into an oasis if we wanted."

Joel grinned. "Maybe we should build a water theme park."

"Ah, to be young again." David laughed.

"Gentlemen, what we witnessed here was nothing short of divine intervention," Ezra said. "Our enemies tried to drive us out, but according to scripture, 'You intended to harm me, but God intended it all for good.'"

The men joined together building a makeshift fence around the chasm, so that the grazing animals and livestock wouldn't wander too close and fall in.

"Well, I think we're done here," Jim said as he brushed dirt from his hands. "It has been a good day."

David, Ezra, and Joel headed back to the town of Arroyo Seco, singing light-hearted praise songs as they went.

"I can't wait to tell Elita what we saw," David said as they pulled up in front of the General Store. "Boys, I think we should celebrate with some sandwiches and drinks. I'm buying."

At the lunch counter, Coco was helping Joy color a picture of a rainbow. A few feet away, David's sister and his wife were having a serious conversation behind the lunch counter. The look on their faces told him that all was not well.

Paige looked at her brother and said with a cynical tone, "We were over at the media center watching Alistair Dormin hold a press conference. Apparently, he has just saved our planet from total destruction!"

"What are you talking about?" David said.

"An asteroid is heading toward Earth," Elita chimed in, "but NASA launched a rocket that is supposed to divert it."

"I hope it works," David said.

"According to our anointed Chairman, the mission was a success, but I just don't trust anything that man says," Paige interjected. "As far as I'm concerned, Alistair Dormin is evil."

Chapter 30

Israel

Jean Pierre looked out the window of the luxury Learjet as it taxied toward a private hangar at the Ben Gurion International Airport in Tel Aviv. Alistair Dormin was on a rant, and the object of his anger was the Director of the European Space Agency, who was seated across from the Chairman.

"So, you are telling me that you've spotted another smaller, unidentifiable object, and you don't know what it is?"

"Yes, Sir, but we do know that it appears to be heading for Jerusalem."

"With all your high-powered equipment, this is the best you can do?! What does it look like?"

"We've never seen or detected anything like this before, Mr. Chairman. The object is an extremely luminous mass with nebulous lights surrounding it. Some of our scientists believe this may be some kind of living organism, an alien life form."

"That is ludicrous! You've been reading too many sci-fi books." The sound of Alistair Dormin's cackle made Jean Pierre cringe.

"Nonetheless, Mr. Chairman, we are treating it as a potential threat."

Dormin stood and glowered down at the ESA Director. "If my boys at NASA can alter the course of a massive asteroid, then surely you or someone can deal with this object."

"Yes, Sir. Some units of the Israeli Mobile Air Defense System, known as the Iron Dome, have been positioned in the Jezreel Valley. I assure you that we are responding forcefully to this situation."

"Fine," Dormin said as the jet pulled inside the hangar. "I don't care what it is. You can shoot it out of the sky and analyze what's left of it later." Alistair snapped his fingers, and his personal aid hurried over with his jacket and briefcase.

Jean Pierre and the demoralized Director of the ESA deplaned and followed Dormin to a helicopter that was waiting on the tarmac. No one dared to speak while the brooding Chairman thumbed through papers in his briefcase. They flew to the Jezreel Valley in tense silence.

Jean Pierre clicked his tongue unconsciously and stared down at the landscape as they flew over Mount Gilboa, banked left, and passed the ruins of Megiddo. In the Jezreel Valley, the helicopter hovered over and then landed on a portable landing pad. Outside, the brass was waiting to welcome Alistair Dormin and Jean Pierre like royalty.

"I want to see this so-called Iron Dome," Dormin said as soon as the formal greetings ended.

"Yes, Sir," the general replied. "I believe that you will be impressed by our Mobile Air Defense System." The men climbed on board an air-conditioned, armored vehicle, and the general played tour guide as they moved through the military encampment.

The Chairman's mood improved when the General mentioned how easily the asteroid had been deflected. "I fully expect these missiles will handle our latest little challenge with the same success."

"I claim the victory over this object." A fleeting micro smile flicked across Dormin's lips. "The people of the globe have faith in me, and I must not disappoint them."

In the back seat of the armored vehicle, an unsettling thought needled Jean Pierre. *Alistair Dormin actually believes that he possesses the power to speak things into existence!*

⸺⏣⸺

North of Jerusalem, Israel

Katrina and Elam had been walking for hours. They kept away from the roadways and ducked behind shrubs to avoid being seen by passing motorists.

"Let's rest for a while." Elam paused to wipe sweat from his face. "Do we have any water left?"

"Not much." Katrina sought shade beneath a tree and rifled through her pack for the last of their water. "What's that smell?"

"This is a Terabinth tree that we're sitting under, also known as the turpentine tree. I learned about it in horticulture class." Elam left a swallow of water in the bottle and handed it back to Katrina. "Do you have anything to eat in that back-pack?"

Katrina split the last piece of pita bread and handed half of it to Elam. "So, you were raised in the States?"

"Yeah, I was born in Scarsdale, New York, but one day my dad was looking through my history book, and he read that the Holocaust was mostly a political fabrication. My folks decided it was time to reconnect with our Jewish heritage, so they yanked me out of school during my sophomore year. I was so pissed at my folks at the time, but now I'd give anything just to see them again."

"I understand how your parents must have felt. My grandmother survived Auschwitz," Katrina said. "She often quoted from William Shakespeare, who wrote, 'What's past is prologue.'"

"What does that mean?"

She finished the bread and brushed crumbs from her fingers. "History molds our perspective of the present."

"Oh, I get it. Like that old saying, 'Those who refuse to learn from history are doomed to repeat it.'"

"That's right."

"So, what's your story?" Elam asked. "Are you married or anything?"

Katrina shook her head as her thoughts drifted to Benjamin and the fateful day when he drowned. She then stood and slipped the empty water bottle back into her pack. "We'd better get going if we're going to find a safe place to stop for the night."

They walked over rocks and around scrub brush until their aching feet broke out with blisters. By the time they'd reached the base of a mountain, the shadows had lengthened. Elam stopped for another breather. He wiped sweat from his red face.

"Just a little farther." Katrina pointed to a narrow trail that snaked up the side of the mountain. "We'll be safer up there, and after resting for the night, we'll be able to look over the lay of the land." As they picked their way up the mountainside, Katrina whispered, "Dear God, we could use some help here."

As they crested the top, a gust of wind pummeled them, and Elam whined, "We were better off down below."

Katrina led them to some rocky outcroppings that provided shelter from the wind, and in the moonlight, Elam cleared away a tangle of prickly brown weeds from a cleft in a rock. "Hey man, come look at this." He showed Katrina a small opening in the rock that was just wide enough for an adult to climb through.

"I'm going to check it out," Elam said as he dove through the opening. He emerged a few minutes later. "It opens into a bigger cave, and you're not going to believe it Katrina, but there are some people in there, and they have food and water to share."

⸺⊛⊛⊛⸺

Arroyo Seco, Arizona

David and his family rose early to prepare the General Store for the upcoming prayer vigil. The gathering had been organized for all who wanted to intercede on behalf of those who faced injustice. The Israeli Prime Minister had been killed by the World Fortress Institute, and all over the world, the streets were stained with the blood of Jews and Christians.

Ezra arrived with his arms loaded with free Bibles for the refugees who had given their lives to Christ. "Greetings, Fillmore family!" he called out as he placed the books onto the counter.

"More ham radio reports have been trickling in," David told him.

"Are you talking about the painful boils that are now afflicting millions?" Ezra asked.

"Yes, but there has been chatter about other nefarious government activities too," David said. "Some compliant citizens are growing disillusioned by Dormin's heavy-handed policies. Poverty is still widespread, but daring to question the ruling class is now a punishable offense."

"The subjugated working class is being tossed crumbs while Dormin and the World Fortress Institute elite live on delicacies and fine champagne." David paused and then added, "I bet a lot of people wish they had seen it coming."

"It's too late now," Ezra said. "Jesus once lamented over his own people who rejected him, saying, 'How often I have wanted to gather your children together as a hen protects her chicks beneath her wings, but you wouldn't let me.'"

"Why does Jesus tell us to pray for our enemies if it's too late?" David asked.

"Because only our God can judge the heart," Ezra explained. "God is patient and slow to anger, not wanting anyone to perish, but we have all been given free will. The Lord wants us to freely choose to love him from our hearts. Anything less is shallow and empty."

"That's right," Elita said as she made her way to the front of the store. "Jesus said, 'I stand at the door and knock. If you hear my voice and open the door, I will come in, and we will share a meal together as friends.' I believe he was referring to the door of our hearts."

Chasha rushed in with Uri close behind. "Have I got things to tell you," the old kibitzer said. "Amazing things have been happening around here. People have been dreaming dreams and having visions from God about what is soon coming upon this world." Chasha elbowed her husband. "Tell them about what you heard."

"It's true," Uri nodded. "Devout Jews who once made fun of our Yeshua are now leaping about like children, saying 'God himself has revealed the Messiah's sacrificial love to us.'"

People began to arrive. There were so many they filled the General Store. The spillover gathered on the porch and in the street out front.

Ezra opened in prayer and intercession, and the fellowship continued for several hours. The roar of their shouts and praises were so loud that it drew others from miles around. Finally, the prayers grew softer, and some fell upon their knees to petition the Lord with tears.

Mr. Mike arrived with an urgent message.

"Can I have everyone's attention," David announced

from the porch and then waited for everyone to be quiet. "We have just received word that Arizona Governor Burns has been assassinated."

Shocked murmurs of panic rippled through the street. Someone shouted, "We're all going to be deported!"

"Don't be afraid!" Ezra yelled. "If God is with us, then who can stand against us?"

Chapter 31

Mount Gilboa, Israel

Katrina awoke with her heart pounding. The same disturbing nightmare that she'd had in Detroit had replayed in her dreams. *She was looking down a cliff, watching helplessly as desperate people tried to claw their way up the side only to fall to their deaths. This dream continued, but this time it contained another disturbing element.*

In the dark cave, Katrina heard the others stirring. Someone lit a candle, and it reminded her of the second part of the nightmare, small torches of fire blazing from the sky and turning the landscape into blackened ash.

A couple of feet away, Elam sat up and yawned. "Man, I don't know what you were smoking last night, but you mumbled a lot in your sleep."

"Bad night," Katrina replied.

"I'm starving," the high schooler said. "Hey, you guys got any more matzo crackers over there?"

"Be patient!" Shalev said as she dumped chickpeas into a bowl and began to mash them. "I am making a paste from the leftovers from last night." She turned to her daughter, Rina, and asked her to fetch the matzah bread.

"I used to hate garbanzo beans when my parents served them," Elam said. "Now, I think they taste pretty good."

"It's amazing what a little hunger will do," Katrina chided. She rose and moved across the cave, trying not to scrape her head on the rocky ceiling. "I'm going outside to stretch my legs."

"Remember what I told you, Katrina," Shalev said. "Don't stand near the edge of the cliff because there are soldiers down there, and you could be seen."

Katrina grabbed the binoculars from her pack and squeezed through the small opening of the cave. She stood and arched her back. It felt good to breathe in the crisp fresh air and to gaze upon the beauty of the landscape beyond the Jezreel Valley.

The morning sun felt warm on her skin. She closed her eyes and tried to recall her past life of ease and worldly success. Katrina realized that she didn't miss any of it! Her new-found faith brought a peace that she had never known before.

From somewhere down below, a sound met her ear. Curiosity drove her closer to the edge of the cliff. Katrina crawled on her knees and then lay flat upon her stomach before she carefully peered down into the valley. She was stunned to see a vast army of World Fortress Institute soldiers camped there.

Katrina retrieved her binoculars for a closer look and then froze as her gaze came upon a man wearing a black suit. He towered over the soldiers like a white-haired giant. *Could it be Alistair Dormin? What are the chances?* Katrina thought. He turned, and she caught sight of his silver eyepatch.

Righteous anger burned inside of Katrina, and she knew what needed to be done.

⸺⧢⸺

Jezreel Valley, Israel

In a large, paneled tent that was furnished like an executive office, Jean Pierre took a seat beside Alistair Dormin. Seated across the long table, the top brass had come to brief the Chairman on the current military operations. General Adamos began with a report on the recent sweep of the historic sectors of old Jerusalem. "Sir, the area has been secured, and the rats have been flushed from the sewers."

Dormin smiled at the general's metaphor for Jews, but Jean Pierre clicked his tongue. In recent weeks, he had found the man's smugness distasteful.

Before the next general could give his report, the meeting was interrupted by a communication specialist who rushed into the tent with a satellite phone. "Mr. Chairman, Director Swindon of NASA needs to speak to you. He says it's urgent."

Alistair Dormin seemed visibly annoyed. "What now?" He snatched the phone from the man's hand and said, "Swindon, this better be good news!"

The Chairman listened for a few minutes. "What? Are you sure? Well, what can be done about this?" The Chairman paused to listen. "That's not good enough Swindon! If you don't fix this problem, your career is over! Do you understand?" Dormin threw the phone down, and the look on his face alarmed everyone at the conference table. "Everybody out, except you, Pierre."

The Chairman thrust his tall frame from the chair and began to pace. His good eye bulged with rage when he looked at Jean Pierre. "Do you know what that incompetent SOB told me?"

Pierre shook his head. "No, Monsieur."

"He said that there is an unforeseen problem with the Space X Falcon Heavy mission."

"Something has gone wrong?" Jean Pierre asked.

"Apparently, their calculations were slightly off. The asteroid was diverted, but it clipped the moon, and this redirected the trajectory. He says that it is now back on a collision course with the earth."

"Mon Dieu!"

"Your feeble little god has nothing to do with this!" Dormin slammed his fist onto the table.

Jean mopped sweat from his brow. "What can be done?"

"He said there isn't time or space enough to redirect the trajectory of the asteroid now."

Jean Pierre reflected on his conversation with the NASA scientist during the launch. He felt the blood drain from his face. "How long until it reaches our planet?"

"According to that imbecile, we have only eight hours until impact." Alistair Dormin shook his fist at heaven and bellowed, "Not on my watch!"

———∞———

Arroyo Seco, Arizona

The excitement in the Sanctuary Community was almost palpable. Joel and Coco stood in the street looking toward the sky. Some of the residents had been up all night long searching the heavens for the unidentifiable object that had the global media centers speculating.

"Jesus is returning, just like He said." Coco laid a hand over her heart. "I can feel it here."

Almost everyone in the community shared her sense of joy and wonder, but across the globe, scientists made wild speculations about the unidentifiable flying object. Some said that it was a mass of unknown cosmic matter, possibly toxic or radioactive. Others were convinced that it was part of an alien invasion.

Panic and a sense of doom had gripped the international community, especially those nations surrounding Israel. Desperate citizens clamored for someplace safe to hide from the brightness of the coming light. But the people of Arroyo Seco, Hope Springs, and the community of refugees gathered with unshakable faith and joy as they waited for the blessed hope of their Lord's return.

A few feet away, a woman looked up with a radiant face and began to sing with all of her heart. The ethereal tune carried softly through the streets, and others joined in.

"Praise the Lord there's sunlight in my happy soul today,
Brighter than the glorious noon.
Christ the light is shining in my heart and on his way,

I shall rise to glory soon…
Precious Sonlight, precious light,
I shall rise to glory soon…"

"Look at that." Coco pointed to the village children who danced in the streets, and Joel was touched to see old men and women joining in the celebration.

Paige and her teenage son arrived in a utility vehicle, and the boy they referred to as Nasi Katan hopped out with his Bible in hand. He climbed the steps to the porch and began to read the word. "He who is the faithful witness to all these things says, 'Yes, I am coming soon!' Amen! Come, Lord Jesus!"

Jezreel Valley, Israel

Katrina made her way down from the mountain using rocks and bushes for cover. Fearing that her movement would attract attention, she moved deliberately and slowly.

To the left, she could see the ruins of the ancient city of Tel Megiddo. According to Shalev, it was once a utopian agricultural community known as a kibbutz. Now, it was flanked by World Fortress Institute military installations.

As Katrina neared the camp, her anxiety grew. "Jesus, what am I doing? I have no plan," she whispered.

Katrina took shelter beneath the shade of a rough-barked tree and waited for the shadows to lengthen. She watched a lizard hunting bugs and a caterpillar spinning silk between some leaves. As dusk neared, Katrina rose to watch the camp through the crook of the tree. Between her and a row of barracks was a latrine and shower house.

Keeping to the lines of the natural landscape, Katrina crept closer. Even in the face of death, something inside compelled her. "God help me," she prayed.

She made it to the canvas wall of the latrine, hunkered down, and listened to the sound of running water. Carefully, Katrina lifted the bottom of the canvas and peeked inside. Only a few feet away she spotted a uniform lying folded on a chair and sitting on top of that was a pistol. Katrina crawled under the canvas and retrieved them with quiet speed. Outside, she quickly donned the uniform, cinched up the belt, and then made her way into the heart of enemy territory.

She walked purposefully like a woman on a mission. She was reminded of the scripture that was etched on her grandmother's wall plaque and now in her mind, "This is my command—be strong and courageous! Do not be afraid or discouraged. For the Lord your God is with you wherever you go." A deep and inexplicable peace filled her spirit as she made her way to the center of the camp where she had first spotted Alistair Dormin hours earlier. Once there, Katrina hung back to assess the situation. It was dark now, but security lighting and armed guards had been set up all around the massive tent.

Suddenly a blinding light shined down on the camp from above. Katrina could see flashes of sheet lighting in the thick clouds. *Is this some kind of World Fortress Institute warcraft?* she wondered. The intense brightness seemed to cause confusion among the guards, and several bolted away in fear.

Alistair Dormin and Grand Apostle Max Nellaf emerged from the large tent followed close behind by a decorated general. They all stood gazing up at the sky.

"Position the Air Defense Missiles," Dormin told the general. "Await my orders to deploy."

"Yes, Sir." The general saluted the Chairman, climbed aboard his chauffeured Humvee, and was whisked away.

In the confusion, Katrina was able to approach the Chairman without being noticed. She racked the pistol slide, and Alistair Dormin's good eye shifted her way. A fleeting look of surprise passed across his face. Suddenly, she was surrounded by armed guards.

Dormin smirked. "I should have had you killed back in New York City."

Overhead, the intensity of the white light in the sky grew until form and color seemed to blur.

Max Nellaf pointed his scepter at Katrina and spewed out a litany of religious-sounding curses, but Katrina kept Dormin in her sights.

He threw back his head in mocking laughter as her finger tightened on the trigger. She was ready to put an end to this evil man who had caused so much suffering, but then something odd began to happen. The hair on her arms stood up from static electricity, and sparks of color danced through the air like lightning bugs.

The sparks turned to blue fingers of electricity that reached for Dormin and flowed across his body. There was a look of terror on his face, and something unintelligible passed his lips. Then, to the horror of everyone around, his body burst into a raging inferno!

The Grand Apostle Nellaf shrieked and dropped his scepter. As he turned to run, a bolt of lightning struck him to the ground. The soldiers began wildly firing random shots into the air, and Katrina closed her eyes and waited for the bullet that would surely end her life.

"Katrina," a familiar voice said. When she opened her eyes, Zeke was standing right in front of her.

He took her hand. "Come with me, Missy. I want to show you something." In a flash, they were transported miles away to the Kidron Valley. Katrina and the old man hovered in the air and gazed down upon the ancient tombs that now lay open on the surface.

Katrina looked on in amazement. "The graves are all empty," she said.

Zeke smiled. "They certainly are!"

Suddenly, it hit Katrina. "You're an angel, aren't you?" She bowed her head in reverent awe.

"Hold on, Missy! Only God deserves your worship." The old man's crystal eyes shined like stars. "I'm only a servant, just like you."

All of a sudden, they were surrounded by multitudes who had gone before them. "Babbeh and Benjamin!" Katrina cried out in joyful communion.

Then, she saw the Lord Jesus standing on the Mount of Olives. The beauty of his countenance was inexpressible. She felt weightless and unfettered as she looked upon the Savior. His hair glowed white, and from His fingers shined rays of light. He looked at her, and though every thought and deed were laid bare before His gaze, the Lord still loved her!

In an instant, she realized that Jesus had always been with her, even from her mother's womb, throughout the abuse she had suffered as a little child. In Katrina's darkest hours, the Lord had been present whispering words of comfort and peace.

"Aren't you glad you didn't pull that trigger, Missy?" Zeke asked.

The Mount of Olives where Jesus stood abruptly split from east to west as the Lord looked upon the city that he loved.

Darkness shadowed the earth. The landscape heaved. Buildings quaked and tumbled as though made of sand, and a fracture formed in the corner of the newly built temple door.

Katrina watched as water trickled and then gushed from the fissure. It formed a rivulet that grew as it passed to the right of the altar where the statue of Dormin lay broken. When the waters touched the Golden Gate, its sealed entrance gave way, and the crystal waters poured into the Kidron Valley. The rivulet became a river that rolled between the now-cleaved Mount of Olives, and it continued across the plains.

From the heavens, they heard a mighty shout and looked to see a huge blazing rock hurling toward the earth. The air concussed, and the impact was so powerful that the earth seemed to rock from its axis. But Katrina and the multitudes watched from the safety of their Savior's shadow.

Not long after the asteroid hit, flames fell to earth like raindrops from the sky, igniting firestorms that roared across the landscape.

Katrina cried out, "Will anyone survive?"

Zeke smiled and said, "That question is a little above my paygrade, Missy, but scripture tells us that mankind will be as rare as the Gold of Ophir. The Prophet Zechariah wrote that everyone who is left of all the nations that came against Jerusalem will come here from year to year to worship the Lord of Hosts." He pointed to the new crystal-clear river that flowed from Jerusalem. "If you really look closely, you can see saplings sprouting on the banks of that river. Their leaves are for the healing of the nations. Mankind has been trying for centuries to build themselves a utopia, but only God can make all things new. That is just what He's doing now, and it's going to be amazing."

As a soft breeze fluttered through Zeke's long white beard, he said, "No eye has seen, no ear has heard, and no mind has imagined what God has prepared for those who love him."

Epilogue

Then I saw a new Heaven and a new earth,
for the old Heaven and the old earth had disappeared.
And the sea was also gone.
And I saw the holy city, the new Jerusalem,
coming down from God out of Heaven
like a bride beautifully dressed for her husband.
I heard a loud shout from the throne, saying,
"Look, God's home is now among his people!
He will live with them, and they will be his people.
God himself will be with them.
He will wipe every tear from their eyes,
and there will be no more death or sorrow or crying or pain.
All these things are gone forever."
And the one sitting on the throne said,
"Look, I am making everything new!"
And then he said to me,
"Write this down, for what I tell you
is trustworthy and true."
And he also said, "It is finished!
I am the Alpha and the Omega—
the Beginning and the End."

Revelation 21:1-6

About the Author

From her Grandfather's tales about Buffalo Bill to the mystique of the West, L. P. Hoffman's imagination was primed at an early age. In her transient childhood, she experienced the dark side of Caribbean culture and survived war in the Middle East. As an adult, the author has traveled the world and moved among Washington insiders. L. P. Hoffman values unique perspectives and believes that culturally relevant stories born of experience are the ones best told.

Read more about
L. P. Hoffman

Visit and "Like" L.P. Hoffman,
Author on Facebook

L. P. Hoffman books are available in paperback and eBook at: Your Local Bookstore
www.Amazon.com, www.BarnesandNoble.com
www.HopeSpringsMedia.com

The Third Peril Trilogy

A modern-day, epic-suspense trilogy about faith, hope, and providence in times of cultural upheaval and national insecurity.

Just imagine what it might be like if the events foretold in the Bible were to happen in contemporary times.

Follow the diverse and complex cast of characters whose lives are intertwined as they each navigate economic and geopolitical changes, natural disasters and wars, and spiritual trials and tribulations. There is mystery, intrigue, drama, and redemption. Be sure to watch for Zeke, the little gnome-like man with a long white beard who drives an old Rambler with a seemingly endless tank of gas as he rolls in and out of people's lives with his joyful sense of humor and divine pearls of wisdom.

Other Novels by L. P. Hoffman

A noble lie or a deadly secret?
Murder in Maine, wolves in Wyoming, and a fugitive-one life-changing summer for wolf biologist, Anna O'Neil. She needs answers. Who shot her father and why? Then, the arrival of a mysterious document forces Anna to examine her own beliefs and gives her the key to restore a divided community. But, first, she must find the courage to confront a hidden evil and catch her father's killer.

- 2009 Indie Book Awards Winner
- 2009 USA Book News Awards Finalist

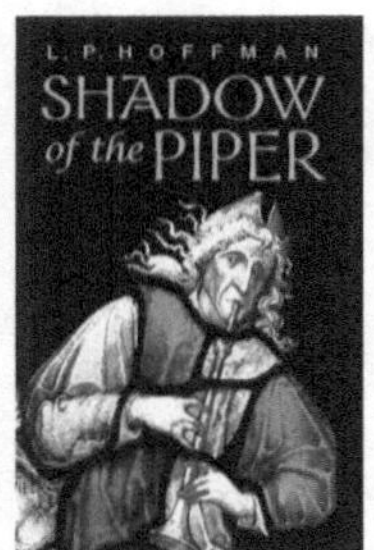

The Pied Piper still plays his tune, and in his shadow, many fall.
When a disturbed teenager arrives at the Pittsburgh Rescue Mission, Cali turns things upside down by claiming to know "secrets" about a young evangelist's shadowy past. The deranged girl lures Jesse Berryacross the country only to slip away after they reach their destination. Hamlin, Montana, is not the quaint mining town it appears to be. Something sinister moves below the surface —the youth are at risk—and someone there wants Jesse dead.

- 2013 Indie Fab Book of the Year Award
- 2013 Indie Book Awards Finalist

www.ingramcontent.com/pod-product-compliance
Lightning Source LLC
Chambersburg PA
CBHW050611170726

48283CB00001B/196